why the River Runs

The Riverview Series
A Novel

I0685837

JoAnna Grace

JoAnna Grace

BY JOANNA GRACE

Divine Chronicle Series:
Divine Awakening
Divine Destiny
Divine Judgment
Divine Encounter
Divine Pursuit
Divine Escape (coming soon)

The Roles We Play

Blake Pride Series:
Pride Before The Fall
Break Her Fall
The Harder They Fall
Divided We Fall (Coming Soon)

The Riverview Series:
Why The River Runs

Omega Office Romance Series: *(Coming Soon)*
Crossing The Lines
Blurring The Lines
Erasing The Lines

A Division of Y&R Enterprises, LLC
PO Box 2283
Lindale, TX 75771

For information about special discounts for bulk purchases, please contact Y&R Enterprises Special Sales at 1.903.251.9511 or info@yandrpr.com.

The Y&R Speakers Bureau can bring authors to your live event. For more information or to book an event, contact the Y&R Speakers Bureau at 903.251.9511 or visit our website at yandrpr.com.

Cover Design by Simply Defined Art
Book design by Champagne Formats

Library of Congress Control Number Data
Grace, JoAnna.
Why the river runs / JoAnna Grace.
Contemporary romance—southern couple —Fiction.2. Romance—Fiction.
Fiction. | BISAC: FICTION / Romance / Contemporary. | FICTION / Romance / General. |
PCN 20179329112017

ISBN: 978-1940460-55-0

authorjoannagrace.com
yandrpublishing.com

Dedication

To Donny,
My partner in business, marriage, parenting, friendship,
and life.
You're my rock, solid and strong, allowing me to flow wild
and free.
We's peas and carrots.

A special thanks to

Parole Officer Golightly for your information. People will only see the tip of the iceberg of information you provided and I'm so thankful for your insight into the process and people.

Fireman Aaron Munn, for comical talks about explosives and bombs. We're both on some government watch list for sure. Hope I can continue to entertain the guys at the station who overhear our conversations. Much love to all of you.

Home builder Nathan Bass and my friends at Cypress for answering my random questions. You've been great to work with and it's a joy getting to know you all.

To my real life construction crew - you guys are awesome! It's not hard to write about Tina's feelings for her employees when I know just how she feels.

Charlie Ray - The kindness you've shown my family is priceless. You are a saint.

To Y&R, my editors, beta readers, formatter, and cover designer: I couldn't do it without you. Thanks again…and again…the second time through.

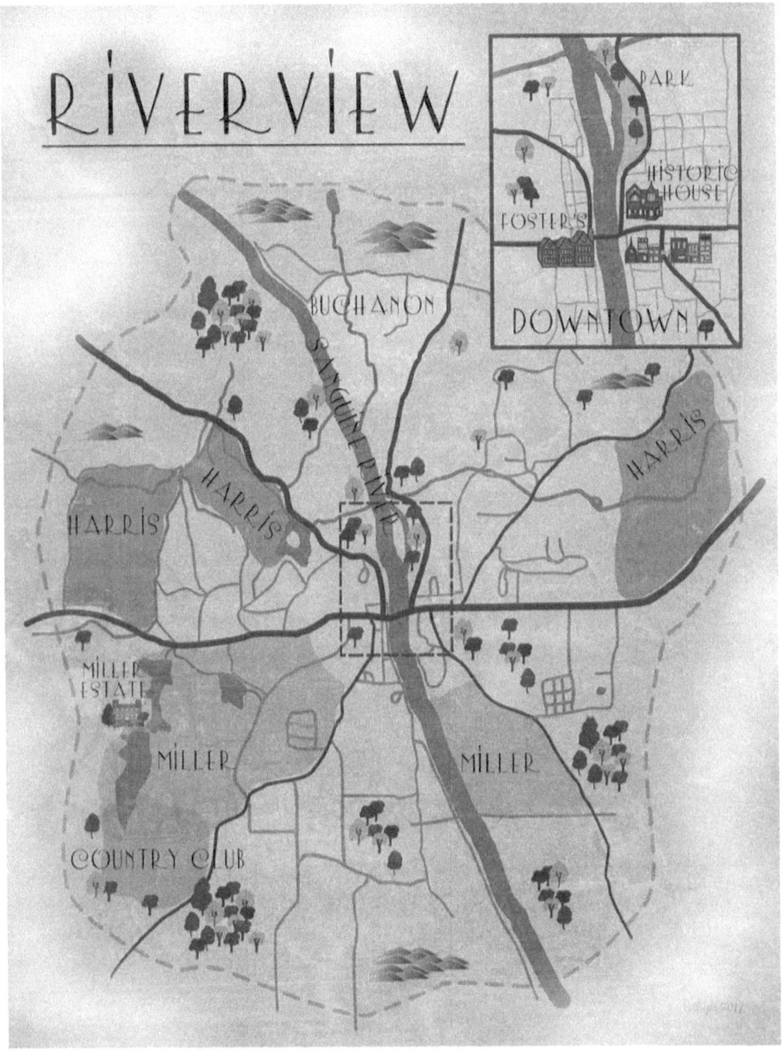
RIVERVIEW
PARK
HISTORIC HOUSE
FOSTER'S
DOWNTOWN
BUCHANON
SANGUINE RIVER
HARRIS
HARRIS
HARRIS
MILLER ESTATE
MILLER
MILLER
COUNTRY CLUB

Chapter One

Bo's foot tapped the floor as he waited for Mr. Foster to read over his resume. The writing on the paper was sparse, seeing how there wasn't much to report for the last four years. This job meant a lot. It was a fresh start, a new beginning, a clean slate. Coming home to Riverview and working at Foster's represented all these things and more. Foster Construction could be his ticket to redemption.

Okay, maybe that was putting too much pressure on one interview. But it would be ideal if he could get in with one of the biggest companies in the county. Especially since his grandmother knew someone who knew someone who was friends with Duane Foster and they might skip the background check based on the recommendation.

"You've done construction?" Duane's thick gray brows rose as he read the resume over the top of his readers.

"Y'sir," Bo answered. Even years in California couldn't

beat his country accent out of him.

"Carpentry, huh?"

"Y'sir."

"Where did you learn?"

Jail. "On-the-job experience."

"With who?"

"The State."

"And who can I contact as a reference over there?"

Bo paused. *My parole officer?* Sweat dripped down the back of his neck. He wasn't prepared for the stare-down. Even the Border Collie sitting beside the desk gawked.

Duane let out a long breath and swiped a hand down his face. He leaned over his beat-up metal desk and braced himself on his elbows. "All right, son, let's cut the bull, shall we?"

Dang it. Here it came. The *I'm sorry we don't hire criminals* speech. It would be the third one he'd received since he got out. Bo looked down at his work boots. His grandmother had bought them brand new just for this interview. She lived on social security and selling produce from her own garden, but she'd spent all her extra money that month for the steel-toed boots. All he wanted to do was pay her back with a little good news.

"I talked to your grandmother already, Bo." There was a hint of affection in his voice. "Sweet lady, right there."

He nodded and glanced at his boots. "Y' sir." As hard as it was, he kept his chin up.

Duane steepled his fingers. "Said you just got out. How long you been home, son?"

"Two weeks, sir."

Duane nodded. "Welcome back to civilization. Have a probation officer?"

"Parole, sir. Got out three years early. Have to check in monthly and prove I'm working, sir."

"She said you did four years. What for?"

Shit. Bo met Duane's gaze. He'd paid his time for a crime he wasn't too terribly sorry for. "Found my step-dad hitting my mother. I returned the gesture. Judge decided since I was a black belt, and I didn't exactly hold my punches, it qualified as assault with a deadly weapon. That's a felony in California."

Duane nodded his head and pursed his lips. "What brings you to Texas?"

"A promise I made to my grandmother and a fresh start."

Duane leaned in, narrowing his gaze. "Do you consider yourself a violent man, Bo?"

How many times had people asked him that question? At least half a dozen. The parole board, his anger management counselor, the judge. This was the first time he looked the person across the table square in the eyes and answered bluntly. "Only when a woman is confused with a punching bag, sir."

"Can't blame you there." Duane's astute eyes narrowed as he leaned back and rested his chin in his hand. He pursed his lips again, studying Bo like he might sprout horns. The dog barked when a door opened and closed down the hall, making Bo flinch. "You have to meet my foreman. Then we'll see."

"Be happy to, sir." Hope lit in his chest. As far as men went, Bo considered himself friendly enough and he knew how to work hard.

Duane's lips stretched into a grin and he huffed. He lifted his chin and hollered, "T, come here. Got some fresh blood for ya."

Bo stood up to greet the other man, uncomfortable with someone approaching the office door from behind him. He turned and locked his gaze with a pair of blue eyes so light and airy, they stole the breath from his lungs.

"Bo, meet my foreman…Tina."

Tina was a good six inches shorter than his six-foot frame, but her presence loudly stated that she had the upper hand. Sun-streaked blonde hair was pulled back into a haphazard bun with strands escaping. The whole twisted mess was held together with a pencil and a band. He had the sudden—and stupid—urge to pluck it from her hair and watch the mass fall. She wore no makeup, but her thick, black lashes almost looked painted on. From many days in the sun, her skin was a golden brown. The great tan was accentuated by the dirty white tank top. Even her brown carpenter pants were stained at the knees and had sawdust on them. Unlike his, her boots were scuffed and marred, painted with a dozen different colors and substances.

Bo couldn't help himself; he studied her head to toe… twice. This was a woman who knew a hard day's labor. She was also the most angelic woman he'd ever seen. Her high cheekbones and heart-shaped face were dusted with bronze, and thin but tempting lips pursed as she looked him up and down.

Bo stirred, his blood heating, his body instantly reacting to her attention.

After an awkward moment of him standing there with his jaw on the floor, Tina held out her hand. "Tina Foster. Who are you?" Her gaze darted from Bo to Duane and back.

It took him a moment to remember anything but how

beautiful she was. *Shit.* "Uh, I, um, I'm Bo Galloway. Nice to meet you, ma'am."

"Likewise. Daddy, we need to deal with a certain painter that's about to burn my biscuits."

Daddy? Of course, this was Duane's daughter. *Double shit.*

"Great," Duane huffed. "Fill me in later."

"You know I will." Tina crouched and rubbed the dog's head, allowing it to lick her cheek. "There's my Dixie girl."

Duane cleared his throat. "Mr. Galloway is Nancy Brewer's grandson. He's returning after far too many years in California."

"The lady who sells the produce, right?" Tina deferred to Duane, who nodded. "Yeah, I thought you looked familiar." She ran her eyes over him once again, her poker face in perfect form. "I didn't realize we were hiring, Dad." She tilted her head at her father.

"We can always use a good hand, you know that."

Tina's lips curled downward. "Everything look tight on paper?"

Duane's eyes met Bo's. For a moment, Bo's heart stopped and he held his breath. One word from Duane and this beautiful, hardworking woman wouldn't give him the time of day—much less a job. Bo pleaded internally. He needed this break.

Duane slid the resume into his desk drawer and glanced at a spot on the wall. "Yup. Looks good on the paperwork end."

Thank God.

"Now you can see if he's worth a darn in the field."

"All right." Tina nodded once, put her hands on her hips, and scowled at him, giving the same contemplating look as her father. "Two things before I let you on my job site."

"Here we go," Duane muttered, turning his attention back to his laptop.

Tina held up one finger. "First off, if you've got issues taking orders from someone with a vagina," she pointed said finger to the door of the office, "there's the door. Don't waste my time. I don't have patience for chauvinistic BS. Two, if you don't like country music, I suggest you invest in noise-canceling ear plugs. You'll work on my site until I see what you can do, then you might be transferred to one of our other crews. When can you start?"

"How fast can you write the address?" Bo said.

"Slow down, son. We have to fill out paperwork." Duane laughed and waved Bo to come sit back down.

Maybe there was a God after all. If so, He was smiling down on Bo at that moment. Bo called his grandmother to tell her he would be busy at lunch.

The country music comment was understood immediately. Bo parked his late grandfather's rusted Ford on the construction site and exited the truck to the local country music station blaring from a radio. He traded his button-down for a company tee-shirt and searched for Tina.

"You the new guy?" A tall man with salt and pepper hair and matching beard gave him a speculative glance. "Duane called me a minute ago."

Bo swallowed and looked upwards. "Yes, sir."

He thrust out a hand. "Great. T's upstairs. She's hanging the sheetrock in the bedrooms. Take this." Terry handed him a box of screws. "I'm gonna get the next boards ready."

Bo nodded, accepting the screws.

"I'm Terry Hicks, her right-hand man. Word of advice: don't argue with her and don't hit on her. You're likely to get your nuts shot off with a nail gun either way."

Instinctually, Bo covered himself, cringing. What the hell did he just walk into? "You give that speech often?"

Terry grinned, his age apparent in every wrinkle on his face. "Every chance I get. I'm her uncle."

Bo nodded and headed inside the gutted two-story ranch house, stepping over tools and wires. Each room was in various stages of renovation. He found Tina and two other guys in an upstairs bedroom.

"Crapballs." Tina let out a guttural growl as she snapped the battery back on her cordless drill. "These things don't last more than five freaking minutes." Tina glanced up and back down once she saw him. "Where's Terry?"

"Down there." Bo held out the box of screws. He didn't know what to think of Tina yet. She walked a thin line between being a total bitch or a total badass. Based on the way she gave him the cold shoulder, he was leaning towards the former.

"You know how to hang?" She didn't meet his eyes as she opened the box of screws and poured them into the pocket of her utility belt.

Bo swallowed hard. His experience working construction in high school only lasted a short while. "A little."

Tina sighed and squinted her eyes at the floor. The two seconds she hesitated felt like two hours. "No time like the present." She checked her watch. "Clocking in at ten twenty. Jason, Bill, this is Bo. Let's teach him how to hang wall, m'kay?"

The two other men nodded and smiled. Not overly friendly but not indifferent either. Tina turned her back to him and finished up the piece of drywall she was working on. Bill was older, at least in his forties, and had thinning hair and a pot belly. Jason looked closer to Bo's age, mid-twenties, and wore his baseball cap backwards. He had tats on his forearms and the back of his neck. He at least gave Bo a cordial fist bump.

Bo observed them place a few boards and became momentarily stunned at the quickness with which Tina worked. It took her spare minutes to screw the whole thing to the studs. Terry came in with her next piece. She situated it on the wall and Bo jumped in to hold it steady so she could anchor it.

She crouched down, giving him a great view of her back and ass. "Damn it, Terry. Get your glasses out, old man." Tina examined where the electrical outlet cut out *should've* been.

"What?" he said, bending over to look. "Aw, hell."

"If you don't start wearing your glasses on the job, I'm going to staple them to your stubborn head." Tina straightened.

"I got it." This was one thing he could do. Bo grabbed the measuring tape from her belt and measured for the outlet, using Terry's pencil to mark it on the drywall. He tossed the tape back to Tina and grabbed the mechanical handsaw on the ground behind them all. He made a precise and even cut, perfectly framing the blue outlet casing.

"Thanks." Tina pointed a finger at him. "But don't touch my belt again."

"Yes, ma'am."

Terry shook his head and laughed. "I'll get him a

tool belt. We don't need another lawsuit." He went back downstairs.

"*Another* one?" Bo stared off after Terry. Jason chuckled, Bill shivered.

Tina merely shrugged and rolled her eyes, returning to her task like it was no big deal. What the hell kind of woman was he dealing with? Lawsuits over tools, nailing testicles, stapling glasses to heads. Dear God. He definitely wasn't in California anymore.

Damn, it was nice to be back in the South. He'd almost forgotten what country girls were like.

For the rest of the morning, he trod carefully around Tina Foster. She had no problems telling him exactly what she wanted him to do and how she wanted it done. Every move she made was calculated and skillful. The woman was all business, except for when certain songs came on the radio. Then the whole crew tried to out sing one another. The only time she stopped working was when she danced over to pick up a tool or twirled around in place to the beat.

The crazy thing was, the chick had a good set of pipes on her. She kept up with the radio singers without breaking her working stride. The guys on the crew couldn't carry a tune in a five-gallon bucket, but that didn't stop them from loudly following along, creating a painful racket.

If there was one thing Bo learned by working construction years ago, it was that men would relate everything to their penises. Everything could be turned into a sexual innuendo, and filters worked best on machinery, not mouths. Cussing was not only standard conversation, it was practically a requirement of the job.

He wondered how having Tina in the mix affected that atmosphere. Throwing a woman in the ring didn't faze them a bit. Hell, Tina didn't hold her tongue either. She gave those guys a hard time every chance she was given. They teased, laughed, cursed, and pranked each other like…well, like one big happy family. Everyone knew their places, knew their roles, and did their jobs efficiently.

He could only hope to carve out a place for himself in this well-oiled machine of a crew.

At the end of the day, Bo was tired and completely satisfied. Just before they'd called it quits, Tina walked him to his truck.

"Not bad, Galloway. See you back here tomorrow at six."

"Six?" He leaned his head in as if he didn't hear her. On the job at six in the morning, he could handle that. He was used to breakfast call at 5:30.

"The earlier we get started, the earlier we can call it a day. Summer in Texas is brutal, Galloway. It's no fun working in the afternoon heat. Get to bed early, bring lots of water." She spun on her heel and gave him a view of her round backside. He nearly dropped his keys.

As she walked away, a song came to his mind. To see her smile, he'd do anything. He didn't care for country music, but if it meant being around Tina Foster all day, he'd learn to love it.

That evening, he pulled up to his grandmother's old farmhouse. Besides the flowers, it hadn't changed since he was a child. The same swing hung on the porch, the screen door still had a hole in it from when his mother kicked it. The paint needed refreshing and the gravel driveway was losing the war with the grass, but the house had never looked better to him.

For three weeks, since his grandmother had driven all the way to southern California to pick him up, she had sat at the dinner table and prayed every night that he would find a job. Tonight, he had good news for her.

Nan came out the front door, her arms up in the air in triumph, a huge smile on her face.

Bo's face matched hers as he climbed the stairs and hugged her.

"See, I told you praying helps. I'm so proud, Bo."

"Thanks, Nan. Now all I have to do is keep it."

She waved a bony arm, dismissing his pessimism. "Nonsense. You're going to excel, I just know it."

Bo held open the door for her.

"You've never been lazy, Bo Allen. You just put that determination of yours to good use and the Fosters are going to be sending me a fruit basket. Just wait and see."

He treasured the confidence she had in him. When it felt like all the world had abandoned him, Nan had stood like a lighthouse in the storm. He had promised his grandfather he would take care of her and he would make good on it.

"I made your favorite, chicken fried steak. There's sweet tea in the fridge and," she bent to pull a cake out of the oven, "I made you a pineapple cream cake." Her face glowed, truly glowed, with happiness for him.

"Dang, Nan. I need to get a job every day."

"Son, we are going to celebrate every little victory we can." She kissed his cheek and immediately spit like she'd licked a lemon. "Ugh, you're dirty. I think I just ate sawdust. Go get cleaned up, working man."

Bo laughed. "Yes, ma'am." If he gave her a million dollars

a day for the rest of his life, it would never be enough to repay her for everything she'd given him. Maybe he could start by working on her house.

Tina fell into her father's office chair with a cloud of dust rising into the air. She was tired to the bones, a good feeling. It hurt to rub Dixie's head, but she couldn't withhold love from her favorite girl.

"How'd he do?" Daddy shut his laptop.

She didn't require an explanation of who he was talking about. "Fine. Didn't say ten words all day and probably thought we're all bat-shit crazy."

Her father chuckled, knowing all too well about their singing rituals and Tina's habitual dancing while she worked.

"That's to be expected. Think he'll stick?"

She shrugged and dusted off her shirt. "Hell if I know. He's awful quiet to fit in around here. What's his deal? We weren't looking to hire anyone."

Daddy shifted in his chair. "It's a favor for an old friend."

Picking up on her father's reluctance to broach the subject, she leaned over and pinned him with her stare. "What's his deal, Dad? I know something's off."

"How can you tell?"

"His boots. You and I know the only time a person in construction has new boots is around Christmas and their birthday. So, unless he blew out some candles recently, he hasn't seen work in a while."

Daddy nodded, the corner of his mouth pulled back into a smirk. "He's had a rough go at it, T. Give him a chance. He needs the work."

Tina tilted her head and nodded. Her father had a soft heart, but she was trying to run a business, not a shelter for the lost and needy. If Bo Galloway didn't pull his weight, he'd be gone. "Dad, I love your heart. But I'm a week behind as it is, and as much as I know you love to take in strays—"

"Dixie was a stray and look how she turned out." Daddy cocked his head to the side.

Tina nodded. Fair point. "What'cha want for dinner?" Joints and muscles complained as she got to her feet.

"It's my turn to cook."

"No arguments here. I hate drywall days. They kill me." She rubbed the base of her back.

Daddy pushed himself out of his chair and grabbed the two canes he required to walk out of the office. If he only needed the canes, then today was a good day. Bad days required the wheelchair. Daddy had broken his back on a job site just after her high school graduation. The surgery to fix his back was a botched job that left him with permanent spinal damage and the inability to walk for more than a few minutes at a time. That was when he and his daughter traded places. Tina had helped in the office. Now, Daddy held the desk job and Tina busted her ass every day.

She wouldn't have it any other way. At least he was alive. The same couldn't be said of her mother, who had died giving birth to her.

They made their way to the back of the building where they lived. The two-story warehouse, formally a cannery, was part of Riverview's history. They loved being able to take care of the building. They'd bought it at auction and renovated every inch of it themselves. Now it stood proudly on the bank of the river as a tribute to the town's history.

Behind the front offices was a one-bedroom apartment

for Daddy. Tina lived upstairs in another apartment. She usually ate with her father, caught a game or two, then headed up to her own space.

"You got plans for the weekend?" her father asked over dinner.

Tina was showered and comfy in her sweats, her hair wet around her shoulders. She shook her head and shrugged a shoulder, knowing what her father was really asking. Did she have a date?

Daddy huffed. "That engineer fellow hasn't called you yet?"

Tina blew it off. "Only five or six times…today."

Daddy speared his pasta and put it in his mouth. "I think he's really smitten with you."

"Smitten?" Tina curled her lip up and rolled her eyes. "Daddy, really. Trey is great, but I don't think I want a guy who is *smitten*. Sounds a little soft, you know?"

Not that she would confess that to her father, but soft was exactly how she and her crew described Trey. He was a pencil-pushing, number-crunching, civil engineer who would happily place himself at her heel like a dog. The attention was flattering, she had to admit. Trey doted on her, praised her with gifts and adoration. She would never have to worry about him cheating or running around on her, which he was capable of doing. He had just enough Asian descent to give him the tear-shaped brown eyes and dark features. As her crew said, Trey was pretty. Tina wouldn't disagree. She'd looked at him plenty in the beginning.

"Don't discount him just because he's not as tough as you are. Not many men are." He mumbled the last part as if he didn't want her to hear it. His eyes said it all. Daddy carried a healthy respect for her above and beyond what fathers and daughters share. They were business partners and friends.

"Why don't you plan something with the girls? Keri or Jayden—"

"Dad," Tina cut him off, "why are you so interested in my social life?" Her knee bounced under the table.

He shrugged his wide shoulders. "Aw, I don't know, baby girl. I guess I saw the way Bo looked at you and I realized how often I overlook the fact that you're a pretty young woman who should be fighting men off with a stick." His blue eyes, just like hers, saw far too much these days.

"I do fight men off with a stick, every day. It's usually because they want to wring my neck, but it counts." Tina grinned, hoping to lighten her father's mood. He rolled his eyes. "Daddy, look." She set down her fork and made sure she had his attention. "Right now, Trey and I are just a casual thing. I don't have time for an all-in relationship and he knows that. He says he's okay with it. Jayden is a freaking mess. We're coming up on the anniversary of Chris's death and Keri and I are arguing over how to handle it."

"What do you mean?" Daddy put his elbows on the table and stared at her.

She pulled her hair back and twisted it, playing with the strands, and settled in for a discussion with her father. "Well, I think we need to usher her out of town, take her mind off it. Keri thinks we need to do some sort of balloon release thing. We agreed to take the weekend and think about it, talk to Bear, talk to Chris's mom, and see what the family thinks. I don't know what the answer is. What did you do after Mom died?"

Daddy pursed his lips and squinted his eyes. "It was a little different. I had you, and you kept me busy. When your mom's birthday came along, you were learning to sit up, so I tried to concentrate on that. The anniversary of her death was your birthday, so we celebrated your birth and her home-going. Jayden doesn't have a baby to keep her mind occupied." He looked down at his plate and his face slipped into sadness. "I guess in some ways, I was lucky to have a piece of your mother left to get me through. All Jayden has is that unfinished house."

"Maybe that's why I don't want to date anyone right now. It's too hard to think about losing them. Besides, I don't need a man. I'm just too busy." Seeing her father's loss and living through Jayden's pain only helped mortar up the cracks that Bo created in her defenses. If she was to save herself the heartache losing the one she loved, it was best not to go down that path at all. Keeping people at arm's length was the simplest solution.

"I know that. You've been independent from your first breath. I know you don't *need* a man, T. I'm just worried that you don't *want* one." Her father sighed, a troubling scowl forming on his face.

"Well, if it makes you feel better, I don't want a girl either." Tina picked up her plate to take it to the sink as her father chuckled, put his hands together in prayer, and mouthed *thank you Lord* to the ceiling.

Tina thumped him in the back of the head as she walked past and he laughed. "What? I want grandbabies."

"You find a man who can keep up with me, Daddy, and we'll talk." She kissed his head as she came back to pick up his dishes. "I have our company to run and that's my priority."

Daddy gently touched her arm. "Loneliness is a sneaky demon, Tina Marie. You work so hard you don't realize it's sitting in the same room with you until it's too late."

"You should practice what you preach, old man." Tina winked at him. As much as she joked about it, she was as worried about her father being alone as much as he was worried about her. Neither of them had a thriving social life, but they had friends. Being single in a small town presented challenges people from the city didn't understand. If you weren't related to half the town, then you grew up with them and already knew them far too well to ever consider dating them.

The only reason Trey was in the picture was because he was the engineer on a job they had done in another town. The clients wanted a tornado shelter dug into their foundation in the garage and Tina contacted his agency. It was all good at first, but they were both so involved with their jobs that an actual relationship was too much trouble. Trey was cute and scratched an itch, but that was about it.

Once the kitchen was clean and her father was properly settled back with a beer and his remote, she retreated upstairs. Her apartment was the entire second floor of the warehouse. Brick walls and support columns, fifteen-foot ceilings, old wood floors complete with all the scars and marks from the cannery, large arched windows, and thirty-five hundred square feet of space all hers. She loved the industrial feel, the way the ducts and pipes ran along the ceiling, the way the length of the building faced the river, affording her one of the best views in town.

Tina fixed herself a glass of iced tea and went out to the balcony to watch the boats go by.

I saw the way Bo looked at you today...

Yeah, she'd caught that too. He'd wavered all day between fear and awe. More than once, she'd caught him staring as if he couldn't tear his eyes away from her. Bo would blink, blush, and turn elsewhere.

The problem was, she was just as dumbstruck by him. Bo Galloway was flaming, smoking, fan-yourself-and-clench-your-thighs hot. He was at least six feet of toned muscle, tattoos, and deeply soulful hazel eyes. Prying her attention from his full bottom lip was harder than she thought possible. Usually, she liked her men to have longer hair, but his dark brown buzz cut fit him just fine. So did his slightly shadowed jaw.

It was all she could do to act normal. The truth was, her sweat hadn't been just from the work site. He'd worn cologne to the interview and she could smell it as he heated up throughout the day. It tickled her senses, made her dizzy. Not to mention that quiet, respectful tone of voice he used with her. The rich, husky texture slid over her like a caress, lighting her up in dark places.

He was brand new to her work crew and yet today he'd been a valuable set of hands. If everything worked out with him, he might help them finish this house under budget. It was a lot cheaper hiring one man for two weeks than to have her entire crew out there for a couple extra days.

Too bad he was such a sexy distraction. Twice she'd lost her train of thought and had to go back inside to re-measure for a cut. One look at Bo lifting dry wall over his head, flexing his bulging arm muscles, stretching out his defined back, and she was like a drooling teenager.

She didn't need this right now. Or ever. Men like Bo didn't stick around and she was dealing with a disastrous dating life as it was. Somewhere along the way, her brain had begun to function more like all the men she was surrounded by. She had a one-track mind; single in focus and hard to derail. She'd given up trying to be overly feminine with makeup and an actual hairstyle, at least from Monday to Friday.

Even her current love interest was more high maintenance than she was. Trey was fond of his expensive suits and his office job. He drove a nice car, styled his dark hair, and his face could stop traffic...except for when it came to her. There was something about him that she couldn't name. Something that made her keep him at arm's length, even though they'd been together for months.

The bigger problem was, as she drifted to sleep, it wasn't Trey on her mind. It was Bo.

Chapter Two

The next morning, Daddy suggested Tina show Bo around the various houses they were working on. At any given time, Foster Construction had six to ten projects going. Some were in the beginning stage with framing, and some were in the finishing-out stage with only paint and molding left.

"I've already called him and told him to come to the office instead of the site he worked yesterday." Daddy sipped his steaming cup of coffee.

"Why would you do that? He did good yesterday on that crew; they're the ones who need an extra hand when I'm not there—like today."

Daddy squinted through his readers at the laptop screen. "Do you know how to tweet? The lady at the inspector's office said I should try to tweet. I can't find it on the Google."

Tina slapped a hand over her face. "Jesus, Daddy,

really? You? On social media?"

"She said it was easier than that face-look thing you like." He pecked at the keys.

"Daddy, focus." Tina checked her watch and stopped her foot from tapping.

"What did you ask me? Oh, yeah, Bo. You don't know what his strengths are. He might be good on Terry's crew, but he might be great on Gary's crew."

She rubbed the bridge of her nose. "Gary's crew doesn't need help."

"Gary wants me to fire his assistant painter too. Guy does sloppy work and it's getting worse. He sent pictures; it's bad. Gary has to clean up after him, he left boot prints on the slab—"

Tina threw her hands up. "I'll give him the grand tour and check on Gary's crew in the process." She checked her watch again, wondering when Bo would arrive. It was still ten minutes until six.

Having him in the truck with her all day made the dream she had last night a bit too prophetic. Her heart had been racing when she'd woken up. Was she seriously nervous about riding around alone with him? Why would she be? This guy was nothing, no one to her, just another guy who might or might not make it with her company. Who was to say he wouldn't be gone in a day or a week? Their company had tripled its customers and crewmen in the last year. They'd lost count of the guys they'd hired and fired for one reason or another. Bo could end up being another waste of time. Until a man proved himself in the field, Tina didn't hold her breath.

However, Bo was the first guy in months who made her stutter and forget what she was supposed to be doing.

Sex was very low on her list of priorities, but yesterday she'd thought of it every time Bo caught her eye. Even now, heat pooled in her belly.

It was going to be a long day.

Her cell phone rang with an incoming video call. Tina melted at the sweet, chubby baby face and walked down the hall from her father's office. "Is that my little Noah-bear?" Her voice pitched up an octave and she gave an exaggerated smile.

Megan, one of her dear friends from high school, held her baby in her lap and made his arm wave. "Say hi to Aunt Tina."

Noah gave a grin and she could count all his teeth on three fingers. He mumbled something unintelligible and tried to grab the phone from Megan's outstretched arm.

This was a phone call they made every week and Tina loved it. She missed Megan terribly. "Tell her, baby. Tell Mama you want to come see Aunt T. I can teach you to play with nail guns and chainsaws." Noah giggled, drool dripped onto Meg's arm, and she wiped it away without even thinking about it. Tina laughed. Man, Megan had made a cute kid. His bright blue eyes shined like the summer sky and it touched her heart. "Did he get my care package?"

Megan laughed and rolled her brown eyes. She held up the plastic hammer and screwdriver. "We did. He loves to eat them. But it's helping with the teething, so I'm not complaining." She pulled her red hair out of his fingers and held up the toys to get his attention.

Sure enough, Noah grabbed the bright yellow and red plastic screwdriver and stuck it into his mouth.

"Funny, that's what I do with mine too." Tina and Megan laughed, which made Noah laugh.

"Tina's so silly." Megan kissed his forehead and moved the phone again so he wouldn't whack it with the toy.

Tina giggled. "That kid is just like you, can't sit still. He's like a little worm."

"No kidding." Megan sighed. "So, how's it going down there?" Meg had moved a few years ago and married Noah's father, Cole, who most of their friends despised because he treated her like total crap.

"Totally great. Business is booming. We just hired someone else yesterday and Dad finally brought the book-keeper on full time to help him in the office. He knows just enough about computers to be dangerous." Tina crinkled her lip. Megan knew all about her father.

"I heard that!" Daddy hollered from down the hall, making the girls laugh.

"He's trying, T, give him credit." Meg pushed her hair back behind her ears. "Have you heard from Lynette? What country is she in this week?"

"Australia. She's studying law there too. She wants a degree in Homeland Security. Who comes up with that shit? What kind of job do you get with that?"

Meg threw back her head and sighed. "That's our girl. She's never thought small, has she?"

"No, but I wish she'd think about the continental United States at least. Jayden hates her being gone; you know how close she is to her cousin."

Megan swallowed hard and set Noah down on the floor beside her. She leaned in close to the phone screen. "How is she?"

Tina let out a breath and bit her bottom lip. "She's okay, most days. She still hasn't really grieved, but her mother is determined to make this some sort of public relations bullshit. The two-year anniversary is coming up and Keri and I are arguing over how to handle it."

"Let me guess, Jayden has to remain *Miller-perfect* at all times?" Meg shook her head, her face frowning.

"Oh yeah. I'd give anything for her temper to overflow the dam and let her get it all out, you know? She's working at the clothing store with her neurotic mess of a mother."

About then, Noah yelled out and Meg turned to check on him. "What's wrong, sweetie? Did you drop your toy?" She faced the screen again.

"Your hair is getting so long." Tina grinned, knowing that Cole hated it. "It's like a flaming beacon of rebellion."

Meg wiggled her brows and suppressed a smile. "It sure is." There was a hint of defiance in her voice that made Tina proud. She turned her head to something in the background and frowned. "Cole just drove up, better go. It's good to see you, T. I love you and miss you. Can I call when he leaves again and we can talk more about Jay?"

"Any time, you know that. I miss you too. Love you and my Noah-bear to pieces. I need to see him again before he turns into a freaking toddler. He's growing so fast."

Meg picked up the baby and Noah focused in on Tina. "Say bye to Aunt Tina."

"Bye-bye." Tina waved at the screen and grinned widely and talked to him in that silly voice everyone used with babies. "I love you, love you, sweet boy. Yes, I do." She blew him kisses. "Take care of Mama for me. Bye-bye, baby."

After she hung up, her heart hurt. Meg was halfway across the country in Boston with that stupid husband of hers. Tina and Jayden had both flown out there when Noah was born to help out, but that was the last time they'd been face-to-face. The distance hadn't lessened their contact or their love as friends, but Tina still rubbed her chest where her heart ached to be closer to Noah. She didn't have siblings and that baby was as close to a nephew as she was going to get. Naturally, she wanted to spoil him, even from afar.

"T?"

She swung around to see Bo standing in the hallway, holding his baseball cap and curling the brim. "Hey." Tina blinked back the emotion and put on her professional face.

His body angled back towards the office and he pointed with his thumb. "I can wait in—"

"Nope. We need to get going." She bustled past him and grabbed her keys.

"Yes, ma'am." Bo was hot on her heels as she grabbed her clipboard of current jobs and notes and headed for her truck.

Being alone in the truck with Bo might not be the best idea. "Dixie, come." Tina whistled for the dog and she came running, her bushy tail wagging with excitement. Even though her truck had a back seat, Dixie would make a good buffer up front. Dixie ran to the door and sat, waiting for Tina to invite her into the truck. Tina opened the door of the truck and snapped her fingers. "Up."

"Someone's worked with her." Bo slid into the truck and buckled his belt. "That's a good dog."

"That would be me." Tina ignored the way the texture of his voice reminded her of leather—thick and rough, like he didn't use it enough to warm up his vocal cords.

She took a call from one of her electricians who needed the status of permits, then had to call Daddy to transfer the message. Tina had a love-hate relationship with her cell phone. It rang all day—sometimes customers, sometimes family, sometimes friends. But that damn thing rang all day.

"I shoulda figured you were one of them." His tone hinted of either admiration or sarcasm, but she didn't know him well enough to judge.

"What does that mean?" It might've been petty to get defensive, but it was too late now.

Bo flicked his finger at the picture Tina kept in her truck. It was from her junior year of high school featuring her drill team. That year, the team took the State Championship in cheerleading and dance, then made runner-up in their division at Nationals. That championship, ten years ago, solidified Tina's relationships with most of her friends, including Meg. But it didn't solidify the meaning of Bo's comment.

"You were one of the girls who went to Nationals."

Tina scowled. "How do you know what that's from?" She backed out of the lot and headed down the road that ran perpendicular to the river.

"The year before that, I was second string kicker on the varsity football team. We used to talk about how the girls on the drill team were—"

"Drones who shared the same brain," Tina smarted. "Yeah, I remember that well."

Bo threw up his hands and grinned. "Easy, easy. It wasn't supposed to be an insult."

Just because she felt bratty, Tina lifted her chin. "I guess you didn't make an impression, because I don't remember you."

Bo turned his face to the window, his shoulders dropping slightly. "I tried not to make impressions."

Now she just felt like an ass. Thankfully, she had to take another phone call.

"I guess you know Bear and Marshall, huh?" Tina tried to make conversation, but she wasn't always good at it.

"Oh yeah, Bear was a beast even as a kid and Marshall Miller was a legend." Bo let out a huff. "I read he was headed to the pros."

Tina turned onto the bridge that connected one side of Riverview to the other. "Marsh played four years of college ball, had sponsors lined up, and was headed to the combine for scouting. Then he had that horse accident and," she shook her head, "well, you know. It messed him up."

"What happened?"

She saw him staring in her periphery but didn't look directly at him. Her cheeks heated under his gaze. The spice of his cologne made it hard to concentrate on anything but how warm and delicious he smelled. She'd caught the scent yesterday, and wouldn't you know, it was part of her dream last night. If only she could hold her breath. "He came home for Jayden's wedding and decided to impress his wife while they were out for a ride. Horse tripped and rolled, crushed his right leg from the knee down. Doctors said the bones looked like a shattered window."

Bo made a clicking sound and shook his head. "Tough break. He was good."

"So you went to Riverview, but did you graduate from here?"

"No, ma'am, I was only here for a few years. My family moved here when I was in grade school, then I moved to California after my junior year. I was gone by the time this happened." He pointed to the picture of the girls holding their trophies.

How could she not remember him? If he was on the football team, she had to have seen him at games. Then again, that was a decade ago and this was no high school boy sitting beside her. This was a full grown, buff and brawny man with a deep voice that made her toes curl. *Not good.*

She racked her brain trying to remember the guys on the football team. "Crazy, I don't remember you. Riverview High School wasn't that big. It's almost embarrassing."

"Don't worry, I don't remember you either."

"That actually does make me feel better." She chuckled and shook her head. He didn't laugh, only nodded.

He put his arm over the back of the seat and rested his hand on Dixie's head, giving her a good scratch behind the ears. Tina took another phone call from her concrete contractor wanting to know when she could go by and approve the slabs they'd poured so the lender would release funds.

Bo pointed, ever so casually, at the cute little white farmhouse on the right side of the road. It was surrounded by patches of gardens and fields of vegetables. "That's my grandmother's house."

"I've talked to Nancy in passing several times at the farmer's market. She seems very sweet and I could eat her tomatoes like apples."

"She is sweet, unless you eat her tomatoes right off the vine. Then, not so sweet." Bo grinned, but not at her, at a memory. His face turned to the window as they passed by his house. When he met her gaze, the affection softened his hard face, making him even more attractive.

God and hormones, have mercy on me.

Her nerves were shot by the time they arrived at their first job. As she exited her truck, she took a deep pull of air that wasn't spiked with his delicious scent. "Dixie, come."

She had to get her head in the game. This was her

inspection day, she had things to do, important things, things that didn't involve getting hot and heavy with Bo in a truck. Tina grit her teeth and flipped the switch in her brain. There was no room for errors or distractions on the job site. If this continued, she would have no choice but to get rid of the distraction.

"Do you paint?" she asked Bo as they approached the nearly completed house.

"Yes, ma'am."

"Cut-ins and trim work?"

"Yes, ma'am."

"Good. Pay attention to the trim-out guy's work." They opened the front door and the chemical scent of freshly spread paint hit her nose. It was one smell she didn't mind. Everything looked better with a fresh coat of paint—even people. It hid so much.

A short guy with glasses came up to Tina. "Hey, T. She's really coming along." He turned his eyes to Bo and they widened a fraction. "Man, did ya hire a bodyguard or what?"

Tina played along with Gary, who had worked for her father for nearly eight years. "Someone has to protect me from all the men I piss off every day."

Gary pushed his glasses up and gave a toothy grin. "What happens when you piss him off? 'Cause it's bound to happen."

Tina examined Bo, dramatically rubbing her chin and squinting her eyes. "I bet I have a nail gun that will fix him right up."

Gary clapped his hands together and laughed. "Take pictures this time."

"I quit." Bo held up his hands and the faintest smile

pulled his lips back. He shook hands with Gary and they joked a bit more about Tina's obsession with nail guns.

She, on the other hand, turned her attention to the work being done before she could get caught up on Bo's lips.

Their trim-out guy was on a ladder in a bathroom, painting crown molding bright white. He had painter's tape across the wall and the ceiling, something she didn't like. The ninety-degree corner cuts looked like hammered horse crap and one of the trim boards had a gap between it and the ceiling where it needed another nail.

How many times do we have to go over this? She could think of two times right off the top of her head.

"Rodman?"

"Whatd'ya want, boss lady?"

"How many times have I personally showed you how to cut corner molds?"

"I don't know, why?" He shrugged, turning on the ladder to look at her. Paint dripped off his brush and onto the concrete floor. Not a big deal, if it wasn't supposed to be stained. Rodman didn't even acknowledge the splatter. Sure, her concrete guys would clean it up when they prepared the floor for staining, but it showed a poor level of workmanship on his part. His familial ties with Trey were the only reason he was even here and, at this point, even that wasn't working in his favor.

"Duane has your quarterly review in his office. Go see him before five." She would just have to deal with the drama when Trey found out.

He nodded and went right back to work, clearly too stupid to realize he was getting canned. Tina moved on to the next bedroom where two of her other painters were finishing up the walls in a soft gray.

Luke and John had the radio playing classical music as they worked. They both seemed off in their own minds most of the time, rarely talking to each other while painting.

"Look who's here to break our silence." John's chubby cheeks balled up as he greeted her with a smile. "How are you today, General?"

"I'm good. How are my two favorite prophets?"

"Good." Luke gave her a high five. He, too, was a heavier set man with a beer gut. "This color is great. It spreads nice."

"It's perfect." Tina glanced around the room, envisioning the final product with carpet and white trim. She'd already picked out charming light fixtures to top it off.

"This house will be ready for Keri to list pretty dang fast...if we don't have to clean up after shit-for-brains in there." Luke winked at her.

"Yeah, about that. It's handled. I found a trim-out guy for y'all to try out." She turned her head to see Bo examining the work Rodman was doing in the bathroom.

Hopefully, *he* didn't lie on his resume.

Chapter Three

B O CLIMBED UP IN THE TRUCK, KNOWING JUST WHAT Tina was thinking. "You want me to replace him?"

She backed her truck out onto the street and didn't look at him. "If you can."

If he *could?* Of course he could. Painting a house required attention to detail and a master's degree in common sense, both of which he had. Was she trying to test him? Trying to see what he was capable of or willing to do? "I can."

"We'll see what your strengths are." She casually shrugged a shoulder, as if she didn't believe him.

"Hmm." He scratched on Dixie, who laid her head in his lap and gave him the most pathetic puppy eyes. "You're a sad one."

"Isn't she?" Tina patted her twice on the rear. "Daddy has her so spoiled. She thinks every time you open the car door, she should go."

"I'm sure your father isn't the only one who gives her that impression." He didn't smile, but she caught his teasing.

"Watch it." Tina gave him a side-grin and then answered her ever-ringing cell phone.

Her phone was turned up loud enough he could hear every word from every conversation coming over the line.

"Hey, sweetie," said a male's voice who was not her father. "Are you free tonight?"

"I have some paperwork to do, but it won't take long."

"Do you want to go see that new assassin movie?"

Tina groaned. "I have no desire to see that movie."

"Oh…well…I really want to go."

Bo didn't have to know this guy to hear the whining in his voice and the uncaring distance in hers. Why in the world would she even give this guy the time of day? The pieces didn't fit in his head.

"I know you do, but it looks like every other action movie out there."

"Well, the guys from work are going—"

"Then go with your friends, Trey. I don't have to go." She stopped at a crossroads and picked up her clipboard, checking off the address of their next destination.

"You won't be offended if I go without you?"

"I would have to care to be offended and I don't." She laid the clipboard down and put on her blinker, completely blowing off the guy. "Go, have fun."

"Well, I guess I'm going with them, if that's okay with you, sweetie."

There was no warmth in her voice and very little inflection to indicate that she was emotionally connected. "Yeah, okay. I'm about to pull up to a job."

"I'll call you later, sweetie. Bye, T."

"Later." She clicked off her phone and turned up the radio, unconcerned with her phone call, and focused on the road.

Bo tucked that conversation into his memory bank. He couldn't imagine a woman as rough and tough as Tina Foster would appreciate being called *sweetie*. Not to mention that she completely lied to get off the phone with him.

"How many jobs do you have going?" Bo asked, knowing she would talk about work.

"Right now, we have the two-story that you met Terry at yesterday, we have that house." She pointed over her shoulder at the place they just left. "We have a renovation that's in the rewiring stage, an older, pier-and-beam house downtown that is currently getting re-leveled before we start renovating, and we recently started pouring the foundations in a subdivision out by the high school. We have five houses in there."

"Cool. Where do you want me?"

Tina froze for a split second and then cleared her throat. "I, um, think taking over for Rodman. Unless you happen to be a licensed electrician?"

"No, ma'am."

"Painting it is. Usually, I float around and fill in wherever I'm needed."

"You could've left me there with them." He indicated the house with his thumb.

"Dad has to fire Rodman first. But I bet tomorrow you'll be sent there." She passed a slow- moving sedan, careful not to linger too long in the other lane.

"You say that like it's no big deal."

"What?"

"Firing someone."

"He's an idiot."

"Does he deserve it?"

Tina glanced over at him. "Do you have a problem with how I run my company?"

Her hard tone took him by surprise. Jail, however, had perfected his poker face. "No, ma'am. Not my place."

"You're right, it's not." She took a deep breath and turned left onto an old dirt road. "Rodman *has* earned his pink slip, just so you know. He lied on his resume, which pisses me off. The only reason he even got hired was because he's Trey's cousin or nephew or something like that." She waved off the connection as unimportant.

"The guy who just called?" Bo tried to hide his amusement for how easily she dismissed the guy. Poor fool.

"Yeah, him. Anyway, Rodman said he had done trim and molding work, and he hadn't. Dad taught him, Terry showed him, and I know Gary has been on his ass for months. He's lucky I leave the HR crap to Dad or I would've chewed him a new one for dropping paint on my concrete floors."

"I'm not questioning your decision." Bo didn't like where this was heading. He needed this job and pissing off a woman with power and power tools was a horrible idea.

"Then what *are* you questioning?" She narrowed her eyes at him and his body stirred at her challenge. Tina's temper was just about as sexy as it got.

"Not a damn thing."

He refrained from asking too many questions for the rest of the morning. They went to various jobs and Tina showed him their current projects. She took phone call after phone call, put out fires, answered questions, calmed homeowners, and lit a fire under lenders to release funds. It was a pleasure to watch her work and listen as her brilliant mind negotiated and dealt her cards like a seasoned pro. Tina knew how to flirt, how to intimidate, and every tactic in between.

Bo slowly learned the various tones of her voice. She was clipped and direct with some people, like her contractors. With others, like her father or crewmen, she was a little more talkative and more prone to joke around. When one of her real friends called, her voice held affection that was undeniable.

"Yes, Keri, bring her over. I don't mind babysitting. What the hell else do I have to do? Besides, Misty loves me. We go on walks and play in shaving cream. It gives me an excuse to binge watch cartoons and eat cereal in bed. I love it." Warmth seeped from her words as she assured her friend that she was happy to babysit.

This was the tone Bo wanted her to have with him… eventually.

To his surprise, when she hung up, she offered personal information about the kid she was babysitting.

"It's Marshall and Keri Miller's daughter, Misty. Oh, she's so adorable. She and Noah are the same age; she's about to be two. Keri always feels bad asking me to give up my time, but it's fun. She's really getting around good now and I like seeing how fast she's growing. I'd love to get Misty and Noah together. They'd have a ball."

"That's the boy you were talking to earlier?"

Tina's affections were written all over her face. "Yes, that's my sweet boy."

"Kids are cute at that age. They go from being crying blobs to real little people." When he lived in California, the couple next door had two children who loved to watch him practice his martial arts. It still warmed his heart to think of the toddler imitating his kicks and falling over.

"Exactly," Tina said, narrowing her eyes. She acted surprised that he understood what she meant, but he did.

That afternoon, they went back to the ranch house and helped Terry's crew with drywall again. They were behind on installation and the tape and texture guys were riding their heels. As much as Tina Foster mastered her phone calls, she mastered her work more. Bo respected the fact that she didn't mind getting her hands dirty.

At five o'clock, Bo washed the sheetrock dust off his hands and gathered up the tools to place them back in the tool boxes. Terry and Tina were in the upstairs hallway talking.

"So is Bo going to stay on with our crew?" Terry asked. "He's quick. I like him."

"No. He's going to take Rodman's place."

"Your boyfriend isn't going to like that."

"My *boyfriend* doesn't run this company."

"We sure need an extra set of hands, Tina."

"I'll work with y'all. I can't do trim work worth shit."

"*Humph.* Fine, but I hope you change your mind. Since Brad left, we've been behind and I know you've got better things to do on this project than hang rock."

"The painters will be done with that house next week and then we'll see. Until then, he goes with them." Footsteps pounded the stairs as Tina and Terry came down. Bo slipped back into the other room until they were outside.

It was nice to know at least Terry liked him so far. Usually, one guy's opinion wouldn't matter, but this was Tina's uncle. Terry worked harder than guys half his age and knew what he was doing. Bo held the compliment in high regard. If only Tina wasn't so determined to put him in a corner.

Dixie came out of the hall and he knelt to pay her attention. "Your mama is a pistol, girl. It's a good thing I know how to handle a pistol, huh? You going to help me?" He scratched behind her ears and under her chin. Dixie licked his arm, then held up her paw to shake. "Deal."

"You making deals with my dog, Bo?" Tina stood behind him, arms crossed over her chest. "She doesn't sign your paychecks."

"Nope, but she does kiss me."

She rolled her eyes and pressed her lips into thin lines to suppress a smile. "Go home, Bo."

"I can't." When she looked at him with a puzzled tilt of her head, he said, "My truck is at your office."

She slapped a hand over her forehead. "Duh. Come on. Come, Dixie."

He stood up and mirrored her stance, crossing his arms over his chest. "I'm going to pretend you didn't just give me and the dog the same command."

Tina's brow quirked up. "And look at who is actually obeying." Dixie took off out of the house. She looked him down and up again. "Hmm." Then turned her fine ass around and went to the truck.

Oh yes, she was a pistol all right. And he knew all too well how to handle a loaded gun.

Tina waved as Bo drove off in the old red and white pickup. As soon as she entered the office, she leaned against the door and let her head fall backwards. What the hell was she thinking, flirting with him, goading him on, and pushing him like that? She'd intentionally put more swing in her hips as she walked away from him. Then she'd put the dog in the backseat just to see if he would stretch his arm over the front bench seat like he'd done earlier. Why? Why would she even go there? It wasn't worth the risk and, for all intents and purposes, she had a boyfriend...of sorts.

"I need a drink," she mumbled as she took her ringing phone from her back pocket. "Hey."

"Hey, girl," Jay said. "I rented a movie; you want to come hang? I want to talk to you and Keri about some stuff too."

Jayden didn't invite people over often. With the two-year anniversary of her husband's death closing in, Tina wasn't going to deny one of her best friends the support she needed.

"Yeah, I just got home, so let me get clean and comfy and I'll be over."

"No rush." Jayden usually said that when she was cooking something. *Mmmm.* Tina's stomach growled with anticipation.

Daddy was already in his apartment, kicked back with a beer. "Hey, kiddo."

"Hey, Daddy. I'm going to head to Jay's for a while."

"Okay. Did you pass Rodman on your way in?"

"No, why?"

"Good. Jerk kid. I figured he would have something to say to you. God knows he had plenty to say to me when I fired him. I'm afraid you're going to hear all about it from Trey."

"I don't care." Tina waved it off. Trey didn't dictate her business decisions. The one time she let him, she ended up with Rodman, for Christ sake.

Later, Tina hopped out of her truck with Dixie in tow

and she could smell the sweet scent of baked goods. Jayden's house was one of her favorites. It was the old Harris homestead, a three-story farmhouse. Built in the early 1900s, it had seen better days, but Jayden was a talented interior decorator and had it accessorized beautifully. The home was a gift from Christopher's parents on their wedding day. As the first son to get married, it was a big deal. Upon his death, Jayden had insisted the home go back to the family. She was willing to move back in with her parents or find an apartment in town, but the Harris family had hearts the size of Texas. They said that the home belonged to her and that Chris would be royally pissed if it was taken away.

Keri's Mercedes was parked in the driveway. Selling real estate and taking the Miller name by marrying Jayden's brother had been good to the Hispanic girl from the wrong side of town. Everything a *Miller* touched turned to gold. That name, paired with her vivacious personality, had helped Keri become one of the top sellers in the county. She had opened her own brokerage agency after working for a local chain. She boasted of being a hometown girl and people seemed to like the fact that a girl from the poorest neighborhood in Riverview had risen to the top.

Jayden and Tina didn't care about where she came from or where she was going. They loved her because she was a loyal and loving friend who would go to the ends of the earth for them.

Tina didn't knock, knowing the door was always open to her. She waltzed into Jayden's kitchen and found the sisters-in-law with their heads over a pot on the stove.

"It needs more pepper," Keri insisted, grabbing for the spice.

"No, I'm not trying to make it burn your internal

organs." Jayden closed the lid before Keri could add more pepper. "Get, get." She shooed Keri away.

"You two are always fighting about something." Tina hugged them both and hopped up on a bar stool. They exchanged the usual small talk—who said what, who did what, the latest family drama, etc.—while Jayden prepared what looked and smelled like gumbo.

Tina set out bowls on the table and filled glasses with sweet tea. Once the three of them were seated and gumbo dispensed, Tina couldn't hold her tongue. "So, are you going to keep talking about your college classes all night or are you going to tell us what's going on? You don't make gumbo on a whim."

Keri twirled her spoon in the air in Tina's direction without lifting her gaze from her bowl. "What she said."

Jayden held up her hands. "First, I want to know who that hunky guy was in your truck today, Tina Marie."

Keri leaned back in her seat, giving Tina a mother's glare. "Hunky guy? Yes, let's hear about the hunk."

Tina waved them off, praying they didn't chase that bone. Jayden and Keri were two people impossible to keep secrets from. They had the ability to gang up on her and get all the information they wanted. "He's just a crewman. Daddy made me show him the current projects. No big deal."

"If you say it's not a big deal, it totally is." Jayden grinned and wiggled her brows. "He's hot."

"How do you even know?" Tina glared at her.

"I was on my way to Mama's when I passed you. You were smiling at him." She was a hound with a scent now. *Crap.*

Tina shrugged and pushed the gumbo around her

bowl. "I was being friendly."

"Lie to someone else, *chica*," Keri said. "You're blushing. Spill."

Tina leaned back and put her spoon down. "Okay." She scrubbed a hand down her face. "His name is Bo, he used to go to Riverview a long time ago, but I don't remember him. Daddy hired him as a favor to Nancy, the produce lady. Yes, he's so damn hot I can't stand it…and he smells good. God, he smells good." She waved off the thought before she dove head-first down that rabbit hole. "That's neither here nor there. He's a distraction I can't afford right now. I've put him to work on a crew I don't have to oversee for a while and, no, I don't want to talk about it anymore."

"You want to talk about it," Jayden deadpanned. "You want to talk about how hot he is."

"No, I don't."

"I remember him." Keri nodded. "Bo Galloway. He was kicker on the football team, his mom was a druggie, they moved in with Nancy, and his mom spent all Nancy's money. But he was a stringy kid, lanky and awkward." She turned up her nose.

"He's not now," Tina mumbled, her thoughts slipping right out of her mouth.

"Ah-ha!" Jayden slapped the table, excited to be hot on the trail, getting Dixie's attention. "You like him."

Tina nearly spit out her drink of tea. "No, no, no. Don't go starting crap. Thinking someone is hot is a lot different than *liking* him. I don't know him. My eyes like him, that's all. The end."

Her dog had come to the table, which was a no-no. Tina snapped her fingers and told her to go lie down. If only people minded as well as Dixie. She'd like to tell Jayden to sit and stay…far away from this subject.

"But you're attracted to him, I can tell." Jayden was too excited about this and there was no denying the heat that crept up Tina's face.

She sighed and turned her eyes to the ceiling. "Fine, Jay, if it makes you feel better, yes, I'm attracted to him. He's hot and he makes me tingle." She said it all sarcastically, trying to downplay the truth. "Here's the problem, I don't need a man putting those thoughts in my head. I have a boyfriend and I have to concentrate on work."

"What thoughts?" Keri asked. Tina shook her head and Keri put her hands together to beg. "Please, humor me. I have a toddler and an eighty-hour work-week. My sex-life is almost non-existent."

The girls laughed and Tina cringed.

"Don't make fun of me." Tina swallowed hard and resigned herself to confess. "I think I've been hanging around construction workers too long. We were talking about the various crews and he asked where I needed him."

"Oh, open that door, son." Jayden smirked and arched a brow.

"And all I could think was, right between my legs, baby." Tina laughed right along with her friends.

"Yeah, that was a very testosterone-induced response." Jayden couldn't stop giggling. "You're such a dude."

Tina hung her head. "Right? Gosh, I need to work with women again. These guys are getting to me."

"What about Trey?" Keri asked.

"What about him?" Tina filled her mouth with sausage and shrimp, hopefully giving her a moment to get over the embarrassment.

"Is that the kind of response you give to him?"

"Hell, no. Trey is…Trey…" What was she trying to say? "Trey is a sweet guy. He's not…"

"Erotic."

"Sexy."

"Adventurous."

"Exciting."

The two of them volleyed back and forth until Tina spoke up. "He's *nice*, okay. Trey is a nice guy."

"And let me guess," Keri raised a brow, "the sex is *nice*." Her tone and downturned lips made that sentence more of an insult than a compliment.

Tina sighed. "Yeah. Not that it happens often."

"Welcome to the club." Keri took a drink.

Jayden tapped her spoon on her lips. "But you and Trey have only been together for a few months. You should still be in the new, exciting, all-consuming stage, not the old married couple stage. That just makes me sad for you, T."

"I don't have time for all-consuming anything." She pushed her chair back and rose to take her dishes to the sink. "Trey is easy. Bo is—"

"Hard?" Keri said, lifting a brow. She and Jayden cackled like hens. Tina rolled her eyes but had to laugh at their antics. Her friends were insane and she loved every bit of it.

"Okay, you've had your jokes." She speared Jayden with a glare. "Your turn."

Jayden straightened in her chair and pushed her empty bowl back. "I know what I'm going to do for the anniversary."

Tina sat back down at the table and glanced at Keri.

"I talked to Peggy and Bruce, I've talked to Bear and he talked to the other boys, and we all agree." Jayden took a deep breath.

"Balloons or Vegas?" Tina asked.

"Neither." Jayden intertwined her hands on the table. "Christopher was an advocate of being financially responsible and he was very smart with his investments. I want to do the same."

"Then why are you as nervous as a cat in a room full of rocking chairs?"

"Because I'm afraid you're going to lose your mind when I tell you...I want to fix up the house."

Tina froze. "This house?" She was still as death, hoping and praying that Jayden would turn her loose on these four walls. She'd dreamt of restoring this house for years. When she was a child, the older generation of the Harris family lived here and were beloved in the community. These four walls were a piece of history, a foundation of Riverview. To put her own fingerprint on such a treasure made her giddy. Christopher had hinted around about it for months, but they had needed to get their finances together. Then he passed and the option was taken off the table because Jayden sure enough didn't have that kind of money to sink into it.

Jayden nodded. "Chris would want you to work on it."

Tina came out of her skin. Finally, she could make the Harris homestead shine. She jumped up and threw her arms around Jayden's neck. "Oh my God! Jayden! I'm so excited. Holy crap." Joyful tears misted over her eyes. "Are you kidding me?"

"I can't breathe, honey." Jayden chuckled and Tina let her go. "It's for real. Chris wouldn't want it any other way. He loved you and Duane."

"But how can you afford it?" Keri asked, ever the responsible one.

"That's what else I wanted to talk about." She took a deep breath and Tina sat back down, her blood humming in her veins. "This stays between us, okay?"

Tina and Keri agreed.

"The Harris family has a trust set up. Technically, this house and all the land belongs to the family trust. Each of the boys, Bear, Chris, Sean, and Donnie, have interests in the trust and they can assign those interests. The Harrises contacted me to let me know that Christopher had an agreement with them that should anything ever happen to him, I would be assigned a certain amount of the money in the trust."

"What are we talking?" Keri dusted crumbs off the table. "A few thousand dollars?" Her tone was speculative.

Jayden swallowed and her eyes darted between the two of them. "Try a few million."

Keri said some blue words in Spanish that Tina echoed in English.

"How the hell?" Tina grabbed at her chest. She couldn't imagine the weight of such a sum of money.

Jayden spread her palms out over the table. "I mean it when I say no one can know. You know how people are and the Harris family had strict instructions."

"Every free-loader in the county will be on your doorstop asking for handouts." Keri rolled her eyes. "Half of them will be my family claiming to be yours." It was already a burden the Millers had to bear. Jayden carried double weight, being born a Miller and married to a Harris. With excessive money came people who felt entitled to it or challenged to steal it.

"And every single bachelor in the county will show up on your door with a wedding ring." Tina nodded, understanding the predicament. Jayden just became a very wealthy widow at a young age. Not to mention, she was the bridge that linked two of the wealthiest families in Texas.

"Bruce and Peggy were aware of Christopher's wishes from the beginning. They said Chris applied the delay because of grieving time." Jayden's lips pulled back into a smile, her eyes filled with moisture. "Even in death, he's taking care of me."

"They're willingly giving you the money?" Tina asked, loving Bruce and Peggy Harris more and more every day.

Jayden nodded. "They want me to fix the house."

Tina grasped at her chest, overwhelmed by the loyalty of Chris's family towards his widow. "Jayden, that's incredible."

"That's not even the best part. The lady who owns the clothing boutique is retiring. She doesn't want the store. Bruce and Peggy want me to buy her out. She rents the space from my parents, so it's not like I would have to move the store. It could be mine." Jayden's unsure smile gleamed. "I think I can do it."

"Of course you can." Tina reached out to touch her arm. "This is your dream, girl. Take it."

Jayden had wanted to own her own boutique since high school. She had worked retail at various places and had planned to open her own shop one day. Now Chris had given her one more gift—the ability to achieve her dreams.

They spent the evening brainstorming about the house restoration, the clothing store, investments, and business. They joked about burying the money in the back yard or moving off to some island and living their life on the beach. It reminded her of the slumber parties they had every weekend as teenagers. Finally, it felt like a ray of sunshine had poked its head through the clouds. Jayden smiled and gave voice to all the dreams she'd had about owning her own clothing store. It gave Tina a sense of hope. If Jayden could overcome her pain, anything was possible.

Since the three of them were all in the same room, they called Meg and talked to her for a while, told her about fixing up the house, and made silly faces at Noah. They tried calling Lynette, Jayden's cousin, who had moved to Australia to study abroad, but she didn't answer and they left her a long message. Holly, the youngest of their group of besties, lived upriver and didn't answer either.

"I'm going to show up on Holly's doorstep and drag her ass back to Riverview." Tina flopped down on the couch as Jayden started the movie.

"She's got to come home. Seriously. Now she's just avoiding us." Keri brought over a bag of popcorn and a package of candy.

"We need to get in the car and go up there one weekend. Just show up and kidnap her."

"I'm in." Tina raised her hand. Holly had her reasons for leaving Riverview after the death of one of their friends, but tonight had made it clear that their group of friends was healing and Holly needed to be a part of that.

Tina grabbed a pillow and settled in to the couch with the girls to watch their movie. They talked through most of it, but at least Jayden had pushed play.

Chapter Four

Two weeks later, Tina couldn't avoid Bo any longer. It had been easy, sending him to Gary's painting crew, giving her time to build up the defenses needed to be around him. She worked with Terry on the other house, didn't have to see Bo much, and only had to hear about what a great job he was doing.

Three days in, Tina had gone over to check his work after hours. The clean lines and smoothness of his work impressed her.

But the paint job for that house was completed. Now he moved to working on the same house as Terry's crew, where she'd been hiding from Bo.

It took less than two days in the new house for him to find his rhythm. He meshed into the flow of men, catching on to the order, the who-did-what and where he was needed to finish out the house. Cabinets were hung, walls were textured, countertops installed, lighting fixtures were wired in, and trim was nailed up.

Tina came in on one of their final painting days to find Bo on a ladder cutting in trim work. She watched for a moment as his steady hands glided the brush over the strip of crown molding, not getting a drop of white on the walls or ceiling. She didn't speak until he'd brought the bush down for more paint.

"Nice job. Not many people have the patience for trim out. None of my guys have steady enough hands. We usually have to tape everything off."

He shrugged those wide shoulders, calling her attention to the way his body moved under his white tank top. "Just takes concentration."

One foot was lifted to the upper rung of the ladder, showcasing the curve of his ass. It was a very nice view from the ground. Tina turned her face away. Lusting over a crew member had caused her trouble in the past. She had to keep that in mind.

"I'm heading out. I have a restoration job to bid. If you need anything, holler at Terry."

"Yes, ma'am."

He never turned around, never took his focus off his work. A trait she could admire, if she hadn't wanted him to look at her.

Stupid. She shook her head and walked out of the room.

The entire drive, she thought about his focus, his shoulders, and the tattoos that she wanted to explore, the way he always had the same stoic expression on his sexy face. Bo was like a rooted tree: nothing moved him. He showed up on time, never complained, worked his ass off, and was respectful to the other crewmen. He'd taken his first paycheck with appreciation, staring at it for a second before turning his gaze to hers. Those mysterious hazel eyes drew her in and held her captive. Damn, he was hot.

And completely in the *not on your life* list.

The house she went to look at was a beautifully decaying Victorian. It needed a lot of work and she practically danced in her seat when she pulled up in the driveway. An older couple met her on the front walkway and described all the work they wanted done to restore their house.

"I grew up here," the woman said fondly. "We've lived with our daughter for about ten years and now we want to come home and live in this house. But it's falling down."

"No problem." Tina smiled. "I have a soft spot for restoring old houses. Why don't we go inside and you can show me around, let me know what you're thinking?"

The Raglands were adorable people. They held hands like newlyweds, but they'd been married over thirty years. Mrs. Ragland gave her the grand tour, complete with stories from her childhood. Tina ate it up, became acquainted with the house, the memory of what it once was, and the vision of what it could be again. She touched the walls, stroked spindles of the staircase, and glided her hand over the dusty railing with affection. The walls had stories; they held the memories and spirits of people who lived here. All they needed was a little love and devotion to bring them back to life.

"I have to say, Miss Foster," Mr. Ragland grinned, "you seem taken with our home."

"I am." Tina, half-dazed, was already planning and figuring costs in her mind. "I love this house. I love most older homes, but this house—you have history. It makes it so personal, so real and intimate to work on." She turned to them. "I'll get you a formal estimate, but I really hope you let me work on this house."

The Raglands exchanged a smile. "We'll review the estimate. If it's reasonable, you've got the job. The other man who came out didn't care at all about what this place means to us. You…get it."

Excitement filled her until she was about to bubble over. She smiled wide and full as her lips would let her. "Really? I'm thrilled. Oh, I can't wait." Being the business woman she was, she filled out her paperwork, taking pictures of the house, and gathered the information she needed to put together a formal plan of construction.

Victory filled her by the time she left. Building new houses was profitable, and there was a flow to the job. But older homes? They were what she loved most. Feeling happy and light, she called Trey out of habit.

"Hey," he answered, distracted. "What's up?"

"I just scored a complete restoration. I'm so excited. This house is 1920s Victorian, it's two stories—"

"Tina, that's great, sweetheart. Do you mind telling me about it tonight over dinner? I'm swamped right now." He rifled through some papers and stapled something. "I can bring something over if you want?"

"Oh." Her balloon deflated. Trey always dropped what he was doing to talk to her. Why was it the one time she wanted to share a piece of herself, he wasn't receptive? "Of course."

"I'll call you when I get home. Is that okay?"

"Sure, okay."

She hung up, wishing Keri or Jayden could understand her fixation with houses. They would listen but not really appreciate the joy she felt. Jayden was into fashion and while she would've mustered up some enthusiasm, it wasn't the same. Keri, a realtor, would've been more inclined, but Tina didn't want to bother her.

At least Dad will care.

Instead of heading straight home, she decided to check on the progress of a current project close by. Only one truck remained on site. The rest of the guys had left, but Bo's rusty red and white Ford remained—with the hood up.

His rear end hung out of the engine compartment. He dislodged himself when she pulled next to him.

"Glad I came by. That looks like trouble." Tina smiled, but it faltered when their eyes met.

Something about Bo's direct stare caused her insides to melt. Her stomach did flips and heat pooled in her belly like always.

Only his flared nostrils gave away that anything was wrong with him. "Damn thing won't start. Sat in a field too long. Now that I'm using it every day, shit keeps breaking."

"You need a ride? A tow? A hand?"

"You know engines too?" One brow bowed up, his skepticism obvious in the down-turned set of his lips.

Ah, he does have more than one expression!

"As a matter of fact, I do." She kicked out her hip.

Bo nodded, wiping his grease covered hands on his jeans. "Really?"

Tina narrowed her eyes. "What's she sound like when she starts?"

"Clanking around. She overheated on the way here." He sighed and stepped aside as Tina bent down to the ground and ran a finger through the liquid pooled under his truck.

She sniffed her fingers. *Hmm.* She went to the driver's side. "Mind?"

He shook his head, slightly amused, if she read him

right. It only took her turning over the engine for a moment before she switched it off. "Busted head gasket, sounds like. You're leaking, overheating, *clanking*."

Bo nodded and chewed on the inside of his cheek. "Yup. That's what I figured. I'll have to remove the heads. You know a shop I can take 'em to?"

"Ray's." Tina took out her cell phone and dialed a number. "Charlie-Ray? Hey there, stranger. Tina Foster."

"Howdy, Miss Foster." They exchanged the typical pleasantries and checked on each other's families. "That pretty new truck of yours can't have anything wrong with it. What can I do for ya?"

"I need a favor for a friend of mine. He's going to need some head work too." She prattled off the address and thanked him in advance before she hung up.

Bo leaned against the truck and rubbed his eyes. "T, I don't really have, I mean, I can't uh…"

"No worries." She shrugged.

"Tina." His jaws clenched when he pinned her with his stare again. "No."

She narrowed her eyes and turned to meet him head on. "You want to know what bugs me about men? They never ask for help. Like it's some sort of damn sin. Bugs the piss out of me. You're not going to bug the piss out of me, are you, Galloway?"

Bo let out a heavy breath and closed his eyes, the muscles in his jaws working. "No, ma'am."

"Good. Because after these last couple weeks of your help around here, it's the least I can do. Besides, you have to get your ass to work somehow."

"I'm not a charity case," he spat out with more than a little bitterness in his tone.

"Damn straight, you're not. You're going to work every dollar of it off." Tina held out her hand and met his hazel gaze.

The moment his hand slipped into hers, the air around them sparked. His eyes widened a fraction and she gasped, but neither let go. Was he as caught under the force of electricity crackling between them as she?

Tina pulled away first, unable to stand the magnetic draw. She knew nothing about Bo. He was virtually a stranger. He didn't even have a Facebook profile, for heaven's sake. Physical attraction this strong couldn't be healthy.

"How'd your appointment go?" he asked, retrieving a couple bottles of water from the cooler in the back of his truck.

"Good. Good. I think, no, I *know* we got the job." Thrilled to have someone—anyone—to talk about the house with, Tina gushed over how challenging and fun this restoration would be. Bo listened, asked questions, even high-fived her when she explained how the Raglands didn't flinch when she called out numbers. "I'm so excited. Working on old houses like that."

"It's like fixing history." Bo gazed down at his boots, which now sported the signs of hard work: scuffs, paint, and dirt.

"Yes! Exactly." Their eyes met again and he smiled. A tingle went up her spine. "You get it."

"Yeah, I get it. It's cool that you're so pumped over the job."

"Well, my excitement guarantees your paycheck, I guess," Tina joked and took a swig of her water as the tow truck pulled up.

Her phone rang just as they reached the mechanic's

shop. She'd followed the tow truck, knowing Bo would need a ride home. He sat quiet in her passenger seat, an awkward silence settling over them.

"Hi, Trey."

"Hi, sweetheart. I am so, so sorry about earlier. Please forgive me. It's usually not that crazy around the office, but—"

"It's fine."

"No, it's not. You're my girlfriend and you should always be first."

"Uh…not really." She took a deep breath, reining in the rebellious feminist inside who hated weak men. "It all worked out. Something came up. Maybe this weekend?"

"Absolutely. Anything you want. I'm sorry, really."

She stifled a groan. "Okay. I'll call you."

"I'll be waiting, sweetheart."

Trey hung up and Tina stared at her phone, not understanding why he suddenly raked on her nerves so much. "I hate being called *sweetheart*."

"Boyfriend?"

Tina pinched the bridge of her nose. "No—uh, yeah, I guess he…is." Before he could open a can of worms, she slid out of her truck and went into Ray's machine shop. "Justin," she called out to the only guy left working at this time of day.

"Tina!" Justin hugged her tight and smiled brightly. "Holy crap, Bo Galloway?"

The two men shook hands and Tina tried to understand how Justin remembered him from high school and she didn't. Justin was a grade behind her, which would've made him two grades behind Bo.

"Tina, this guy was like the freaking Karate Kid. I'm

not joking." He slapped Bo on the back. "You still into martial arts?"

"A bit, yeah." Bo nodded.

"Of course you are, look at you. Man, I bet you can whip some ass." Justin laughed and did some horrible karate impressions. Bo shrugged, grinning as if the compliment embarrassed him. "Well, either way, with those guns, I want to stay on your good side. What can I help you with?"

Bo made it clear that he was capable of taking out the heads and replacing them, but since the truck was already sitting there, Tina insisted on allowing Justin to do it. That earned her a deep scowl from Bo.

He was fuming by the time they left and she drove him home.

"Spit it out, Bo. Smoke's coming out your ears."

"Believe it or not, Tina, I know what the hell I'm doing with an engine. Why would I pay someone to do something I'm perfectly capable of?" He kept his face turned towards the window.

"I don't doubt your skills. But you need to get to work, right? You need that truck as fast as they can get it to you. Charlie-Ray's the best around. Be happy I'm help—"

"You need to stop bossing me around when I'm off the clock. I don't want a warden."

It was the most he'd said to her in the two weeks they'd worked together. Every word dripped with contempt. His words hit her twice as hard as they should've. She didn't understand the intensity of the impact, but Bo's anger towards her cut deep.

"Message received," she whispered, turning her attention to the road. She was an absolute fool for allowing him to have that much power over her emotions.

Bo's big body sank back in his seat and he leaned his head against the headrest with a sigh. "Tina, I'm—"

"I don't care." His head whipped around, but she continued without looking at him. "Handle your shit however you want to." She came to a screeching halt in his driveway and put the truck in park, still keeping her eyes straight ahead.

His grandmother's simple farmhouse was cute and well-loved. A couple of the windows were lit with a soft yellow glow and she could see the television as the old woman pulled back the curtains to see who'd driven up.

"I didn't mean to be a dick." Bo opened the door and slid out. "Thanks for the ride and all your help."

Tina simply nodded and put the truck in reverse. She would not let him get to her just because she was physically attracted to him. Things had been better with Trey and she needed to concentrate on a guy who sincerely wanted her.

Chapter Five

B O HESITATED TO ENTER THE HOUSE. TIRES SQUEALED down the road and the sound of Tina's truck coming back caught his attention. The blue Chevy truck sped by his house like the hounds of hell were behind it. Gravel kicked up when she took the corner, her brake lights illuminating for only a split second before she accelerated again.

"What the hell?" Bo didn't know what he should do. Follow her? Call her? What was the emergency?

"Bo Allen?" his grandmother called from inside. "You've got a phone call."

He opened the door to the house, but he kept his eyes on the road.

"It's Mrs. Robin." Nan handed him the phone. This was one call he had to take.

"Hello, Mrs. Robin," he said into the phone, Nan giving him a questioning look. The weekly phone call from his parole officer wasn't anything new, but his lateness was.

"Hi, Bo. I'm just checking in. How are things going?"

Bo sat down on the couch. "Good, ma'am. Real good."

"I see you've been working for the Fosters. That's wonderful."

Not at the moment. "Yes, ma'am. Duane has been good to work for."

"He's staying in contact with me. He says you're doing a good job, making friends."

"Yes, ma'am." He answered all her questions, but his mind was on Tina. What if she was in trouble? Was she that mad at him? What if she had a wreck, driving crazy like that?

"Have you had any trouble? Anything we need to talk about? Heard from your mom?" Mrs. Robin's voice was kind and soft, proving once again she cared. That was her job.

"Not a word, and I'm glad. She can keep her drama in California."

"You're still angry?" she asked with a heavy sigh.

"No, ma'am. I've had four years to be angry. Now I'm just trying to move on."

"Good, Bo. I think you're going to be just fine." Mrs. Robin confirmed their face to face appointment for the next week and hung up.

Bo leaned back on the couch and rubbed his eyes. Talking to Mrs. Robin every week wasn't a big deal and it sure beat jail. He just didn't want to have to tell Duane he had to take off work to meet at her office. He sure didn't want Tina to know.

"You okay, son?" Nan sat a plate of food in his lap. "Where's the truck?"

"The truck is in the shop having the heads worked on."

Nan sat beside him. "Oh no. Do you need money?"

Bo patted her knee. "Thanks, Nan. But I can handle it."

She nodded and let him eat. Nan always knew when to give him space, like she had a sixth sense to know he didn't want to be around anyone. Part of his adjustment to the outside was getting used to having people around all the time. He stayed a loner in jail and only made a peep when he had to. Now he had men he worked with all day, Nan at home always wanting to talk, a parole officer asking him twenty questions every week. Sometimes he wanted solitude.

"Hey, Nan? Did you keep Grandpa's tools in the barn?"

Nan tried to hide her smile. "They're all still out there. You're welcome to them."

Bo made his way to the barn behind the house where his grandfather did woodworking. Most of the wooden benches in downtown were carved by his grandfather. He was a master at his craft and he had shown Bo how to do a lot of it. It had been years since he'd even picked up a carving knife, but it would be something to do in the evenings that could help bring in money to the household...if he was any good at it.

Before he cleaned up the workshop, he texted Tina. He just had to know she was safe.

Chapter Six

NOT HALF A MILE FROM BO'S HOUSE, TINA'S CELL phone rang. The temptation to let it go to voicemail burned strong, but when she saw Jayden's face on the caller ID, she answered.

"Please come," Jayden sobbed on the other end of the line. "I can't do this. I don't know who else to call."

"I'm on the way." Tina whipped her truck into the bar ditch and turned around before she could hang up. She drove past Bo's driveway and sped north to the gravel road leading to Jayden's house in the country.

It took her half the time than usual. She jumped out of the truck and took the stairs up the porch two at a time. Knocking was unnecessary.

Jayden was curled up in the fetal position in the middle of the living room, sobbing like a baby, an empty bottle of Jack beside her.

"Oh shit." Tina dropped to her knees in front of Jay.

"How much did you drink?"

"I can't do this," Jayden cried. "I can't pretend like I'm okay." Her body shook with more sobs as Tina picked her up and laid her head in her lap. She took a deep breath and tried not to get sucked into her friend's emotional grave until she knew if this was a medical emergency or not. Jayden had been on antidepressants since Chris died and they didn't mix well with hard liquor.

"Jayden, I need to know how much you drank. Did you take any pills? Do I need to be calling an ambulance?"

Jayden hugged Tina's waist. "No, just hold me."

Tina sighed and did as her very drunk and very upset friend asked. Everything about this situation sucked. It hurt to think about the root of Jayden's breakdown, the loss of her husband. Christopher died a hero, saving a woman and child from the river, but he still died. A wife lost a husband. A mother and father lost their son. Bear, Sean, and Donnie lost their brother. Chris was all of this and more. He was one of Tina's friends, always the life of the party, and she missed him terribly.

Now, at the two-year anniversary, the pain of the loss came back for everyone, especially Jayden. Time had not dulled her aching heart.

"It's not supposed to be like this," Jayden cried. "We're supposed to be celebrating birthdays and anniversaries, having babies, living the life we planned. I'm not supposed to be a widow at twenty-six. I don't want the money; I want my husband back. It's not fair."

"I know, honey." Tina's lip quivered when she spoke, but she kept herself together. Only one of them could fall apart at a time. "It's not fair and you don't have to pretend like it is. You don't have to pretend to be okay."

"Yes, I do. Everyone expects me to act like I'm proud of his sacrifice, and I am. But I'm also fucking pissed. He left me. He risked his life, our life together, and he lost."

Tina had no words. She let Jayden cry it out while she stroked her hair and hummed to her. It was all she could do not to grab the bottle of Jack and sip the few drops that were left. As much as her heart had broken when Chris died, as much as she'd wept and missed him, she couldn't imagine what Jayden was going through. The two of them had been inseparable since grade school, a true storybook couple. He played football and she was a cheerleader. Then, the prom king married the prom queen and joined the two most prominent families in Riverview. They moved into the house Chris inherited and were supposed to have kids and live happily ever after.

Until the waters of the Sanguine River claimed him for their own.

Tina closed her eyes and grit her teeth. She couldn't lose it, she couldn't break down, not right now, especially since Jayden was finally running out of steam. "Okay, honey," she coaxed her softly. "You need to rest. You need to get up off this floor, okay? It's time for bed."

"Not in our bed."

"I know, the guest room." Tina helped her up off the floor. Jayden was wobbly and so drunk, her legs gave out twice before Tina finally got her to walking. She took Jay to the first-floor guest room, glad she didn't have to lug her tall ass up the stairs. Jayden hadn't slept upstairs since the accident.

Tina helped her get into pajamas, crawl into bed, and cover up. "How's that? Better?"

She grabbed the trash can out of the bathroom in case

Jay was sick at some point during the night.

"Tina?"

"Yeah, hun?" She sat down on the edge of the bed.

"You're always strong for me. No one else is ever as strong as you are. No one else can handle it."

"I'm always here for you. You're my friend; that's what we do." Tina smiled, her heart clenching at the raw emotions.

"Will you talk to me until I can sleep?" Puffy red eyes pleaded with her.

"Yep." Tina kicked off her boots and crawled right over Jayden to sit on the other side of the bed on top of the covers. About that time, her cell phone buzzed with an incoming text.

I saw your truck fly by, you okay?

Tina took a deep breath and bit her bottom lip. Bo. She texted him back. *Yes, friend needed me.*

Everything okay? You were in a hurry.

It will be. She watched her phone for a second before another text made it jiggle.

Can I help?

Not unless you can raise the dead.

No, but I can bring ice cream or chocolate.

Oh, Bo. All her anger from the ride home dissipated. If Bo could make her that mad and then make her this warm and fuzzy in the same day, he was dangerous. His next message only made her feel more inclined to forgive him.

I'm sorry about earlier.

You had a rough day, I understand.

Not an excuse to be an ass.

Tina bit the inside of her lip to keep from smiling at the graphic of a donkey that accompanied his text. *I wasn't going to say anything…but since you mentioned it…*

Ha ha. Have a good nite, T. Hope your friend is okay.

You, too. She tucked her phone away, glad to have some closure of that issue, at least.

Jayden sniffed and pushed her mass of brown hair off of her neck, rolling on her side to get comfortable. "Tell me who put that smile on your face? Trey?"

Tina took a deep breath and blew it out of her mouth. "Okay, well, since you're so sloshed you probably won't remember this in the morning, I'll tell you about Bo."

"The hot new guy?"

"Yep." Tina sighed. "The hot new guy." With a shake of her head, she unloaded what she found enticing about Bo and every reason under the sun she didn't need to find him attractive. "I have a boyfriend, you know? I…I can't date someone who's on the payroll. It never works. And it's not like he's put out any vibes. I mean, I think I see things, but what if I'm making that up?"

"You don't love Trey. Everyone knows it." Jayden sniffed and adjusted her pillow.

"He's a nice guy."

"Yeah, so is your Uncle Terry and your dad. Nice guys are everywhere."

"Trey puts up with me, though. That's not easy." Tina shook her head. "Not too many men can keep up with me."

"Can Bo?"

"Maybe." *Yes.*

Jayden reached out and grabbed Tina's hand, gripping it so tight it scared her. "Listen to me, please. I would give anything, *anything*, Tina, for one more day with Chris. The one thing that we did right was not to wait. We didn't listen to anyone who told us we were too young to get married."

A ghost of a smile crossed her lips. "We didn't listen when our families tried to talk us out of it. We just knew. As sad as I am now, I can at least say I gave it everything I had. There are no regrets when it came to our marriage or our decision to be together." Tears crested over her eyes again. "Don't waste time. Don't make room for regrets. That's the one blessing I have in all of this. I gave Chris everything and we were happy until the very end." She pressed her lips tightly together and smiled through her tears.

Tina angrily wiped away her own tears and leaned her head back against the headboard. "I don't know if I can give that much to anyone. I'm not made that way. I'm not able to let go of my heart like that."

"But when you find the person who can take better care of your heart than you can, don't let that go, okay?"

"I won't." Tina hugged Jayden close and thought about the kind of love she had shared with Chris. It knew no borders, acknowledged no boundaries, and lit up the world. She could only hope to find a man who inspired such deep love from her.

Chapter Seven

ONE MONTH INTO HIS JOB, BO AND THE REST OF THE crew celebrated another finished project. Tina announced that since they came in under budget and on time, which was rare in construction, drinks were on her that Friday night.

Jason happened to live close enough that he'd given Bo rides to work while Ray's fixed his engine heads. As much as he hated to admit it, Justin Meyers had done a great job and hadn't charged him an arm and a leg either. In fact, he knew the bill was considerably lower than what it should've been.

When he hit Tina up about it, she shrugged it off. "He's like family. It's what we do."

That only made him feel more indebted to her—an unwelcome sensation. He didn't like owing people, especially women. Being under obligation to someone gave them power and he didn't like anyone holding things over his head. It led to trouble and complications and he'd just as soon steer clear of such. He'd learned those lessons behind bars. Too many debts in jail and you don't live through the payoff.

It was hard, adjusting to the outside again where people did nice things simply to be kind to their fellow man. He kept looking for the catch, waiting for the other shoe to fall. Accepting that Tina and Duane were good people took time. Over the last four weeks, he had watched them with their crewmen, their customers, and through other business dealings. Tina might be a pistol, but she was also generous and fair, just like her father.

Friday night, they met up after work at Bear's Bar and Grill. He'd ridden with Jason and they were kicked back when Jake "Bear" Harris came towards them. He was aptly nicknamed, at least six and a half feet tall and as wide as a barn door. Guys that tall usually appeared lanky and lean, but Bear was a giant among mortals.

"Damn, Bo Allen Galloway." He shook his head and extended his hand. Bo was shocked when Bear pulled him into a man hug and slapped him on the back. He didn't remember Bear being so...*big*. "It's good to see you on this side, you know?"

Bo's gaze darted to Jason, who might be a new friend, but he didn't know about Bo's past like Bear did. "Yeah, it's good to be on this side of the country again. California was rough." He begged with his eyes that Bear catch his drift. Jason was about the only friend he had and he really didn't want to ruin it.

Bear's face softened. "I know. But you're home now and Riverview can wash the California right off." A huge smile stretched across his face. He was a massive man, but he was also one of the friendliest people Bo had ever met. Even in school, they had become fast friends. Bear made the point of including Bo in the social scene, recognizing that Bo was naturally a loner.

"How long have you been in town?"

"A couple months."

"Months?" Bear's eyes widened and his mouth hung open. "And you haven't come to see me, you prick. What the hell?" Bear punched him in the arm.

"My boss is a slave driver." Bo chuckled, fondly thinking about Tina.

Bear nodded. "I get that."

"You've been busy too." Bo looked around at the restaurant. It was just like Bear. Rustic, country, huge, and welcoming. "This is great, man."

Bear glanced around like a proud papa. "It's my baby." He took another good look at Bo and held out his hand once more. "Well, now that you're done hiding from me, we should hang, catch a game or go shoot something."

"Deal." Bo clasped his hand and smiled. Bear had that effect on people. He just lit up the atmosphere.

"Have a good time and your food is on the house."

"What about me?" Jason said, nursing his second beer.

"Jason Tucker, you'd put me out of business with your hungry ass." The two men shared a laugh, but Bo got distracted by the beauty walking through the door.

Tina sauntered in, wearing her hair down over her bare shoulders. She had on another tank top, baby pink, that brought out the blush of her cheeks. Her short, tight denim skirt was frayed around the bottom and cowboy boots came to her knees. It was the first time he'd seen her dressed like a chick with jewelry and makeup, like she'd really taken time getting ready.

She was so damned beautiful it made his chest ache. He rubbed the spot, wishing like hell it would ease up. "Damn."

"I heard that," Jason said around his beer. He wiggled his brows at Bo and chuckled low in his chest. "You're so screwed."

"You didn't hear shit." Bo waved him off, but Jason had figured out his fixation with Tina a week ago and had been giving him hell.

Jason wasn't the type to open his mouth and start drama. So far, he was the only guy at Foster Construction who made an effort to befriend him outside of work. "I hope you fare better than the last guy." He shuddered, still laughing.

Bo sat down but kept his eyes on Tina.

A tall man with dark hair and olive skin followed behind her. He put his hand on her lower back and Tina flinched as if he'd surprised her. Then she gave him a tight smile that didn't reach her eyes.

This was the boyfriend. He was respectable-looking, clean cut, and fancily dressed in his slacks and sweater-vest combo with those shiny shoes. But Tina walked through the crowd in front of him, uncaring of where he was or if he kept up. Trey was a prop, and Bo mentally brushed him off.

Bear grabbed Tina up in a hug that lifted her off the ground. She smiled freely at him, her joy at his presence written all over her happy face. Bo felt the blurred edges of jealousy in his gut. As much as it had kicked him in the balls for Tina to take care of his truck, he'd never liked a woman more. He'd shown it by being a complete asshole and, for the last couple weeks, she'd kept her distance.

"What brings y'all in tonight?" Bear addressed the table of crewmen.

"Just finished a new house, starting a restoration Monday, and we need to celebrate." Tina gave Jason a fist bump and solicited cheers from her co-workers.

Bear laughed and clapped at their success. "Done. I'll get a waitress over here to take your orders and I'm going to whip up something special to start you off." He headed to the kitchen while a waitress handed out menus that featured everything from steak to fried green tomatoes and salads. The beverage list had mainly Texas beers and the staples.

Tina and Duane were consistently surrounded by people. They knew everybody in town. She could hardly keep up a conversation with one person without being greeted by another. Trey leaned out of the way, chatting with Duane, allowing Tina to be the smiling face of the family.

Every few minutes, Bo would glance over to meet her gaze. He couldn't help but look at her. He couldn't keep his thoughts off of her. If Tina Foster was hot as hell covered in sawdust and sweat, she was drop dead gorgeous with her hair curled down her back and her eyes smoky and dark with shadow. Why the hell she kept glancing at him when she had a pretty-boy next to her, he'd never know...but he could hope.

As they both tried to converse with other people, their stares kept meeting, holding a heartbeat, and bouncing away again. Each time, his heart ached a little more. Every glance made him long for the next.

Bear's waitresses kept the food coming and the beers full...except for his. He was allowed to drink, but with his parole officer being well-known in the county, he didn't want anything getting back to her. There were too many people in this place.

"You play pool?" Jason leaned over and asked. "I think you need a distraction."

Bo nodded. They took their beers across the massive log cabin-style building and waited until a table opened.

A waitress with kinky golden curls and a friendly smile came by with a tray of beers balancing on her palm. She stopped when she saw Bo.

"Hey, Jason, introduce me to your friend." She gave him a wink that had surely lured many drunken men.

Names were exchanged, not that he remembered hers three seconds after Jason said it.

"You're new to Tina's crew, huh?" She appraised him from head to toe, smiling in approval. "Don't be a stranger, good lookin'." She winked again and sauntered off.

Bo followed the exaggerated movement of her hips until he glanced up to find Tina again. A thin wrinkle formed between her brows and she turned away. She was talking to a couple of women he didn't know.

"Bo, table's free. Quit staring at the boss lady," Jason teased and handed him a pool stick.

Bo shook his head. "It's not weird to you, seeing her...I don't know, like a *girl*."

Jason threw his head back, laughing. "I guess I'm used to it by now. But yeah. Hard to believe that little cutie pie could be the same slave driver you're used to seeing on the job site." Jason shrugged. "She's just one of the guys to me, ya know?"

They played a couple rounds, and the whole time, Bo wondered how Jason could possibly get one-of-the-guys vibes looking at Tina in that skirt and tank top. God knows, he didn't.

Chapter Eight

Tina loved coming here. Bear had successfully established a restaurant and dance hall that attracted tourists and felt like home to the locals. After everything that had happened in the last two years, it gave her pride to see Bear flourish. He'd worked on the restaurant as a way to deal with the grief of losing his little brother and turned a tragic accident into motivation to live his life to the fullest. If only all the Harris boys had done the same. Donnie, the baby, was in the military trying to make a career out of it—mainly to avoid Riverview. Sean, the next youngest, had gone off the deep end when he lost his best friend and then his brother so close together. Now he preferred the company of druggies and drunks over his real friends.

At least Bear was doing well.

He came by and dropped a mixed drink in front of her.

"Oh no, no, no, no. Not tonight, Bear." *Not with Bo here.* The thought of singing in front of Bo gave her a sudden and alarming case of stage fright. The way he was looking at her tonight had her insides quivering.

"Come on, T. The house is packed and people started asking the moment you walked in. Please?" He put his hands together in front of him, begging. How could she turn him down? She loved Bear so very much.

"She said not tonight, Jake. Maybe some other time." Trey casually pushed the drink away from Tina.

A shiver of defiance crawled up her spine. No man dictated what she would or wouldn't do for her friends.

"Oh, come on, Miss Foster!" One of the other patrons sitting behind them tapped her shoulder when she would've snapped at Trey. "I have family in from Denver and it would be a real treat."

Tina smiled at the table of people and nodded. "Okay. Give me a minute and I'll sing." She stood up to that table cheering and went to the bathroom to check her makeup and hair and take a deep breath. As she came out, Trey stood by the door, his face drawn tight.

"Why do you let him do this to you?" He crossed his arms over his chest and shook his head, grinding his teeth like he always did when he was aggravated at her.

"Do what? He asked me to sing, not dance topless." She went to move past him and he stepped in her way. Trey wasn't a dominant man. For him to bristle up meant he must be angry. "Trey, I don't mind."

"Yes, you do. You have to drink the whole time you're on stage just to keep from throwing up. I know you and you don't want to be up there."

Tina raised her chin and narrowed her eyes. "Apparently, you don't know me, because I love to sing. It's just a minor case of nerves because the place is packed."

"And you'll be drunk by the time it's over." He pursed his lips and shoved his hands into his pockets, backing down.

"You've never complained before." Tina kicked out a hip and raised a brow. Usually, when she was tipsy, he got lucky.

Trey sighed, his eyes turning to the floor. "My girlfriend shouldn't have to be drunk to want to have sex with me."

"It's not like that, and this is *seriously* not the place or the time to have this discussion." Dear heavens, she didn't have time for his emotional drama. "I'm going to go sing now." She pushed past him.

Trey squared his shoulders, mustering up what courage he had. "I can't watch this."

"Then don't." She threw up her hands, letting him know she didn't care if he left or stayed. Sure, it was bitchy. But her first love was calling her name and Trey would never give her the buzz that being on stage did…which was usually why she had to be tipsy to get into bed with him.

Bear had the karaoke set up on the stage and waved her over. She requested two more shots from her waitress. The impromptu performance wasn't a shock. Bear took advantage of the live entertainment when he could, which was why Tina never paid for her meals at his place.

"I hate it when you do this, brat," she whispered in his ear.

"You love it." He kissed her cheek. "And you're so damn good at it, baby," Bear said, all smiles and wicked grins. He was far too handsome for his own good. He had long, dirty-blond hair, bright blue eyes, and a smile that could melt the panties right off a woman.

Too bad he was like a brother to her. He'd make the

perfect date.

Bear smacked her butt, right there in front of God and everybody. "Ladies and gents, the lovely, the talented, the sweetheart of Riverview—Tina Foster."

Tina took the microphone and smiled at the applause. Turning on her performance mode was as easy as slipping on her favorite jacket. She wore the spotlight with comfort and familiarity. "How y'all doin'?" She adjusted the stand to fit her short frame. "How many first timers do we have tonight?"

A large percentage of the crowd cheered. Riverview was one of the few leisure and tourism focused towns along the river in this area. The town brought in a lot of visitors looking for an inland beach getaway.

"Fantastic, welcome to Riverview and welcome to Bear's Bar, the hang out for the in-laws, out-laws, and every poor sucker in between." She smiled and found Bo to her right, leaning against the pool table with Jason, watching her impromptu show. "I know Bear loves to hear me sing, but he also likes it when I do impressions of some of our favorite singers."

Her dad and uncle let out a whoop, encouraging her. Better than their applause was the grin on Bo's face as he watched her on stage.

"If you've seen these before, just laugh really loud and pretend you haven't. So, uh, okay, this is one of America's favorite divas. Yell it out when you know who it is."

Chapter Nine

TINA LET LOOSE A COUPLE STANZAS OF *I Will Always Love You*, full on Whitney. Bo's mouth fell open. This little country girl, no bigger than a minute, sounded just like the famous star. The crowd at Bear's ate it up. Hell, *he* ate it up.

"And if you prefer the other version…" Tina said, changing her voice entirely to sound just like Dolly.

Bear called out another big name from behind the bar.

Tina laughed and waved him off. "Patience, big man, I'm getting there. Someone smack him."

Bo grinned. Tina was a natural on stage. She took a swig of the mixed drink in her hand and then busted out with the first verse of *Fancy*. After a couple more impressions and a happily entertained audience gathered around, Tina had seemed to settle in to her surroundings.

"Now, here's my impression of me. I happen to do this one very well." She laughed and pressed play on the karaoke machine. The familiar strands of *Fancy* came on again. The song was considered a Southern classic and every red-blooded country girl knew it.

If he had it his way, Tina Foster would re-record that song and release it today. Tina crooned the lyrics of heartache and seduction like it was her personal story. She worked the people who gathered on the dance floor twirling each other around.

She did three fast, old-school country hits and a couple newer ones. The girl was amazing. If he hadn't already been mesmerized with her, he was good and falling for her now.

"You're a sunk ship, man." Jason leaned against the other side of the cedar beam, where Bo had moved to get a better view.

"Not a word." Bo's threat held no heat; he was too enraptured by Tina.

"Funny, you staring at her like that, the boyfriend staring at her like...*that*." Jason motioned across the room with his beer. Bo swung his gaze to Trey fuming at the table. He said something to Duane and the two men exchanged words. Duane's brows lowered and he motioned his head toward the door. Trey stood up and headed out.

"He didn't last long. I lost that bet." Jason removed his ball cap and scratched his head. "I owe Bill a twenty, don't let me forget. I didn't give him much longer."

Good.

"He doesn't like her singing? Is he stupid?"

Jason shook his head and tilted back his beer. Bo's attention stayed on Tina. "Not singing, the drinking. You might not realize it, 'cause she's so good, but she's tipsy as hell right now. Trey doesn't like her to drink." Jason pointed to the stage. "He's a damn fool to miss out on this." He grinned as Tina danced around on the stage doing some fancy footwork in her boots.

Jason was a good-looking fellow. Dark hair, dark eyes, friendly smile with dimples, and construction worker's tan lines on his buff arms. It made Bo wonder.

"Have you ever, uh, you know?"

Jason's brows rose to his forehead. "Are you kidding me? She's hot, but I'm not that stupid."

"What do you mean?"

"Last guy she dated seriously, besides the pretty boy," Jason took another drink, "ended up with his pants nailed to a two-by-four…at the crotch…while he was still wearing them."

Bo's mouth hung open and Jason laughed at his shocked expression.

"In her defense, no physical harm was done, and she gave him the chance to shimmy his balls out of the way before she shot the nail gun, but still. I like my jewels attached and unperforated." Jason saluted him with his beer and finished it off, turning the bottle up.

Terry hadn't been making idle threats on Bo's first day. He had given him a serious warning.

Tina finished up a song, holding out the last note for an unbelievably long time. She was his dream woman, nail guns and all.

"Now y'all join me on the dance floor for the Riverview anthem." Tina swayed her hips along to the beat of *Pontoon*. "My brother from another mother has to come help me."

The crowd started cheering as Bear made his way to the stage. Compared to Tina, he was massive. He removed his black jacket, revealing a tank top in bright red—about the same color his face turned. Everyone around here lived like they were in the Caribbean, not Texas. Flip-flops and tanks were perfectly acceptable attire for any occasion. Bear's Bar was no exception.

"Payback, baby. Let's do this." Tina chugged back some beer and sang the opening lines.

The crowd kept time, clapping at her command. Bear was quite the comic himself. He danced and sang right along with her. His talent paled in comparison, but he put on a show.

Unfortunately, he had no boundaries and Bo had to watch as Tina rolled her hips against him. It might be in good fun, might just be for show, but Bo clenched his hand around his beer so tight his knuckles hurt. He threw the bottle away, using any excuse not to watch.

Thankfully, Duane flagged him down, back to the table he and Terry never left.

"Hey, son. Here's Tina's keys. You mind making sure she gets home? You can either take her truck or leave yours here. We can come get it in the morning." He tossed the ring at Bo.

"Y'sir. You sure about this? Jason can—"

"You're fine. Jason's working on his sixth or seventh beer. You've had what, two all night? You might have to drive them both."

"Didn't her boyfriend drive her, sir?"

"Eh." Duane waved him off and muttered something about corn cobs up asses.

Bo nodded. Guess that meant he couldn't order something stronger to wash the images of Tina's fine body out of his mind tonight. *Damn it.* That also meant he had to be alone with her.

"Us old men are going home." Terry slapped his bloated,

full belly and pushed out of his chair. He handed Duane his canes and they headed out.

Bo stuffed the keys into his pocket. It humbled him that Duane trusted him not only with a vehicle, but his daughter. Maybe that wasn't a good thing. If Duane thought for one minute that something would happen between him and Tina, he would've picked someone else.

There was a kick in the balls if there ever was one.

Bo joined Jason and the crowd just as Bear and Tina launched into a duet. He'd never heard the song, but it instantly made him itchy. They sang to each other about playing games, how it was too late to turn back.

He had enough of the stage romance and the one-night-stand song until Tina surveyed the crowd and found him. A stone settled in his gut as she met his stare and sang. Blood pooled to his groin as she crooned directly to him about starting fires and how she'd never say goodbye.

If she wasn't three sheets to the wind, he'd believe she meant it. The conviction with which she sang was Oscar-worthy. He blinked twice, wondering if she meant to stare at him with those bedroom eyes, hoping and praying she did.

"Damn, bro. I think she's singin' to you." Jason took a step to the left, away from him.

Tina's eyes didn't move.

"Yup. Boss lady has the hots for you. Guard your nuts."

Bo ignored him. He was too captivated by Tina's voice, too turned on by her words.

Unfortunately, Jason wasn't the only one who noticed her serenading him. Bear put his hand on the small of her back, getting her attention and breaking their connection. Tina smiled up at her partner and they finished the song.

All smiles and giggles, they took a quick bow and he led her off stage.

Bo casually turned around and engaged Jason in another game of pool. The last thing he needed was an altercation in a bar, centered around his boss.

"Um, Bo?"

Her voice sent warmth over his skin. He turned, keeping his eyes averted. "Yes, ma'am?"

"Do you know where my dad went? He had my keys."

Bo cleared his throat, noting that Bear was a step behind her. "He asked me to make sure you get home."

"I can do that," Bear volunteered.

"You don't leave until midnight or after," Tina dismissed him. "I'm tired and my buzz is wearing off."

"We can leave whenever you're ready." Bo put down his pool stick, earning him a sneer from Jason.

"T, can I talk to you?" Bear pulled at her arm and Bo's instincts were to swipe his hand away from her. But he wasn't hurting or forcing her. They had a couple words, she smiled, he smiled and kissed her cheek, and they came back to Bo. "You guys drive careful." Bear stuck out his enormous hand. "Bo, nice to see you again. Take care of my girl."

Bo clasped his hand. This guy meant a lot to Tina and Bo didn't want to piss off one of her friends. Bo smiled and forced sincerity into his words. "Thanks for a great time and some great food, man. See you again soon, I'm sure."

"Count on it." Bear smiled, but it was more of a predatory grin than a friendly gesture.

He asked Jason if he needed a ride, but he was flirting with a girl over by the pool tables and she was more than willing to give him a ride…and take him home after. Bo and Tina bid their friends goodbye, receiving many raised brows and pursed lips.

"How you want to do this?" Bo asked. "I can leave my truck here."

"Okay. If you don't mind coming to get me in the morning—" she yawned, "—we can come back and get it."

He nodded and flashed the lights of her Chevy. Bo was downright lustful over her truck. Four doors, extended bed, tool boxes and lumber scraps in the back. Even her truck was sexy. Damn, he had it bad. He opened her door and waited. She had some trouble getting her boot on the running board.

"I must be buzzed more than I thought." Her giggle fell on his ears like a caress.

"Here." Bo gently turned her to face him and lifted her by her hips. She gasped when he set her in the truck seat with no effort.

"Thanks." Her wide eyes darted away from him.

His attention lingered on her sexy legs and the way her skirt shifted for a teasing glimpse of her thigh. Tina was like explosives—a lot of impact in a tiny package. Bo closed the door before he reached out and touched something that might blow up in his face.

He didn't know what the hell to say to her. Thankfully, they had a short drive. Besides work, he didn't know what they had in common. Neither had their mothers in the picture, but it was not like he was going to start with that shit. He'd made her uncomfortable by lifting her into the truck. He could tell by the way she leaned close to the door. If work was the one thing that linked them, that was what he needed to go with to bring her back.

"You excited for Monday?" He turned over the engine, loving the way it purred.

"Yeah," she said quickly, looking at him for only a moment. "I'm going to love working on this place. They have this wallpaper in the dining room that I'm going to have to scour the internet to find. I'm afraid that once we start cleaning and messing around in there, it's going to come off. But it's a great print, and the owners want to keep it." She pulled out her cell phone and flipped through her pictures. "See, it's totally retro, right?"

He couldn't tell much by the small picture, but the slate blue wallpaper had a silver floral design. While she was talking about things she wanted to do in the house, he texted the picture to his phone. If there was one thing he could do, it was research. He had a lot of free time in the evenings when he wasn't working on the truck or in the wood shop.

"Sounds like a cool project." He handed her back the phone, trying desperately to ignore the way the air charged when their fingers brushed. "Can't wait to get started."

Tina turned to look at him. "Are you just saying that because it means you get a paycheck, or do you really mean it? 'Cause I know I'm a freak about houses. The guys make fun of me and my house-gasms all the time."

"Your what?" He couldn't have heard her right. How many drinks did she have?

"House-gasms." She rolled her eyes. "They say I get overly excited about old houses. Like it's my only turn-on or something. They're pervs. Answer my question."

Bo scrubbed a hand over his face. His mind went to forbidden places. Places where Tina was naked and on top of him in the middle of a half-constructed house. Being alone with her was a test in constraint and self-control.

"Uh, yeah. Yeah, I think older houses are much more interesting than that cookie-cutter thing we just finished.

Work is work, I'm not complaining. But I like the older construction."

She smiled, pleased with his answer. "Cool. Okay." Her head bobbed up and down. "Trey doesn't get it," she confessed in a tight tone. "He likes modern everything: modern houses, modern cars, modern technology. It's fine, don't get me wrong. It's just, the one thing he doesn't like is modern women." She ran her hands over her hair, playing with the ends.

Her phone jingled with a text and she glanced at the screen. "Speak of the devil and he shall appear." When she opened the app and read the text, her mouth dropped open. "Oh my God."

"What?"

She held out her phone as if he could read it and drive. "He just fucking broke up with me over text. Text! He didn't even have the balls to call me."

Good. "What did he say?"

"It says, 'Tina, sorry I left early but I can't do this anymore. You are self-destructive and don't seem to appreciate the people who care about you the most. I've given you my heart and all you give me back is half your attention. I saw you watching B—'" She stopped reading aloud. "Um, yeah, he's insane." She skimmed down the mile-long message. "Ugh! He called me manly."

"He's a pussy."

"He called me manly!" She clearly needed to get this out of her system. "Do I look like a man tonight? I shaved my fucking legs for this."

Bo could barely hold in his amusement as she lifted her boot-covered foot up in the air. He wanted to run his hands up her legs and thighs so bad it stole his breath, but she was most certainly not as sober as she thought. "You cuss a lot when you're drunk. It's pretty funny."

"What the hell does he know anyway? He sits behind his fancy desk, building his company on his parents' money. He's never had to do manual labor a day in his stuffy life. He gets fucking manicures, for heaven's sake."

Bo curled up his nose but didn't say anything. His expression made her laugh. She had a great laugh.

He put his foot on the brake, easing the truck to a slower speed and milking the short distance between the bar and her house.

"I do cuss a lot when I'm drunk, *wow*." She pointed a finger at him to make a point. "I am a construction worker." She threw her head back, laughing, and rolled down the window, her long blonde hair waving in the air. "Maybe he's right. Maybe I'm the dude in this relationship and he's the chick. Maybe that's why it's worked this long. All I need is a dick and we'd be the perfect gay couple."

Bo coughed, choking on air and laughing at the same time. Tina popped him a couple times on the back and laughed right along with him. "Oh jeez, I do have a potty mouth."

"Let's leave that train of thought alone," Bo said, still chuckling. He pulled her truck into the parking lot of Foster Construction, where she lived and worked all-in-one. Lights were still on downstairs and Duane's shadow moved across one of the back windows of the two-story metal structure. The building was right along the river, across the bridge from downtown, a drive that was far too short.

He got out of the truck and went to open her door, surprised that she let him.

"Thanks for the ride, Galloway." She gave him a fist bump and strutted towards the front door. Just before she entered, she cast him a sleepy sideways grin that stole his breath. "Take care of her, she's my baby."

Bo swallowed hard at the trust she'd placed in him. "Yes, ma'am."

He drove her truck carefully to his house. It was far too late for his grandmother to be awake, but she was up warming herself a glass of milk.

He kissed her head of long gray hair and touched her shoulder. "Can't sleep?"

Nan patted his cheek. She was a tall woman, like her daughter, like her grandson. Her wise eyes showed the seventy years of her age. She was his personal guardian angel. "I always worry when you're out late."

"It's time for you to get over that."

Her head tilted. "You think your age diminishes my concern? How come you came home in the wrong truck, smarty-pants?" She hit him on his chest with the back of her hand.

How could he not love her? She still gave him hell every chance she got and gave him love every day.

"I had to drive Miss Foster home. She had a couple too many, I think."

Nan pushed back the curtains to eye the truck. "Nice vehicle. I could've sworn she had some kind of sports car. A woman drives that big ole truck?"

Bo didn't try to hide the affection on his face. "She's not like any woman I've ever met, Nan. Keeps up with the best of 'em."

"You like her." Nan put a hand over her heart.

Bo nodded but didn't say anything. He didn't know

the words to describe how much he liked Tina Foster. He would gladly work seven days a week for the rest of his life if it meant being around her every day.

"She's your boss, Bo. Do you think it's a wise idea to allow yourself to go up that stream? You might find yourself without a paddle, as they say."

"Yes, ma'am, I know. I'm trying. I need this job. I like the work, like the people."

"Like the boss?" Nan arched a gray brow and puckered her lips. They sat down at the dining table, a set that dated back to the seventies. Nan was meticulous about caring for her home and her belongings, never taking them for granted.

"You'd like her. She's tough, Nan. Won't let a man wipe his feet on her."

"You mean like your mother would?"

Bo leaned his elbows on the table and scrubbed his face. There was one rule in his grandmother's house that she'd instituted when he got out of jail. He had to confide in her like he had opened up to the counselor who talked to him. Dr. Barker was back in California, meaning their sessions were done over the phone. Nan insisted that talking out his emotions was the best way to keep him grounded. Sometimes her attempt to be a shrink was overkill, but tonight, she had a point.

"Yeah, Nan. Tina's nothing like Mom. She knows who she is; she grabs life by the horns and hangs on for the ride, you know? When her old man was injured, she didn't hesitate to step in and take up the slack."

"You respect her?" Nancy sipped her warm milk, watching him.

He nodded. "A lot."

"That's a good place for things to start."

"She's not interested in me," Bo said, not knowing if it was true or not. She'd sung to him, he was sure of it. And then there was that thing in the text message about her watching him. It wasn't enough, though.

"Did she say that?"

"I'm not her type, Nan." He leaned back in his chair and crossed his arms and legs.

"What's her type?"

"Someone without a record and a history of violence."

Nan rested her hand on his arm. "Bo Allan, you listen to me. You're not a violent person. Don't you dare hide behind labels that your mama slapped on you just because she's a dimwitted flake. It's not like you run around beating people up all the time, even before you went to jail. One time," she held up a bony, weathered finger, "you lost your head one time and that was in the defense of your mother. You don't get to punish yourself for the rest of your life because you messed up once."

Bo studied the texture of his boots, unable to meet her eyes. He nodded, wishing he had as much faith in himself as Nan did.

"Say it, Bo."

"Yes, ma'am. I know."

"No, I said say it, just like Dr. Barker told you."

"I am not the sum of my mistakes, but rather the product of lessons I do or do not learn from." He cast her a narrow-eyed glance. "Happy, Dr. Nancy?"

She stood and walked by him, dropping her hand on his shoulder. "You're a great man, Bo. You simply need to see it for yourself."

He brought her hand to his mouth. "I love you, Nan."

"Oh, baby boy, my cup runneth over." She let out a yawn. "And my eyes droopeth shut." She giggled and left him to his thoughts.

Tina rolled around in his head all night. When he closed his eyes, he saw her. Her sky-blue eyes, those tempting lips, and her messy blonde ponytails. He loved the way she put her heart into everything she did—work, singing, friendships, family. There was no half-way with her; it was all or nothing. That was the real reason her relationship with the engineer wasn't working.

She didn't have faith in Trey. Bo could tell by the way she talked to him on the phone before their breakup. When Tina spoke to her crew or her father, people she trusted, she had authority and confidence that no matter how crass or blunt she sounded, they'd accept her. Trey couldn't deal, that's all there was to it. Tina was an unbroken horse, wild and free, but desperately wanting someone to risk everything for her.

He was more than willing to try, but he had to make sure this wouldn't be a huge mistake for them both.

He rose early the next morning to return the truck. Going down his white gravel road had left a layer of dust over the navy blue. Bo debated, should he take the truck straight back...or do something a little special for Tina?

Bo drove into town and went through the car wash. He scrubbed it clean and vacuumed out the inside, cleaned all the glass, and wiped down her leather seats until they shined.

Soon, he knocked on the Foster's door, nervous to see either Tina or Duane.

"You're up early," Tina called down from a balcony on the side of the building.

Bo stuck his head around to see her leaning over the railing and his heart kicked into fifth gear. All that hair was up in one of her famous messy buns, her baggy shirt fell off one shoulder, and the cotton shorts showed more leg than her skirt last night. Tina's legs were sexy as hell: muscular, tan, and perfect.

"Shouldn't you be hungover or something?" He grinned, wishing, needing more of her.

"Oh, I am. Don't you worry. I only got up to close the curtains and I heard you knocking."

"You should get some rest."

"I won't argue with you," she said and rubbed her forehead. "Thanks for driving me home last night and, you know, making light of a breakup. It helped."

"Yes, ma'am."

She lifted her hand to wave and stepped inside as Duane came out the front door.

Duane rode with him back to the bar to get his truck. They talked sports, work, how his grandmother knew the Fosters. Duane didn't seem to worry about what did or didn't happen with his daughter and Bo on the way home. Not that anything happened, but most men would at least ask. It was a sign of confidence in his daughter. Tina could take care of herself.

With nothing more than a "see ya Monday," Duane left. Bo got in the truck and tried to start it up. Dead. Dead as a doornail. Again.

"Damn it!" Bo pulled out his phone and called Duane before he got too far down the road. "I'm sorry, sir. I know my car troubles are a pain in your ass."

"It's fine." Duane waved him off. "Pop the hood."

Right there in the middle of Bear's parking lot, they

examined his truck. They fiddled with the battery and starter, found a loose wire.

"Bring it over to the house, son. We'll get our hands greasy."

"Yes, sir."

Bo spent the rest of the day up to his elbows in the engine of his truck. Duane was talkative and chipper, happy to work on something, even if he had to take frequent breaks. Bo found him easy to talk to and relaxing to be around. A rarity. Usually, father figures didn't mesh well with him. Hell, parental figures period didn't mesh well with him. Duane was different. He listened to Bo, genuinely listened, and asked his opinion on whatever subject they were on.

Around lunch time, Tina came out of the house wearing a long, straight dress with flip-flops and black sunglasses. "Mornin', men-folk. More car trouble?"

"Yes, ma'am." Bo was dumbstruck that she could make everything from dresses to denim to dirty tank tops look like high fashion. "Feeling better?" he asked, needing any reason to talk to her.

"Yeah, thanks."

"Going out with the girls?" Duane asked from his perch in the driver's seat.

"Keri and Jayden are meeting me for pedicures." She grinned at them. "Pick up your jaw, Bo. Believe it or not, I do like girly things."

"Never doubted it, ma'am." Bo bit his inner lip to keep from smiling like a fool.

She stopped and tilted her head at the shiny blue Chevy. "Did…did you wash my truck?"

"Yes, ma'am." Bo could barely meet her gaze. She did things to his insides he didn't understand and wanted to feel all day long.

Tina opened her mouth twice before she finally smiled widely at him. "That's...thoughtful."

Bo shrugged. "Well, you're kinda dirty, so..." He grinned, hoping he could hear her laughter once again.

She popped out that slender hip and pointed her key at him. "You almost had brownie points, Bo. Not so much now." She hopped her little ass up in that big truck and started the engine, giving them a wave goodbye.

After she left, he shook his head. "That's one hell of a daughter you got there, sir."

Duane shook his head. "You're preachin' to the choir, son. Preachin' to the choir."

Chapter Ten

"HE BROKE UP WITH YOU OVER TEXT?" KERI'S booming voice got the attention of half the salon. Jayden hushed her, and Tina covered her face.

The three women sat side-by-side in the massaging chairs while their feet were buffed and their toes painted.

"For the love of Pete," Tina leaned over, "why don't you get a freaking billboard next time?"

Keri held up a freshly manicured finger. "I can. I have one." A six-foot version of Keri's face greeted people coming into Riverview from the main highway, advertising her as their homegrown realtor. Everyone knew her, and she knew everyone…and all the gossip that came with them.

"Keri," Jayden scolded. "Control your mouth. Maybe T doesn't want everyone in here knowing her business."

"Yeah, what she said." Tina motioned with her head and pretended to read last month's issue of a magazine.

"Well, Trey is an idiot. What's up with Bo?" Keri persisted.

"Nothing."

"Bullshit," Jayden coughed.

Tina gave a one-shouldered shrug. "I don't know him that well. He's nice. Quiet. Dependable. Friendly."

Jayden threw her hands up and deadpanned, "Great, he's a golden retriever. Awesome. Does he play fetch too? Shake his leg when you scratch behind his ears?"

"She'd like to scratch that itch. Look at her blush," Keri teased.

"I bet he'd be good." Tina sighed.

"I'm living vicariously through you," Jayden said. "Go scratch that itch and then call me with the dirty details." The three of them laughed.

"Moving on," Tina said. After feeling the heat of Bo's hands on her waist last night, she didn't think it was wise to go down that road. Instead, she focused on ideas that Jayden had for the Harris house.

Her heart sank when she arrived back home and Bo was gone. She wanted to see him again, which was a strange sensation. The last time she actually longed to see someone was… Well, it was so long ago, she couldn't remember.

Meg called that evening and since Cole was at work, they were able to talk for a long time. Noah was resting in her arms and every now and then let out precious little noises and sighs.

Tina told her all about Trey and his oh-so-brave texting breakup. Part of her story included Bo, so then Meg began the inquisition as to who he was and what Tina thought of him.

"I miss you guys so much," Meg said softly into the

phone. "I have no friends up here, at least not anyone I can talk to. Cole's secretary is about the only woman I talk to and I'm not too fond of her. His mother is a crazy bitch who pretends to like me."

Tina sat out on her balcony and marveled at the sunset with Dixie lying by her feet and watching the ducks play in the water below. "Come visit. I'll buy your ticket. Noah is old enough to travel and he needs to see his Aunt Tina. He misses me, I just know it."

Meg giggled. "He does. He told me so. I'm afraid Cole would crap a brick if I told him I was coming for a visit. He's in the middle of a huge project and he comes home tired and grumpy a lot."

"Even more reason to come," Tina huffed.

"How is everyone there?" Meg quickly changed the subject.

Tina went down the list of their friends. The anniversary of Chris's death was this week and Jayden was dealing with that by focusing on the house. Keri had just closed on a multimillion-dollar ranch transaction from which she was ecstatic. Holly had sold some of her paintings to a local gallery that featured river-inspired art. She worked all day at the bank and then painted all evening, far too busy to visit, of course.

"How is Bear?" Meg's voice tightened as it always did when she asked about him. She'd been head over heels for him in school, but he was already in the military before she graduated. Meg met Cole when she was in nursing school and moved with him to Boston. Meg was ready to leave his ass and come home when they got pregnant with Noah.

Tina always wondered if Meg made the right decision. Not that it mattered now. Noah was a gift from God and despite Cole's flaws, he loved his son.

"Bear's good," Tina said. "The bar is doing very well, especially since it's right on the river. He makes me sing every time I come in, so naturally, I hate him."

Meg laughed. "You love him and you know it."

"I'll neither confirm nor deny."

They caught up and planned a visit, maybe for the summer. Tina could take Noah swimming. "Kiss him for me."

Meg inhaled. "He's the most angelic thing in the world. Especially when he's sleeping." She sounded happy and light. Things must be going well at home.

"Love you, Meg. I'll see you soon, even if I have to come up there."

Tina hung up and felt the sting of missing her friend and Noah. She texted Jayden to pick a weekend they could fly up and visit.

Monday morning came with a flurry of people gathered at the Ragland house. Tina went over her playbook for the project, taking the crew through the home and pointing out who would be focusing on what—not that she needed to, these guys knew the drill. Their morning consisted of floor plans, schematics for new electrical wires, and taking a look at the utilities and plumbing. Assess the house, find its weaknesses, fix the issues, and start taking it apart and build it back better.

She spent the most time with her head carpenter. Kevin was making custom cabinetry and doing a complete overhaul of the kitchen and bathrooms. Updated fixtures and appliances were going in, so they started removing toilets and sinks.

"The one sink in the upstairs master is staying because it's a fabulous antique. Do *not* mess that thing up." She moved on to the demolition of the current downstairs sitting parlor, which was going to be opened up to create a larger formal dining room.

There was something satisfying about the whole process. She was the commander of her ship and her crew, confident in what she was doing, comfortable to take charge of their heading.

The dumpster was delivered at noon, two hours behind schedule. But that didn't slow her down. She jumped on the front-loader and scooped up the trash and boards that had been removed by the crew, dumping the debris into the huge container.

Her happily inflated balloon sprang a tiny leak when she jumped off the machine to find Trey's car pulling up to her job site. He'd never bothered her at work and had no reason to be at this site.

Removing her work gloves, she met him at his car. "What're you doing here?"

One of her pet peeves was people bringing their personal drama to her site. Working with mainly men, that was rarely an issue. The occasional spouse dropped off lunch or forgotten tool belts; that was fine. Nevertheless, the personal drama needed to stay at home.

Trey kept his chin lifted and his hands fisted at his side. The way he stood didn't look natural, as if he were playing a part, purposefully doing something out of the ordinary. "I need to talk to you. Duane gave me the address."

As if that justified interrupting her day? She would have a serious talk with her dad later.

"I'm working." Tina crossed her arms and popped out

a hip, casting him an impatient look. "Didn't you break up with me via text? I'm pretty sure I don't have anything to say to you."

"You owe me an explanation. I want to know why you didn't fight for our relationship? Is this about me not talking to you about this house?" He waved his hand dismissively at her current project.

"Not hardly. You're right, Trey, I can't give you all my attention and I never will."

"Why the hell not?" He ground his teeth together.

"Because when it comes right down to it, I don't want to. It's not worth the effort."

Trey's eyes widened and his lip curled up. His shoulders tensed and moved with each heavy breath.

Tina didn't care how angry he was; he didn't intimidate her. "My job is to give this house the attention it deserves."

Trey took an aggressive step closer. "Are you saying your attentions are for sale? Because they have words for that profession. I didn't know I needed to pay you." For the first time in their relationship, he actually showed some spine. Too bad he was about to get his face beat in for it.

"Screw you. I'm done here." Tina turned to leave and Trey reached out, snagging her arm hard enough to yank her backwards, nearly causing her to lose her balance.

"I'm not done with you," he said through gritted teeth. "I've done everything for you. I've given you everything I have and you've spit on it."

Tina struggled in his hold, feeling his fingers dig into her muscle. *This is going to leave a mark.* Thank God she had a shirt on over her tank. No one would see it.

She met Trey's eyes, letting him see her anger. "I suggest you let go if you want that hand back."

Trey growled at her, his nostrils flared and his teeth clenched. "And I suggest you remember who wears the real pants in this relationship. I'm not your dog."

Tina didn't have a problem meeting him eye to eye and challenging him. She wouldn't cower to any man. "We don't have a relationship, never did. But I guarantee I filled out the pants better than you ever will."

"You'll never find a man who puts up with you like I do. You're making a huge mistake. I'm the best thing that's ever looked at you twice." He glared at her with pure hatred in his eyes. This side of him was altogether new and must have been covered up well for her not to have seen it.

"Let. Me. Go." Tina glared at him and her body tensed with every second he kept his hand on her arm. She eased her hand to the hammer hanging from her tool belt and gripped the head, ready to beat the living hell out of Trey if he tried anything.

"Problem, boss?" Bo stepped up behind her, casually wiping dirt off his hands with a rag. He stuffed it in his pocket and crossed his massive arms over his chest.

An eerie silence fell over her job site. Hammers ceased pounding, saws turned off, even the generator and air compressor went dead.

Trey surveyed the scene behind her and swallowed hard, slowly releasing her arm. "Not at all. Tina and I were just talking. Right, T?"

"Leave." Her body shook with anger and her chest pumped with every ragged breath. How dare he lay a hand on her, especially in front of witnesses.

"We'll continue this later." It was more of a warning than a promise.

"Naw." Bo kept that casual drawl and confident attitude.

He narrowed his eyes and shook his head. "I don't think you will."

"You took my cousin's job and now you think you're going to take my girl? No. Haven't you caused enough problems?"

"If you don't leave, I'll cause another one… And I don't mind going *back* to jail."

Trey's entire body went rigid as he assessed Bo, looking him up and down. If it came down to a physical altercation, Trey didn't stand a chance. Bo was pure muscle from head to toe and Trey had gotten far too comfortable behind a desk. One of Bo's biceps was bigger than Trey's leg.

"Fine. I don't need this shit." Trey yanked his car door open.

"That makes two of us." Tina turned her back as he spun gravel backing out of the driveway. She didn't meet Bo's eyes as she passed him. She couldn't. This was embarrassment to the Nth degree, not to mention highly unprofessional.

Her entire crew stood around the house, on the porch, and even leaned out of the upstairs windows. It was all hands on deck today. Twelve sets of eyes waited to see how she handled herself.

Can I please die now, Lord?

She forced a cheeky grin on her face. "Crazy bastard. Nearly had to get my nail gun."

Her guys laughed, some shaking their heads, and went right back to work. Tina chuckled and ducked inside the house, hoping none of her guys followed her.

Chapter Eleven

H E MIGHT'VE HIDDEN IT WELL, BUT ADRENALINE coursed through Bo's veins. There was something about a man laying his hands on a woman that sent him into a blinding rage. That pencil-pushing asshole had a lot of nerve.

When Tina brushed by him without a word, he felt the tension rolling off her shoulders. She could crack jokes to the crew all she wanted. She didn't fool him. He sensed her frustration, her embarrassment. He let her go, let her walk it off the best way she knew how.

He, on the other hand, needed to find somewhere to cool off for a moment. This old house had a basement in the back corner and that was where he headed.

He passed Terry and the older man stuck out his fist. Bo bumped his against it as the other man nodded once. He received the same thanks from all the men he passed; silent approvals for having T's back. By the time he reached the basement, the red edges were gone and he was breathing steadily.

There stood Tina, illuminated by a thin, wide window of sunshine. Her hands were braced on the concrete wall, her head hung down between her arms. She stood straight and rubbed at her left arm, the one Trey latched on to, turning to find him there.

Their eyes met and froze them in place. Red rimmed her eyes, but no tears or tear tracks.

"The, uh, hot water heater needs to be replaced." She pointed to the heater in the far corner. Tina made for the stairs, but he stopped her, gently pressing his hand to her stomach as she passed. "Don't, Bo."

Ignoring her command, Bo pushed the sleeve of her shirt from her shoulder and saw the beginnings of bruising. Finger-sized stripes of angry red and blue. He took a deep breath, closed his eyes, and went through at least two breathing reps before he could think clearly.

"It's not a big deal," she said, pulling away from him. "You're not going to make it one either. I can take care of myself."

"It is a big deal, and I know you can. That doesn't mean I'll sit back and let shit happen."

Her blue eyes held his without flinching. "I don't need or want a white knight, Bo."

Leaning down, right in her personal space, he whispered, "I'm hardly a white knight." Unable to resist, he leaned further towards her and placed a soft kiss on her shoulder, lingering just long enough to hear her gasp before he stepped back. He'd either planted a seed or signed his pink slip, he didn't know which. "I didn't mean to cause issues between you two—"

"You didn't." Tina clenched her jaw and wrapped her arms around herself. "Trey is making something out of nothing. He thinks he saw something, but he didn't."

Bo nodded, understanding exactly what she was saying. Trey only *thought* she was attracted to Bo... They were both wrong.

"And really, Bo, going *back* to jail? That was a little dramatic, don't you think?" She rolled her eyes and shook her head. Duane must not have told her yet. Tina thought he was bluffing and he wasn't going to correct her just yet.

After a long day of work and awkwardness, he finally got up the nerve to talk to Duane about what happened today. Mr. Foster was no fool, sending Trey to the site like he did. He'd taken a gamble and this time, it paid off. Next time, it might not.

However, when he stepped into the old brick building that housed the office and the Fosters' home, he could hear Tina cutting her dad a new one.

"This is your fault," she said louder than usual. "I can't believe you pulled that."

"What was I supposed to do, T? He wanted to see you face to face." Duane's voice was calm, even though his daughter was irate.

"You could've told him to kiss your ass. You could've told him to go fly a kite in an electrical storm. You could've told him to take a long walk off a short cliff, *anything* besides sending him to my site. You know how that pisses me off."

"Did you two have words?"

"Did we have—" She laughed bitterly. "Yeah, Dad, and the whole fucking crew saw it. I was ready to take a hammer to his thick head, but Bo stepped in—"

"What?" Now Duane reacted. "What happened?"

"Nothing, really. What was Trey going to do when faced with Mr. Muscle and twelve angry construction workers?" Tina paused, and Bo cringed as she screeched. "Oh, my God! You did that on purpose. You sent Trey out there *knowing* he would make a scene in front of the guys." Something slapped down on the floor, possibly a file or a stack of papers. "I don't need you interfering with my love life."

"Tina, that dumbass needed to see that not only can you handle yourself, but if he were to piss you off, you have a crew of pseudo-brothers and fathers that would shove his fancy degree and hybrid car right up his ass. He's lucky Bo didn't let loose on him. Hell, I'd like to see that."

Just as he thought. Duane had set Trey up to face Bo.

"Dad? Seriously?"

"Bo's a black belt, T. It would've been a nice show."

There was a long beat of silence. "Bo's a *what*?"

"He's into karate."

"Yeah, and?"

"He's upper level black belt or something like that. Impressive."

"Good to know if I ever need a bodyguard. Oh wait, I can handle my own shit." Tina stormed out of the office and ran right into him. "Jeez, you're everywhere I turn."

"I'm sorry." Bo lowered his gaze and had a sinking feeling he'd worn out his welcome.

Tina sighed, her shoulders dropped, and she clenched her eyes shut. "Thanks for not kicking his ass ten ways to Sunday…since apparently, you can actually do that."

"Don't thank me. I wanted to." Bo met Duane's gaze over her head. He stood in his office door, leaning on his cane. "And that wouldn't have been good for anyone."

Duane frowned, but nodded, getting his point. The last thing Bo needed was a fight. His parole officer could only do so much.

"I have to get some air."

Bo stepped aside and let Tina pass. He and Duane stayed in the hall. "He bruised her arm."

"I saw."

"Don't put me in that situation again, sir."

"I thought karate and martial arts were all about self-control and discipline?"

"I was controlled. But if he would've hurt Tina, I would've let it slip… for her."

Duane's face went slack as he realized what Bo was willing to risk for Tina. "I see."

Bo left him with that thought.

Chapter Twelve

BO MADE EVERY EFFORT TO KEEP HIS DISTANCE FROM Tina that next week. It wasn't difficult. She was all business to everyone. She didn't even bring Dixie to work with her, and that was rare. The Ragland house became her primary focus and she gave Bo a wide berth.

When he wasn't at work, Bo was in the woodshop. There was a peace in creating things from raw lumber. He tested the various types of hard woods: mahogany, walnut, even a soft cottonwood. His grandfather had left a legacy that could be seen all over town. Bo did his best to copy the craftsmanship. He took pictures of all the benches and introduced himself to all the people who had bought from his grandfather, hoping they would also buy from him.

Nan had a picture hanging in the hallway of the house of a horse standing in the river, rearing up on its back legs. It was one of his grandfather's horses and she'd captured it in the perfect moment. Bo made a copy of the picture and hung it in the shop. It reminded him of Tina—wild, unfettered, and magnificent. He practiced carving it on a small piece of wood when he went on his lunch breaks, hoping to one day create it much larger.

When he wasn't working with his hands, he was working his mind, researching and watching videos on the craft. He also searched tirelessly for the wallpaper that Tina needed for the Ragland house.

On Memorial Day, he and Jason went to Bear's for a drink and walked into a gathering of sorts. It seemed like half the town had shown up and there was a huge portrait of Christopher Harris by the stage. That was when he remembered it was the anniversary of the man's death.

Jason and Bo took a seat in a booth on the opposite end of the restaurant.

"Man," Jason shook his head, "it's hard to believe it's been two years. Seems like yesterday."

"What happened? I heard he died, but not how."

The waitress came by and took their drink orders, then Jason spoke. "He was a firefighter. We had a crazy storm come through and this car hydroplaned right off the bridge into the water. Chris was first on the scene and went in for a water retrieval. He got the little girl out, but the mother was unconscious. He went in to get her." Jason's eyes stayed on the table. "The woman floated to the surface and the other firefighters were able to pull her to shore. We nearly lost her. She had a bad concussion, didn't hardly remember a thing. Chris never surfaced. He just…disappeared." Jason shook his head and glanced over at the group of people raising a toast. "They searched for a long time, all down the river in three counties. He was just *gone*."

"You knew him?"

Jason took the beer from the waitress and wasted no time drinking it down. "I was one of the EMTs that worked on the little girl."

Bo didn't hide his shock. All this time he'd worked with Jason, befriended him, ate lunch with him every day, and he'd never said a word. "You were there?"

"Yeah." Jason took another drink and a deep breath. He met Bo's eyes. "That damn river is a reaper, Bo. I've never been a superstitious person, but I'm telling you right now, don't fuck with the Sanguine. It took Chris Harris and seven months before that, Lance Smith. Those two guys ended up in the water and only one of them was ever found."

About that time, Bo's heart hammered in his chest. Tina and a pretty brunette headed their direction. Jason slid out of the booth and removed his baseball cap. Bo followed. Again, Tina was radiant. Her jeans fit her just right and her black button-up created a contrast against her blonde hair, which fell on her shoulder in a braid. Her blue eyes, looking bigger than ever, were covered in shadow and ringed in black.

"Jayden." Jason extended a hand towards the woman, who smiled kindly at him.

Jayden shook his hand. "Hey, there. You guys want to join us? We're just having a beer and telling stories."

Jason glanced to Bo, pleading. "Um, thanks but, um—" He twisted his cap in his hands.

Bo had never seen Jason nervous or fidgeting like he was. He stepped in. "We don't really want to intrude." He met Tina's gaze and fell head first into those blue eyes.

"It's not intruding." Tina's red lips pulled back on one side. "Come on."

"Yeah, okay." Jason nodded and put his cap back on.

They grabbed their drinks and took a seat on the outskirts of the crowd. Jayden and Tina went back into the heart of the group. Bo tried to remember the names of all the people there. He recognized the mechanic who worked on his car's heads, Justin Meyers, Bear and his parents, and another of the Harris boys, who had seen better days. The kid looked high as a kite and ended up leaving right after Bo started eating. The famous Millers were all in attendance, making toasts to Chris' heroism and bravery. That was Jayden's family; everything seemed to be an opportunity to show the constituents how gracious they were.

A thought struck Bo as he watched the people talk and mingle. These were the founders of Riverview—the elite, top percentage of the town's population, and he was a jailbird. He might've known Christopher Harris, but they hadn't traveled in the same circles. No wonder Tina didn't remember him. Even in school, she had been in a different stratosphere. In spite of their differences, her blue eyes constantly found his in the crowd. Even with all these people around, her friends and colleagues, people she'd known forever, she still sought him out.

"I'm about done. You?" Jason asked, peeling the label off of his beer. He was clearly uncomfortable and had taken all he could take. This wasn't normal behavior for Jason, who was almost as outgoing as Tina.

"Yeah." Bo grabbed Tina's attention and motioned towards the door. She came towards him. "Jason and I are out. Thanks for the invite."

"Sure." Tina pushed her hair behind her ears, then shoved her hands in the back pockets of her jeans. Her eyes darted around like she couldn't figure out where to look. "Daddy said you were coming over tomorrow to work on guy stuff." She grinned at the term.

"He's going to show me some tips on molding and banisters. Nan has some things on her porch I need to fix."

"Cool, cool." Tina finally met his stare. "Well, I'll see you around then." She rocked back on her heels as if she didn't know how to act around him.

Bo made the decision for her. He leaned in and put one arm around her lower back, giving her a gentle hug. "Call me if you need me."

Tina discreetly gripped his arm, clinging for dear life. At least that was what it felt like to him. "I will." She gave Jason a casual smile and awkwardly hugged him from the side as if that would make things normal. "You okay to drive?"

"I've only had one." Jason cleared his throat. "Tell Jay goodbye for me, okay?"

"Sure."

Once he and Jason were out of the bar, Jason let out a huge breath. "Well, that was awkward as fuuuck." He chuckled, grinning like the Cheshire cat. "Boss lady has the hots for you, Bo Allen."

Bo punched him in the shoulder. "Just because Nan calls me that, doesn't mean you get to."

"You'd let Tina call you that."

Bo sighed and shook his head. "Tina Foster could call me whatever the hell she wants as long as she calls me hers."

Now that he was out of there, Jason laughed out loud, the happy sound filling the parking lot. "You're so screwed."

Let him have his laughs, Bo would get Tina one way or another. He had his heart set on that girl and all he had to do was wait until that wild filly came to him.

Thirty days later, the summer heat set in with the force of hell behind it. The Ragland house neared the turning point from demolition and repairs to actual construction and re-modeling. The crew was happy to work inside the house instead of under the June Texas sun. On Friday afternoon, Bo went to the office to collect his paycheck and to show Tina what he'd found the day before.

"Mind if I use the laptop?"

Tina shook her head and popped a potato chip into her mouth. The electricity between them had amped up higher in the last month. More than he ever dreamed possible. Bo played his cards using a cool head. He didn't want to spook her, but he had the winning hand, and Tina would come around once he played it. Timing was everything and the time was now.

He clicked onto a website with victory running through his veins. "I found your wallpaper. It's called Lovebirds, and there's a place in England that produces it."

"No way." Tina bent over his shoulder.

He pulled up the picture of the slate blue paper with gray floral print. In the center of the design, two doves framed a cage. "It's damned expensive, especially the shipping. But it's—"

"Perfect." She let out a gust of air, her mouth hanging open. "It's perfect."

He nearly choked when she threw her arms around his neck from behind and hugged his head to her chest. "I can't believe you found it. I didn't know you were even looking. This is fantastic." She laughed and drummed her hands on his chest, spiking his pulse. "I dreaded telling the Raglands they couldn't have the same paper on the walls. You saved my ass, Bo."

He didn't move. Her hands were splayed on his chest and there was no way she could miss the rapid beating of his heart. When she stilled behind him, he knew she'd realized how much physical contact they had. Her hands slowly slid over his pecs, up to his shoulders, and off.

Tina cleared her throat but couldn't hide the excitement in her voice. "Good job, Bo. I'm, uh, well, you did good. Leave that page up and I'll order what we need."

"Yes, ma'am." His skin tingled where she'd touched him. Even after she walked out of the office, he could still feel the heat of her body. Two months. For two months, he had worked with her five, sometimes six days a week. It was torture. Pure, damn torture. And bliss. Pure, unadulterated bliss. Every day, he fell harder and deeper for her.

"Hey?" She stuck her head in the door again. "I'm getting together with some friends at Bear's later. It's, uh, not a company thing. You in?"

"Sure." *Hell* yeah, *I'm* in. He'd walk barefoot through the desert if it meant spending time with her at her request.

Tina bobbed her head once. "Okay. About eight."

"Yes, ma'am."

She slapped the door frame and disappeared.

He was going to need a serious shower if he was going out with her tonight. Bo's smile lasted all the way home.

Nan was out in her garden pulling weeds, her wide-brimmed hat flopping with her movements. She tended her garden like she tended everything else in her life, strong and fierce, loving it so much, it grew healthy and happy.

Bo went right up to her, picked her up, and twirled her around. Nan squealed and giggled. "Bo Allen, what has gotten into you?" Her face lit up when she looked at him.

"I have a date. A real date."

Nan's eyes sparkled and she covered her mouth with her gardening gloves.

"Got to get ready." Bo winked at her and she ushered him to the house. He peeked out the window to see Nan with her head back to the sunshine, her eyes closed, her hands in the air, and her mouth moving in prayer.

"From your lips to God's ears," he whispered to himself.

Chapter Thirteen

TINA FIDDLED WITH HER HAIR FOR HALF AN HOUR before she finally let it go. It would just have to be wild and free tonight. There was no taming it. Her hands were sweaty and her foot tapped restlessly as she sat at her vanity.

God, did she really invite Bo out with her friends? Not the crew, but her personal friends. She picked up the phone and video-called Meg. She had to keep her cool with Jay and Keri tonight, but Meg wouldn't be there to meet Bo.

"I asked Bo out," she gushed as soon as Meg answered. "I mean, not officially, but kind of. He's coming to Bear's tonight."

Meg's eyes went wide. "Hold on, I have to check the temperature in Hell. I think it just dropped off."

"Meg," Tina whined, gnawing on her bottom lip. "He makes me nervous, you know? I'm around men all day and none of them have ever made me nervous. I mean, Jason is cute, Trey was handsome, so I know it's not just because

Bo is hot. It's more." Tina kept babbling and Meg nodded, listening to her argue with herself. "He just does things that keep me off balance. Like when he drove me home and then washed my truck. He didn't have to do that. No one asked him to. He's always going above and beyond for me. I've been such a bitch to him too. Like, trying to run him off because there's no way this can end well."

"So you asked him out?"

"I'm crazy, right?"

"No, sweetheart. You like him. That's okay. You've talked about him for months. I can tell you like his personality. Don't be scared, T. He might be the love of your life." Meg grinned and cupped her hands over her chest. "Look at you, I've never seen you so affected by a guy."

"I don't know what to wear. Even worse, I actually *care* about what I'm wearing."

"Last time I checked, men didn't really care about the clothing, T."

"*Meg.* You have to help."

There was a mischievous chuckle on the other end of the phone and Meg's brows shot up. Tina tried on a couple outfits and showed them to Meg. "The white sleeveless top with ruffles and your black shorts. The white and black boots with crosses on the sides. Leave your hair down, it looks beautiful as always. Minimal make up except for your eyes."

"You're the best. How's my baby boy?"

Meg pointed the phone to the baby asleep on the couch. "He has a fever. I don't know what's wrong with him. When Cole gets back with the car, he's going to take us to the pediatrician. I told him if he didn't get his ass home, I would have no choice but to take Noah on the bus and Cole hates the very thought of *his* wife using public transportation."

"Oh no. And here I am bugging you with my stupid fashion issues."

Meg waved her off and smiled. "I needed to see your happy face. Have fun tonight and tell Bo if he hurts you, I'll kill him and send his body down the river."

Tina slapped a hand over her face. "This is the one and only time I'm glad you're in Boston."

Meg laughed and blew her a kiss. "Love you, girl. Go get your man."

"Kiss Noah for me." Tina hung up and said a quick prayer for Noah. Sick babies were no fun.

Tina left her house, telling her dad not to wait up. Bear's was packed on a Friday night, but it didn't take long to find her friends. Keri and Jayden argued over what to play on the jukebox next. Marshall, Jayden's brother and also Keri's husband, tried to play referee. One day, he would learn not to get in the middle of his sister and his wife. Bear hung around, off work, judging by the lack of his black chef jacket. His hair hung loose to his shoulders, his wide smile shining.

Tina liked it when Bear and Jayden hung together. He was the brother of her deceased husband and their relationship was nothing less than a rock-solid friendship. They leaned on each other when memories of Christopher's death rose to the surface.

"Hey, hotness!" Bear greeted her with a kiss on her cheek. "Why didn't you tell me you were alone tonight. Donnie's in town and he's dying to see you." He referred to the fourth and youngest Harris brother.

"Actually, I think Bo is coming." Tina stretched a forced

smile on her face like it was no big deal. "I'm not sure, though."

"Well, he's an idiot if he misses out." Marshall hugged her. "How's my favorite contractor?"

"Awesome." Tina's smile was real that time. Even if Bo didn't show up, she was among her favorite people in the world.

They sat down in a booth and ordered beer and appetizers, laughing and joking like they always did. Bear was dealing with a mouse problem in his house; the one thing he couldn't stand. He lived right in the middle of hay fields. Once the first cut of the summer was harvested, the mice scattered from the field, trying to find a new place to nest. It was one of the things people in the country dealt with all the time. The humor was how a big man with the nickname Bear was petrified of tiny field mice.

"They carry diseases, so just kiss my ass, Marshall My-shit-doesn't-stink Miller." He laughed and knocked back a beer.

Marshall was dealing with a crazy woman who insisted on boycotting the public library because they had a popular erotic romance series on display. Not that he could do anything about it, but she'd come directly to him, making it his issue.

"Maybe if she read the damn books, she'd be in a friendlier mood," Marshall joked.

Keri was exhausted because a crazy couple from Florida decided they wanted a house in the Texas countryside. The problem was, they didn't realize they would have to live *in* the countryside. She showed them eight properties all over the county. They hated every one of them because they were too far from the nearest indoor shopping mall, which was nearly an hour away from Riverview. They complained that Texas didn't smell anything like Florida, which was even more annoying.

"If people don't like Texas, they need to stay the hell out." Keri shook her head. "It was all I could do not to offer to drive their Winnebago right back to Florida." She prattled something unintelligible in Spanish, her accent growing heavy with her excitement. "Do you know what kind of hell *mi familia* had to go through to get citizenship? I'm a proud Tex-merican and those uppity people don't need to be ruining my state."

Jayden was—as always—dealing with her crazy mother. Jayden was thinking about leasing out the land around her house to help balance out the property taxes on her three hundred acres. She'd inherited the land when Christopher died, and out of respect, always consulted the Harris family when making decisions about the property. Bear was all on board for whatever she wanted to do. Her mother, on the other hand, was concerned that some serial killer was going to lease the land, kill Jayden, and toss her body into the river, never to be found.

"She's convinced that I need to do a full background check on whatever poor old rancher takes the lease. If it was up to her, I'd procure a DNA sample before the ink was dry."

Tina couldn't help but be entertained by the stories of her friends. She also couldn't help but notice that eight thirty rolled around and there was no sign of Bo. Her heart dropped with every minute that passed. Had he ditched her? Had she been too distant over the last few weeks? Maybe he decided she wasn't worth the risk? There were so many things that could go wrong.

Then again, what if Meg was right? What if she'd finally found the one who could handle her wild heart?

"T?" Jayden pointed to a man who just walked through the door.

Tina's breath caught when she saw Bo scanning the restaurant. He had on a pressed, black button-up with white pinstripes. She was used to him in white tank tops or dirty cotton shirts. The man cleaned up nice—*damn* nice.

"Oh, that's him. She's drooling," Keri whispered to Marshall.

Tina turned to them. "It's not a big deal, okay. He's my crewman, for crying out loud."

"Sure."

"Yeah, right."

"Whatever you say."

Tina waved them off and walked forward to get Bo's attention. The moment he saw her, a small smile curved his lips up. His smooth, shaven jaw was razor sharp and his hazel eyes locked on to hers with the force of a lightning strike.

"Hey. Sorry, I'm late. Damn truck was giving me fits."

"Again?"

"Had to hitch a ride."

"Bo, why didn't you just call me? I would've come—"

"Pride is a bitch, sometimes, which is why I'm all sweaty. The old man who gave me a ride didn't have air conditioning in his car."

Tina touched her lips to keep from laughing. It almost didn't work because he was really aggravated about his truck and at himself. As she tried not to hurt his ego, his eyes warmed and the tension in his neck faded.

"Go ahead, laugh. You're taking me home. Damned my

pride and damned if I'm walking in this heat."

Tina cut her giggle free, reached out, and offered her hand. "Come on, macho man, let's get you a cold beer." Her whole body shivered when he laced his fingers through hers, and they locked eyes. It was as if they were suddenly two different people, not a boss and her employee, but simply a woman and a man. A rightness settled in her chest even as butterflies took wing in her belly. The sensation was all new, so innocent and fresh. Tonight started a new chapter in their knowledge of one another and the possibilities excited her.

They slid into the round booth and she introduced him to her friends, who sympathized with his vehicle issues.

"If my boss wasn't such a tight ass, I'd get another one," he joked, a rarity for him. "She works me like a dog."

"I'll remember that on Monday." Tina poked him in the arm. Her friends thought it was cute.

His arm came up over the back of the booth behind her shoulders, but not touching her. It was odd how natural it felt to lean in just enough that she was sheltered by his body, but not enough to touch it.

Once Bo relaxed and cooled off, he easily fit into the conversations. Not that he said much, a word or two here and there, but his presence was like the final piece to a puzzle, rounding out the big picture. He talked cars with Bear and sports with Marshall. He was incredibly knowledgeable about the housing market in the area, mentioning he researched it once he was hired on with Tina's crew. Somehow, he even talked to Jayden about her boutique and her crazy mother issues. For a man who said so little, he connected with everyone at the table.

When Jayden mentioned her side job teaching dance

aerobics at the gym, Bo asked if they had any martial arts classes.

"Bo is a black belt," Tina bragged, loving the way he humbly accepted it.

"Really? That's cool," Jayden said. "I've always wanted to learn karate. There're so many styles. You'd never get bored."

"I'm going to make him teach me some moves." Tina elbowed him and he grinned at her.

"We are still talking about karate, right?" Keri raised a brow. Tina waved her off and rolled her eyes, but heat crept up her neck.

Marshall slid out of the booth and pulled Keri with him. "The only *moves* you need to worry about right now are on the dance floor." The couple loved to line dance together. They practiced at home and liked to show off whenever they had the chance.

Tina was distracted watching them and she barely noticed Bo lean over to whisper in her ear. "Just so you know, I'm not nearly that coordinated."

She shrugged one shoulder. "No big deal. My feet are killing me anyway."

"And one more thing." He ran his fingers along her bare shoulder. "You look amazing."

Tina smiled up into his hazel eyes. "You clean up pretty well yourself."

His eyes were so intense, so focused on her and her alone, that it made her pulse kick up.

"Oh, dear Lord." Jayden pounded her head on the table and held up her cell phone. "It's Mama." She swiped the screen and put it up to her ear. "Hey, Ma... Yes, Marshall is with me... Where else would Keri be, Ma? You've got their kid. It's not like she ran off to Vegas… Yes, ma'am, I'm sorry I'm being overly sarcastic." Jayden pointed her fingers at her head and pulled the trigger. Tina and Bo both chuckled. Bear shook his head. "It must be the alcohol… Yes, Ma, I know what the Bible says about alcohol. I'm not selling my soul for beer… No, Mother, I don't need you to come get me. I plan on going home with Bear tonight and having a hell of a one-nighter."

Bear held his hands in the air. "Score." That earned him a kick to the shins from Jayden.

"Yes, I'm kidding, Ma. If I'm too drunk to drive, Tina is taking me home." Jayden rolled her eyes. She would never get drunk in public; it would be such a scandal. However, she loved to push her mother's buttons. "Have to go, Ma, hard liquor is calling my name. Mother, if you call me again in an hour, I'm going to turn my phone off. Oh, yeah, love you too." She ended the call and banged the phone on her head while her three friends laughed their asses off. "This is why I will forever be single. Only Chris could brush my mother off. No other man would even try."

Tina couldn't stop braying with laughter, turning her face into Bo's shirt to cover the noise. Maybe her life was crazy, but compared to Jayden's insanity, Tina was sitting pretty.

A slow song came on and Bo pulled her hand, leading her to the dance floor. "This is about all the dancing I know how to do." A sweet blush crawled up his cheeks as he hooked his arm around her waist and pulled her close. "I'll follow, if you lead."

Tina sucked in a breath. His eyes were intense, his words conveying more than simply what was happening on the dance floor. "I don't always have to lead."

"But you like to."

"I've always had to." Tina moved in close but kept her eyes focused on him. "I don't trust anyone else to do it."

"Then you need a new dancing partner." He pulled her close to his chest and Tina naturally melded to fit right where he wanted her. She laid her head on his shoulder and closed her eyes, breathing in the scent of his cologne. It felt right. It felt perfect. Bo held her firm and steady, with their hands laid over his heart. He moved her fluidly around the dance floor, nothing spectacular, but soft and gentle and in control. Her body was in his hands and the thought sent a chill up her spine.

She'd never given in this easy.

As if he had felt her tense up, Bo put his lips to her ear and whispered, "Relax, I've got you."

He knew... And that scared her even more. She gripped his shoulder and buried her head in his neck. Bo's arm tightening around her stole her breath. For the first time in her life, she felt like a man understood her internal battles.

When the song ended, Bo smiled down at her and stole her heart. Everything within her knew that asking him out had been a good decision.

"I like your friends," Bo said as they walked through the parking lot to her truck a couple hours later.

"They're great, right?"

His approval shouldn't have made her so happy, but it did. She'd wanted to see if he would fit inside her circle; she needed to make sure the attraction she felt for him wasn't just because they were thrown together at work. Bo proved that not only could he fit in, but he could keep up with some of the most important people of her life. Bringing a guy out with them was a big step for her. Trey never made it that far and she'd dated him for months. He came out with the crew, but not like this.

"Let's go down by the park and meander around?"

Bo nodded, seeming happy to do whatever she wanted. It was painfully clear he was making an effort to keep his distance. He didn't try to hold her hand or touch her back. He'd been the perfect date so far. Even when a strange guy asked her to dance after seeing Marshall spin her around, Bo told her to go have fun. He paid for her meal, even when she argued. He held the door and had impeccable manners. If only he would say more than a couple words at a time.

"You really need to get a grip on your talking habits, Bo. I couldn't shut you up all night," she teased, loving the way he blushed around her. "Seriously, your jaws are always flapping."

The cute grin on his face turned into a full smile. She'd never seen him smile, not like that. Her blood heated up.

"I'll control myself."

They walked along the rows of shops facing the river, across Main Street and down to Conner Memorial Park located right on the water. The water lapped at the bank below. In the distance, a couple of boats motored by, their lights shining in the darkness.

God, she was nervous, which made no sense. She'd worked beside him for two months, perfectly aware of him as a man. They talked about jobs, figured out problems, made jokes. Tonight was different, though. She was hyper-aware of his gait, the confident but casual way he walked, the way his body moved under that pressed black shirt. He'd worn tank tops to work all the time and yet tonight she was obsessed with the way his shirt stretched over his wide, hard biceps.

"Can I ask you something?" he said, breaking her concentration.

"Sure."

"Why'd you invite me out tonight?" He stopped walking and angled his body to face her, stuffing his hands into his jeans pockets. "Seems like you've wanted to keep your distance lately. Why now? Why tonight?"

That was a loaded question, one she couldn't answer right off the top of her head. Her gaze touched the features of his face—his thick brows, the soft warmth of his eyes, his straight nose that had a small break at the bridge, his full lips and defined jaws, and that stubborn chin.

"I can't figure you out, Bo." She laughed nervously and bit down on her lip when he didn't respond. "You surprise me at every turn. About the time I think I don't want to get closer or get to know you better, you blow me away. Like finding that wallpaper; why'd you do that? How did you even know what you were looking for?"

He shrugged his broad shoulders. "I texted the picture to my phone the night you showed me. Thought I'd help."

Tina tilted her head to the side. "You didn't have to. None of the other crewmen tried to find it, not even the guy who was supposed to."

"I did it for you," he stated. She heard the words but couldn't wrap her mind around them. Bo remained physically closed off, hands in his pockets.

The air left her lungs in a rush. "You confuse me."

"I think that's pretty clear."

"Clear as mud." She laughed, shaking out her long hair and turning her eyes to the heavens for answers. "About the time I think you might be interested, you shut down."

"So says the woman who constantly reminds me that

she doesn't want my help, except for on the job and sometimes not even then." Bo pursed his lips and rocked back on his heels.

Tina walked over to the railing and focused on the way the water rippled and reflected the moonlight. "I guess you're not the only one sending mixed signals or no signals."

"No." He shook his head. Bo leaned his elbows on the rail. "Your signals were loud and clear… until tonight."

Tina's whole body deflated. Was that truly how she was? No wonder none of her relationships worked.

"You're different with them." He motioned his head back in the direction of Bear's. "You open up more. It's nice."

"I guess I'm oblivious. My head is always at work, you know? Even tonight, I was thinking about Jay's house and what needed to be done." She sighed. "I'm surprised you even showed up."

He stood and tugged her hand, bringing her flush against his body. Tina felt tiny compared to his broad frame. Heat rippled off of him and flowed into her. Bo was raw power, harnessed, then again, barely controlled. "Let me clarify. I want you. What do *you* want?"

Those three words sent her head spinning. *I want you.* "Bo," she whispered, placing her hands on his chest. The strength under her palms frightened her. The steadiness of his pulse frightened her more. His words were as steadfast as his body.

"Here's the deal, T. The job site, well, that's your domain and I'll follow orders all day. But if we start something beyond the job site, then I'm in control. You're used to men fearing you, obeying you. I won't. Make sure you understand; I'll take you over. I won't give in. You'll be mine and only mine. I'll give everything I have and take everything you give. Neither of us do anything halfway, and I'd rather we cleared this up tonight before I fall even harder for you."

Tina didn't speak. She couldn't. Bo hadn't spoken that many words in the two months they'd worked together. He'd kept this side of him under wraps, hidden from her. Damn, it was sexy. Her chest rose and fell with each labored breath. His words rooted their way into her mind, branded there in a way that made her body shudder with need. She closed her eyes, breathed him in, and let his masculine scent fill her head. She didn't know how to answer. Bo was absolutely right; she'd always dated men who were submissive to her demands. She'd worn the pants in the relationships. Up until this moment, she assumed Bo would be the same way.

She was wrong.

Now she understood. Bo respected her authority as his boss, but as his woman, he would be the dominant personality. The shy, quiet, obedient man who came to work would not be the same man who would court her. Could she deal with that? Was she able to give in and let a man take control?

He tilted her chin up until their eyes met. "You need to think about it. Don't answer tonight."

Good, because she didn't think she could answer coherently. Bo's passionate declaration scrambled her brain.

"There's one other thing." His brows dipped low and his lips pinched together. "Let's head back to my place first."

"Why?"

He touched her cheek, studying her features as if he might forget them. "Because you might not want me around at all after I tell you."

Chapter Fourteen

TINA ALLOWED HIM TO DRIVE, WHICH ONLY CONFIRMED that she was capable of letting him take some control. A woman like her would either have issues with a man taking her over, or she would secretly desire it. He had been brutally honest about his intentions because that was what she understood: no bullshit, no sugar coating the truth, cut and dry, this is how it is, can you live with it or not?

"Talk to me, Bo," she commanded in her boss tone, as he liked to think of it. She didn't use that tone around her friends.

He took a deep breath and let it fly. There would be no secrets between them, at least not from him. His mother had kept lots of secrets and he would have nothing like that with Tina.

"I did four years in California for assault with a deadly weapon." He didn't look at her; if he saw pity or fear on her face, it would break him. "My mom was—is—an addict.

We lived here in Riverview with my grandmother until I was a junior and Mom couldn't take it anymore. Nan is the person who started me in karate. My grandparents wanted to teach me discipline and honor. They were the only ones who ever gave a shit. My mom hooked up with this asshole, married him, and he moved us to California. I grew up in a house where I didn't come out of my room after seven at night, because my mom would be high and my step-dad would be, well, you don't want to know." He gripped the wheel until his knuckles hurt. "When I was old enough, I started working and used my money to take more karate lessons. I was good. The instructors went above and beyond to help me because I won lots of awards. My grades were high. I took honors classes. I had scholarships lined up, grants, the works. I was all set to get the hell out of there and my mom flipped out. She begged me not to go, kicked my step-dad out, and even tried to clean up. She helped get me into college, handled all the paperwork and everything." He sighed, remembering how different he was back then, how determined he was to reconnect with his mom, prove he was a good son who could take care of her. He wanted his mother to be as proud of him as his grandmother was. "It all went well for about a year or two. I had a good job, making money teaching karate to kids. I went to college right out of high school, made the football department proud for two seasons.

"Halfway through my last semester at that college, I got called into the dean's office. I thought we were going to discuss football or my grades, or what university I would transfer to. Instead, I found out my mom and the step-dad, who was never really out of the picture, were funneling money from my scholarship fund. They'd taken all my grant money, thousands of dollars."

"Oh my God," Tina whispered.

"Needless to say, school was over for me." He huffed out a bitter laugh. "My Nan, she begged me to come home. Told me I belonged here and sent me a bus ticket. So I quit my job, packed up my stuff, and waited until my mom got home from wherever she'd run off to that day. They were late, so I went to tell this friend of mine I was leaving and say goodbye. On my way home, I could hear the screaming from down the block. I ran into my house, found my step-dad standing over my mom, his hands around her neck." Bo gripped the wheel, the scene still far too vivid in his mind. "I lost it. The anger, at how they'd both intentionally screwed me over, just broke loose inside me."

"Oh, God, Bo. I can't imagine."

He'd pulled the truck into his grandmother's driveway and turned off the engine. They sat there in the light coming from the porch.

"My mom threw me under the bus. She told the police I was trying to kill my step-dad, that I was a trained killer and how dangerous I was since I had a black belt. They believed her, 'cause I messed up my step-dad pretty good, nearly killed him, or so the police said. Mom begged me to take the punishment, she cried and told me how much of a danger I was to myself and others. She told me I had scared her to death and how I'd become nothing more than a violent thug. By the time they got done with me, I didn't have any fight left. Nan came out to California. She tried to help, but I was so fucked in the head, I gave up. Pled guilty and spent the next four years trying to figure out where I went wrong."

"You didn't. Don't you see, Bo?" Tina placed a hand on

his arm, turning in her seat to face him. "Your mother manipulated you with every turn. Sure, there were things you could've done differently, but in the end, they still would've found a way to hurt you. They're selfish, messed up people, Bo. You can't punish yourself for their actions."

"Yeah, well, the State of California didn't see it that way." His bitter retort came out harsher than intended. "Anyway, I think it was the wakeup call I needed. There was this head doctor who talked to me. Barker. Kind of helped me see a lot of things I couldn't before. We still talk every other week." He looked over at her, prepared for whatever rejection she might pass. "So there you have it. I have a record, a parole officer, and an anger management therapist."

Tina's shoulders moved up and down with her deep breath. "Did my dad know this when he hired you?"

"Yeah, he did. Don't be mad at him. No matter what, I'm grateful for that."

She nodded her head, her eyes darting around the cab of the truck. "I guess you've given me a lot to think about."

Bo gritted his teeth. He'd wanted her to understand, to accept that while he might have made a mistake years ago, he wasn't a dangerous person. He wanted her ultimate trust.

"Do you regret it?" she asked.

He inhaled and let the air sit in his lungs for a moment before replying. Were there things he would have handled differently, sure. But he'd come out stronger on the other side. It had taken something drastic to open his eyes to his mother's level of depravity. It had made him more cautious, more guarded. It had taught him what he *didn't* want in a marriage or in a woman. He'd learned to deal with his guilt and anger in a healthy way. If he hadn't gone to jail and been forced to take anger management therapy, he wouldn't have met Dr. Barker and gotten the resources he needed. "No. It's made me who I am."

"Do you like who you are?" she asked softly, her voice shaking.

"I'm getting there." He gave her a half-hearted grin. "I would like to point out that *you* have a repeat record of assault with nail guns. I honestly think I'm taking the bigger risk here."

He was relieved when Tina's jaw dropped and she laughed outright. She pointed a finger at him. "You might have a point." Her smile lit up the night and they shared a moment. "You're the best surprise I've had lately, Bo. Even when you piss me off with your macho-man crap, I feel like I'd be stupid to turn you away."

"I want you to take your time, T. Being with me won't be an easy ride or a short trip." Before she could answer, he opened his door and came around to open hers. She slid out of the truck into his arms and put her hands on his chest. He didn't hesitate when he bent down and took her mouth, claiming her with one passionate kiss. Her fingers dug into his chest, grasping his shirt. His body hardened painfully when she licked at his lips, giving as much as he was.

He tunneled his hands in her hair, tilting her head for better access. She tasted damn good, *too* damn good. She moaned and melted deeper into their kiss, hanging on to his neck and pulling him closer while she rose on her tiptoes. Her tiny body drove him mad, rubbing on his, creating friction and heat until he had to come up for air.

"Damn, baby, I just wanted to kiss you goodnight." He rubbed his nose against her cheek and tried to steady his breath. She tore him up inside, made him raw and needy. He couldn't decide if it was a good feeling or not. In his experience, being vulnerable to a woman led to trouble. But this brand of trouble, he'd take all day long.

"That was no goodnight kiss. That was a mission statement. And you started it." Her words were light and airy, as if she couldn't catch her breath either. She let loose of his shirt.

Once again, she coaxed a smile out of him when least expected. "Maybe. I hoped that kiss would swing your vote. I need all the help I can get."

"You don't need as much as you think." She tiptoed up and kissed his cheek. "Would you like me to walk you to your door?" she teased, a gleam in her blue eyes.

"My balls would prefer you didn't." He slapped her butt as she rounded the truck and hopped up in the driver's seat, adjusting the seat for her shorter legs.

Bo leaned his elbows on the passenger side window sill. "Think about what I said, T."

She turned over the ignition. "I asked you out tonight for a reason, Bo. Even after everything you said, that reason hasn't changed."

Thrilled, he nodded his head. "Okay." As her truck backed out of his driveway and disappeared into the darkness, a sense of peace settled over him. Tina knew his darkest secrets and she hadn't peeled out of the driveway in fear. Hell, she'd kissed the shit out of him. For the first time since he was in college, his life had a heading. Things were running well... All except his truck.

Just before he dozed off to sleep, his cell phone chimed with an incoming text.

Thinking about that kiss.

So was he. No doubt his dreams were going to feature a beautiful blonde with bright blue eyes and a great ass.

Since Tina wasn't staring him in the face, he felt bolder in his reply. *I want u.*

I need time. Is that a problem?

Only for my... ego.

Lol. If it makes u feel better, I do wish u were here.

It did make him feel better. This was what he wanted, for her to think about him as much as he thought about her. He wanted her to need his presence the way he craved hers.

I can't sleep either, he replied, knowing her mind was racing if she was reaching out to him at midnight.

Want me to come tuck you in? ;)

Baby, u have no idea how sweet that sounds. But it's a bad idea.

He grinned when his cell phone rang and her number was on the screen.

"Why is that a bad idea?" she asked, her voice sleepy and husky, filling him with images of her naked in bed.

"Tina." He sighed and ran his hand over his face. Didn't she understand what kind of a cliff she was jumping off of by getting involved with him?

"Talk to me, Bo." This time her words were whispered, a sexy plea that nearly tore him apart.

"I'm starving for you."

She gasped on the other end of the phone but didn't speak.

"Desperate men do crazy things." He closed his eyes and bit his bottom lip. "You, *you* make me want to do crazy things."

"You know what kills me? You haven't said this many words to me in the entire two months we've worked together.

And now everything that comes out of your mouth makes me want to be with you more."

"Keeping my distance for two months has been hell. I can't keep it up. That's why I'm not holding back now. I want you with me. There won't be any hiding it either. I won't pretend you don't belong to me while we're in front of the crew. The workplace is your domain; that will never change. You're the boss and the drama stays at home. I know your rules. What we do after hours, that's mine. I'll consume you, baby. I'll be greedy with you, but I'll worship you in return. You have to make sure you want this."

She made a whimpering sound. "Are you going to make me wait until Monday to see you again?"

"Tell me what you want."

"Tomorrow night. My dad and Terry are taking his boat upriver for an overnight fishing trip. I want you here with me. I'll cook."

"Yes, ma'am."

Tina lay in bed after they hung up, contemplating the depth of what Bo offered. He was the kind of man who didn't do causal. This would be nothing like Trey. If Bo let a woman in, she would be the only woman in his heart. That woman would be the center of his universe, the one person who would see inside of him, be treasured in his life.

That woman would be the luckiest woman in the world. Was she ready for that level of commitment or devotion? Hadn't she just told her father when the right man came along, she wouldn't wonder *if* he wanted her or not?

I'm starving for you… I'll be greedy with you… I'll worship you.

"Dear God." Tina sighed and pushed her hair off her face. His words sent thrills and chills down her spine and she knew he would haunt her dreams in the best of ways.

The next morning, she had a minor headache as she headed downstairs to have coffee with her dad. Her mind was still reeling over Bo. For a man of little words, he sure had some nice ones.

"Mornin', honey," her father greeted her from the living room as he packed up his fishing gear. "How was your night?"

"Fine." She grabbed a mug and poured some coffee. Gathering up her courage, she confessed to her dad. "Bo came."

His hands faltered for a second. "Did he, now?"

"He's a nice guy, don't you think?" she asked as inconspicuously as she could.

"Yup."

"Quiet but nice."

Daddy picked up his coffee mug and narrowed his eyes over the rim as he sipped. "Was this a date or a co-worker thing?"

Tina sat down and put her feet up on the coffee table. "A date."

"Do you think that's a responsible decision?" He sat down across from her in his recliner.

"Did you think it was a responsible decision to hire him and not say anything to me about his record?"

Daddy narrowed his eyes, not the kind of man to cower to her challenge. "The risk factor was low. If it didn't work out, I'd simply fire him. Relationships are different. Much higher risk factor."

"I think the risk is great, but the payoff is greater."

This must've surprised her daddy. His mouth came open to speak, but he said nothing.

Tina studied the way her black coffee swirled in her mug. "He told me everything last night. About his parents and going to jail." Her father sat quiet, waiting for her to continue. "He told me a lot last night." She smiled to herself, remembering the way his words wrapped her up and made her feel wanted.

"Which goes to prove that until recently, you didn't know him very well."

"Not true. I know he's responsible. He's respectful and prompt. He keeps his head under most circumstances. When we have an issue at work, he's the first person to offer solutions or options. He's pleasant to the other men. They respect him. Jason seems to think he's a riot, based on how they go on all day. He fit in with my friends last night, something Trey never did. He's kind and thoughtful. He's talented and not afraid to learn new things. I also know that he talks to a therapist twice a month."

"Good for him. Maybe he should pass on the number; you're sounding crazy."

"Dad!" She threw a couch pillow at him.

"I'm teasing."

Their conversation was interrupted by a knocking at the door. Dixie barked and headed to see who was there.

"Speak of the devil," Daddy muttered. "It's too early for Terry. Twenty bucks says that's him."

Tina met his eyes. "He's... he's special."

"I agree. He's a good guy, honey. He's just had a rough life, made some poor choices. I think he's all right." He patted her leg and gave her a reassuring smile. "Go answer the door."

Tina's stomach fluttered at the thought of seeing Bo. Then she realized she was in her cotton pajama shorts and a baggy shirt with no bra on. Oh well, let him get an eyeful.

Bo stood with his hands in his pockets, patiently waiting. When she opened the door, he looked her up and down, then met her eyes. The rhythm of his breathing changed. Had she not been catching her own breath, she might not have noticed.

"Mornin', beautiful," he said softly, melting every cold, dark area of her heart. He knelt to love on Dixie, scratching her ears and kissing her head.

"She likes you."

"Dogs have good judgment." Bo petted Dixie's head and stood, once again shoving his hands in his pockets.

Tina leaned her head against the door and smiled. "So I didn't imagine last night."

Bo shook his head, a kind smile playing at his lips. They stared at each other, her nervously fidgeting, him still as death, fixated on her.

"I think I fixed the truck… again. Just taking it out for a test run."

"And you came all the way over here? On a test run?" Her chest constricted. Did that mean he missed her?

"Something like that." He reached up and rubbed his chin. "Truth is, I couldn't wait. I've been up since six working on the truck and trying to keep busy for the last two hours."

"I know the feeling." She smiled. "We were just having coffee. You want to join us?"

"I'm supposed to be giving you space." He looked down at his feet for a moment.

"I don't want space." Tina rocked back on her heels and took a deep breath. "Can we spend some time together today? Just the two of us? Maybe the three of us?" Tina glanced at Dixie, who stared up at Bo like he was made of dog treats.

"I'm all yours."

Those three words hit her hard. She drummed her hands on her thighs, resisting the urge to fondle the hard body in front of her, and invited him into her home. He cussed behind her and turned. "What?" His eyes were low, as if they'd been on her butt. They popped up to her face. Her jaw dropped open when he blushed. "Were you checking out my ass?"

Bo showed no remorse and shrugged his broad shoulders. "It's a nice ass."

"Behave. My father is in there." She held her smile until he couldn't see it. She was giddy. Good God, it was like being a teenager with a crush all over again. Her heart fluttered when their hands brushed. She sat down in a wide comfy chair while Bo sat across from her on the couch.

"Morning, Bo," Daddy said from his recliner.

"Morning, sir."

"Did you have fun last night?"

Tina's pulse spiked when Bo cast her a quick but heated glance.

"Y'sir. I was hoping to see Tina perform again, but no such luck."

Tina rolled her eyes and shook her head. She reached down and ran her hands through Dixie's soft fur.

"She got that from her mama," Daddy said, eying them both. "Angie could out sing the birds in the trees. When we were dating, all I had to do was take her somewhere with a stage and a dance floor and she was happy. Nothing fancy, just let her sing and dance."

"Apparently, I got my looks from her too, right, Daddy?" Tina loved to hear her father talk about Angie.

Daddy smiled wide and put a hand over his heart. "Dear Lord, that woman." He shook his head and looked over at Bo. "I loved her from the first moment I saw her. No doubt about it. She was singing, imagine that." Daddy went back in time, telling Bo all about the night he met her mother and how they were head over heels in love from then on.

Her father might be lost in the memory, but Tina was lost in Bo. His lips pulled back, just a fraction, just enough to let her see that hidden affection. His hazel eyes were soft and warm as they held hers. Even though he was sitting across the room, he might as well have been right beside her, touching her face. A warm blush rose up her neck and she used her coffee as an excuse to look away. But Bo kept his eyes on her, burning into her, telling her he knew exactly what Daddy meant when he mentioned instant attraction.

"Maybe one day, you two will be lucky enough to find the kind of relationships Angie and I had," Daddy said, finally back in the present. He looked back and forth between Bo and Tina. "Or maybe you have," he muttered into his coffee cup and took a sip.

"I should get dressed." Tina hopped up, not ready to have this discussion with her father. Bo stood up too, an old-fashioned sign of respect. "I'll be right back." She bounded up the stairs and closed her apartment door before she let out her breath.

She'd just left Bo alone to deal with her father. Talk about throwing him to the lions. "Crazy, Dixie," she said to the dog, who had followed her upstairs. "I'm bat-shit crazy." She shook her head and fished for shorts and a shirt.

Chapter Fifteen

B O BLEW OUT A DEEP BREATH THE MOMENT TINA WAS out of sight. He didn't realize he'd held it.

Then he was left alone…with her father…who was assessing him like he was buying a used car, looking for problems.

"You're playing with fire, son."

"Yes, sir."

"She'll eat you up and spit you out if you're not careful."

Bo met Duane's hard stare. "That's a hell of a thing to say about your daughter."

The man gave him a knowing look, one that told him he liked Bo sticking up for Tina. "But true. She won't stick with a weak man, Bo. That's why that engineer didn't last long. A real wuss, that guy was."

"I caught on to that, sir."

"Think you can handle a woman with balls as big as yours?"

"I don't like weak women. Never have. Don't like needy women either. Tina's neither."

"She's still a woman."

"I caught on to that too, sir."

"You realize if you piss her off, I'll fire you right after our crew kicks your ass?" Duane crossed his arms over his chest.

"That was abundantly clear the first day, sir. Along with the fact we should never argue around a nail gun, sir."

Duane huffed and rubbed his temple. "And you're still pursuing her?"

Bo made sure his face and eyes conveyed his conviction. "With everything I have."

"Humph." Duane shook his head. "You've got gumption; I'll give you that. And if she turns you down?"

"Then I'll find another job. I won't make her uncomfortable." Bo leaned over, put his elbows on his knees, and linked his hands. "The thing is, I know she can do better, a shit-load better than me. That doesn't matter because I know exactly what you mean when you talk about loving her mom from the moment you saw her."

Duane's eyes widened for just a moment before they narrowed, his lips curving up into a smile. "In that case, best of luck to ya, son." He held out his hand and the two men shook.

Tina came back downstairs and Bo rose again and didn't sit back down until she was perched on the arm of her father's recliner.

"You need me today?" She kissed the top of his head.

"Not that I know of. I can dial a phone if I do. Terry should be here by one."

"I hear Ms. Patterson is having another open house

at the art gallery. You should go see her on your way out." Tina nudged him with her arm.

"We'll see."

"Love you."

"You too."

Tina tugged at Bo's sleeve and he bid Duane a nice day. On the way out, she snatched a tote bag and tossed it over her shoulder and snapped for Dixie to come.

Once again, the effortless beauty of Tina Foster stole his breath. She was wearing a red plaid shirt that curved into her waist, the open button at the bottom giving a peek at her flat stomach, the open buttons at the top tempting him beyond comprehension. Her blue jeans shorts hugged her hips and accentuated her toned legs. Even the simple ponytail was sexy without meaning to be.

He was far more gone than he thought possible.

He opened her door and helped her into the cab of his old Ford. It wasn't nearly the luxurious ride as her truck, but it worked for now. It had sat for over ten years before he came back and got it running again. Now he just had to be patient while the kinks worked their way out.

"Where to?" Tina asked happily.

"Let's just drive."

"Perfect." Her smile was radiant as she slid on her sunglasses.

They drove around the country roads of Riverview and Tina pointed out houses she'd worked on, places where she knew people lived, and places she'd like to get her hands on. He didn't have to speak much; she was a talkative person. It took the pressure off him, another thing he liked about her. Bo wasn't full of happy stories and funny jokes like she was. The last four years of his life had been a daily battle.

There was no joy there or exciting things to reveal to her. It was all hard lessons and more close calls than he cared to think about.

Throughout the old downtown area, Tina told him all about the latest drama, the town gossip, who was mad at whom and who did what since he'd been gone. The streets looked the same as he remembered. Driving down them today, with a beautiful blonde by his side, the world seemed happier, fuller than it did yesterday.

They ended up north of town and past the home of one of his old school buddies, the only one around this town who had any contact with him when he went off to California. The Buchanan place wasn't at all what he remembered. It seemed, since the death of Mrs. Buchanan, the place had gone downhill.

"So sad," Tina said, shaking her head and examining the scene. "He's drinking himself to death and no one can stop him. Daddy reached out to him, you know they used to be friends. But Mr. Buchanan turned him away. The Millers offered to buy his cattle and land. He refused. I guess he's going to let them starve to death because of his pride."

The old farmhouse sat up on a hill, falling down and decrepit. Close to the road was a dilapidated singlewide the old man had moved into after his wife died. The cows that roamed the bare fields were emaciated, their ribs visible under their hide.

"I need to let Drew know what's going on," Bo said.

"You know where he is?" Tina was surprised. "No one has heard from him in years. Someone said he works for national security, someone else said he was a spy. Who knows?"

Bo did. He couldn't say what all he knew about Andrew

Buchanan, but he could get a message to him about how far downhill the family homestead had gone. Maybe Bo could do something to help in the meantime.

They doubled back and crossed the river headed to the west side of town. Tina rolled down her window and propped her feet on the mirror. He loved the way she entertained them both. She would talk, he would listen and laugh. Perfect.

"See that gate right there? Pull in." She was already unbuckling her seat belt.

"What is this place?" He examined the tire path through the woods.

"It's the back entrance to Jayden's land." She slid from the truck to unlock the combination gate, calling over her shoulder, "There's a lake that's fed by river water. It's beautiful. We can go swimming."

"We didn't bring extra clothes," he yelled from his window.

She pushed the gate open and cast him a mischievous, sexy glance over her shoulder. "*I* did."

He actually shivered in anticipation of what that filly had in mind.

Tina was right. The Harris place was rolling hills, running creeks, pasture land, and patches of forest. Once they finally found the lake, he felt like they were in another zip code.

"That's a big island right in the middle." She pointed across the lake. "The two creeks go all the way to the main river. The Harris family cemetery is on that island."

"Creepy."

Tina elbowed him in the ribs but grinned, so it was worth it.

He parked near a wooden pier that stretched out into the water. Tina grabbed the tote bag and unloaded a blanket. She spread it over the ground under a shade tree and flopped down, patting the spot next to her. Her bag was full of apples, oranges, chips, nuts, and water.

"How the heck did you pack this and get dressed in the five minutes I talked to your dad?"

"I'm fast." She shrugged a shoulder. Dixie ran around, checking out the water and the pier.

Bo took the apple she offered and leaned back on his elbow. Right there on that blanket, Tina made herself at home. She took off her flip-flops, spread out, and sighed as she relaxed. "I've been swimming in this lake since I was a kid. Had many picnics under this same tree."

"Is this where you bring all your boyfriends?"

Her forehead crinkled as she thought about it. "Actually, no. I've never brought a guy here. You're the first."

He shouldn't be so happy about that, but he was.

"The Harris family and the Miller family are like icons of the city. Their ancestors founded the town back when Moses was alive. I've been friends with both families since grade school. When Jayden and Christopher married, you would have thought the damn Queen was coming to town. Finally, the Miller and Harris families would be joined. It was a citywide event, ya know? Biggest party this place has ever seen. The Harris boys were like my brothers to me. I grew up with them, spent the night at their house all the time; hell, their mom taught me how to cook and Chris taught me how to sing. Chris was best friends with Jay's brother, Marshall. I didn't know if we would ever get over Chris' loss. Some days it feels like we still haven't."

"You miss him."

Tina nodded. "I do. Jayden was so different back then. Not nearly as neurotic as she is now," she said and smiled. "I don't know why I told you all that. Or why you even care." She shook her head and lay back down on her back.

Bo curved his body around her and looked down at her lovely face. "I care because you care. This place is special to you, and now it's special to me. I'm also interested in the nail gun thing."

Her eyes widened and her mouth opened to speak before she clamped it shut. She averted her gaze. "Well, you just get right to it, huh?"

"The first thing Terry said to me after 'take these screws to T' was 'don't hit on her unless you want nails in your balls.'"

Tina burst out laughing and covered her eyes with her hands. "Oh my God. I didn't know that." She laughed until he was smiling along with her. He was learning to love that laugh, love the way it reached deep down into his soul and warmed him. "That sounds like Uncle Terry." She sighed and closed her eyes. "Steven," she groaned. "We dated for a couple years. The first year was before my dad's accident, right out of high school. The last year was after. He was part of the crew."

"Ah." Bo nodded, immediately understanding what went wrong.

"It was one thing when he worked with my dad and had a man as his boss. It was something totally different when I stepped in." Tina rolled over onto her belly, propped up on her elbows to look down at him. As she spoke, she absently shredded a few blades of grass. "See, I've been working with my dad since I was a little kid. During the summers, if I didn't go to my grandparents' house, I went to the job site.

Not much choice, ya know? Daddy didn't know what else to do with a little girl, so I was right there with him, swinging a hammer and sawing lumber. By the time I graduated high school, I'd helped him build over twenty houses. It was cool, I loved it. I started college to get my business degree just so I could help Daddy. It's all I've ever wanted to do." She met his gaze. "He's all I have. I might not be his son, but I can follow in his footsteps."

Bo reached up and ran his knuckles down her cheek. He didn't need to say anything.

"Anyway, Steven was hired, and we hit it off immediately. Daddy warned me about dating guys I work with, but I didn't listen. He was on the crew, I was in the office. It worked. When Daddy went down, it changed everything. I went to the field, he took over the office. It was very clear right away that Steven didn't like having me around all day. It was too much. Not to mention, he thought he could boss me around."

Bo grinned. "Idiot. I knew right off the bat you have authority issues."

She laughed and threw grass at him. "So what?"

"I'm not complaining." Bo folded his arms behind his head.

Tina frowned and bit the side of her lip. "He cheated." Her blue eyes flashed over to his and then away again. "I mean, he was with me during all Daddy's surgeries and he stayed at our house to help out while Daddy was in therapy." She shook her head, balled up the grass, and pinched it between her fingers. "I know people say there are things that lead up to men having affairs. I've heard it all. You've proven I can be oblivious, maybe I'm stupid too, because I never saw it coming. Hell, if I hadn't seen it with my own eyes, I never would have believed he was capable."

"Damn. You caught him?" His heart ached for her. There was nothing worse.

"It was the end of the day. He said he was going to finish out some stuff and meet me at home. An hour later, he was still gone. I went back to the site to make sure he was okay and help him finish up. Surprise," she said with a bitter huff. "I might have lost it for a minute. The bimbo immediately ran off, screaming that she didn't know he had a girlfriend. She hid in the car. Steven tried to pull his pants back up and tripped when he saw me go for the nail gun. I put three nails right in the crotch of his pants while he crab-walked on his bare ass across the floor."

Bo chuckled, shaking his head. "Bastard deserved it."

"I made him leave without pants. Then I nailed his jeans to a four-by-four and stuck it out in front of the house so the guys would see it the next morning."

"Please tell me he didn't show up to reclaim them."

"No. He didn't even try to get his final paycheck." She cast him a half-hearted smile. Bo could see the pain she tried to cover. "I went home and cried all night. By that next day, I was so damned angry. For a long time, I thought it was all my fault. I changed the dynamics of our relationship. I...changed. We were young; what the hell did we know? Neither one of us was in our right mind."

He leaned over and gently kissed her shoulder. "Even if he couldn't deal, cheating is a choice, not something you're forced into. That's all on him."

"It took me a long time to figure that out."

"For the record, I think the nail gun was a nice touch."

Tina's awe-inspiring grin spread wide. "Steven told me I was a crazy bitch. I told him to suck my dick."

Bo fell over on his back laughing. He nearly choked on air. Man, he loved the strength and resilience he saw in her. Sure, she might have been heartbroken, but she didn't apologize for being who she was. She'd made a lot of sacrifices so she could care for her father and that kind of love and loyalty made him respect her all the more.

"I need to know something." She angled her body towards him. They both lay on their sides, heads propped up, smiling at each other. "You said that things wouldn't change at work. But I have a hard time believing that. How could they not?"

"Because unlike that asshole you're currently comparing me to, I love the way you command your troops. In jail, it's survival of the fittest. I had to be as mean and as hard as I could just to get through the day. I didn't make waves, tried not to draw too much attention to myself. At the same time, I made damn sure no one fucked with me. I know how to keep my head down and follow directions but still be strong enough to hold my own. You won't walk all over me, baby. And I don't feel the need to assert my manhood over you. It will be a give-and-take for us both." He shrugged a shoulder. "We can handle it. Besides, I'd follow you to the ends of the earth if it meant I could stare at your ass all day."

Chapter Sixteen

THIS MIGHT JUST WORK. TINA GAZED INTO BO'S SEXY eyes. There was always something just below the surface in his stare. Something dangerous and intense. In that moment, she realized Bo Galloway might just be the man she needed.

Tina leaned forward and pressed her lips to his. He had amazing lips, soft and warm. He knew how to use them too. Their mouths slid across each other, coaxing and stroking with a seductive gentleness. She'd wanted to kiss him for so long, it felt good to finally do it.

He'd be so easy to love, so easy to depend on. Bo was a pillar of strength and stability. He'd demonstrated that in his work ethic. Her biggest fear was losing herself to someone else. Then again, Steven had never promised her anything, much less to protect and guard her heart. Their relationship had been all guess work from the beginning, whereas Bo laid it all out in the open. He wouldn't make her step blindly into the dark, then get upset when she didn't know where she was headed. How nice would it be not to always have to lead? How would it feel to have someone take care of her for once? She desperately wanted to find out.

"You realize I brought you here with the intention of getting you naked and wet." She grinned.

"Uh, baby, I think we should go over how this works. You get wet, not me," he replied in a dry tone.

Tina chucked and nudged him as she got to her feet. "I meant in the lake. You do swim, right?"

"I wasn't exactly expecting to take a swim today." Bo tugged at his jeans and shrugged.

Tina shimmied her hips out of her blue jean shorts to reveal her bikini. "I guess you can just watch me swim." She unbuttoned her shirt and sashayed over to the pier with him hot on her heels. Tina didn't have a confidence issue. She was blessed with good genetics and a job that kept her physically fit. Her mother had been tall and thin, and Tina at least got the thin part.

Bo rubbed his jaw and watched, his eyes holding a predatory desire. His darkening stare simmered her blood. He peeled off his shirt, kicked off his shoes, and emptied his pockets. "It's a good thing I live fairly close. Is this lake pretty deep out there?"

"Yeah, why?" Tina dropped her shirt on the wood.

Bo picked her up and jumped right off the end of the pier while she screamed and Dixie barked.

The cool waters of the Sanguine River kept this lake circulating and cool all year long. The water hit her skin and washed away all the summer heat. She surfaced but kept her eyes closed, soaking up the sun. Some called this river a taker of souls, a reaper. Sanguine was the Spanish word for blood and God knew plenty had been spilled in its murky depths. As Tina floated on her back, she couldn't help but feel it was more of an artery, giving life to its limbs, such as this one.

Bo surfaced a couple feet away from her. "Damn, that feels good."

Water dripped off of every curve and ripple of his muscles. Trey might have had a pretty face, but he was nothing compared to the raw strength of Bo Galloway. Tina shook her head, trying to snap out of her trance. "Yeah. This place is perfect for swimming. Come on, Dixie. Come, girl."

The Border Collie hesitated only for a second before leaping off the pier and into the water. She swam around to Tina, then Bo, and then to the bank. She shook off and then went right back to the pier.

Bo liked to play with Dixie and Tina could understand why. Dogs didn't ask questions. Dogs didn't judge people on their past. Dogs were the perfect example of unconditional love. No wonder Bo had bonded with Dixie.

Tina wanted to learn more about him. "Let's see some of that kung-fu mojo you're so proud of."

He resisted, until she walked out of the lake and went to the pier. They took turns jumping off into the lake. Tina got fancy, doing cartwheels and flips. It was too easy to one-up her with his own flips and kicks. He took a running start and did a somersault high above the water, splashing down close to her. When he came back up, she was clapping and whistling.

"Perfect ten," she said and laughed merrily. "That's some badass stuff right there."

"That's your man, a real badass." He rolled his eyes but smiled as he swam towards her.

"Yeah." She wrapped her arms around his neck from behind. "That's my man. Are you hungry?" She kissed his cheek, her lips trailing downward.

"You have no idea." Bo groaned when she bit his neck.

"I meant for food, Captain Hormones."

"Food. You. They both make me happy."

Tina threw her head back, laughing. "Come on, badass. Let's go eat. *Food.*"

Bo shook out the blanket and spread it over the tailgate of his truck. They munched and talked. Well, she talked. He answered direct questions and stared at her. Tina didn't mind railroading the conversation. It was not like he was chatty and there was so much she had to learn about him.

"Can you still teach?" Tina noticed the way his jaw tensed.

"No." His hard tone took her by surprise. "I lost all my belts and titles upon conviction."

"I'm sorry." She wished she'd never even brought it up.

He shook his head. "It's my own fault. I trained for years on how to avoid fighting, how to defend not offend, and all that training went out the window in a moment of anger."

"He was hurting your mother, Bo."

Hard eyes met hers. "And I could've rendered him unable to do so quickly…without causing him a hospital visit." He examined the bag of chips in his lap. "I lost control and that brought shame to my teachers and my dojo. I'm out."

Tina treaded lightly, but she wanted to see how far he would let her dig. "Do you miss it?"

"Every day."

"Did you *want* to hurt him?"

"Yes." Bo took drink of his water. "Keep asking questions but be sure you really want the answers."

She didn't back down from his threats. His answers didn't scare her. "Do you hate your mother?"

He shook his head. "I don't *hate* anyone. I'd be perfectly content never seeing her face again, though. I have Nan and she's all the family I need."

Tina leaned over and touched his knee. "You have me."

Bo lifted her hand to his lips and kissed it. "Then I have more than I need and much more than I deserve."

He could make her heart rate spike faster than anything she'd ever experienced. "Teach me something. I'll be your student."

Bo's eyes lit with a spark of something that had her thighs clenching together. To think she'd thought for so long he was unexpressive. She just hadn't been paying attention. Bo expressed everything in his eyes.

They hopped off the back of the truck.

"Can you throw a punch or twist out of a choke-hold? Every woman needs to know how to break the nose of a pervert if necessary."

"Seriously?" She put her hands on her waist and leaned on a hip.

"All right, Mighty Mouse. Show me what you got besides nail guns." He waved her forward.

Tina braced her feet, bent slightly at the knees, and raised her fists. Looking him right in the eye, she swung.

Had he not been a damn trained martial arts master, she might have whopped him a good one. She had force, a good arc, and she didn't hold back. He was fast and prepared to block her. The expression of shock on his face was a welcome sight. "Nice. Okay. Good. Kick me."

Her kicks, not so much, and she didn't mind laughing at herself. They spent the morning dueling. He taught her some beginner moves, basic self-defense. Each time he got her close enough, he kissed or nipped at her or blew raspberries against her skin. He moved with grace, almost dancing around her with dexterity that amazed her. With each spin or twist, he showed her exactly how he'd earned his belts and his awards.

After the lesson, they played like young kids, playing fetch with Dixie, splashing about, and trying to catch each other in the lake. Tina hadn't had this much fun in years. It was rare for her to let go of the responsibilities that weighed on her constantly. Usually, her brain was in the next work week, mentally distracted by all the tasks ahead and plotting them out. Yet all her thoughts were right there in the moment. She focused on the incredible man in front of her and was able to relax more than she had in far too long. Bo swam over and closed the distance between them. He pulled her into his arms, her legs wrapping around his waist. She nuzzled his neck and closed her eyes, loving the way their bodies felt together and finally having the freedom to touch him as she wanted.

"Can we stay just like this for the rest of the day?" He kissed her hair and held her close. "I haven't been this content in a long time, Tina."

That rawness in him, the way he put all his cards on the table, sometimes took the air right out of her. No games. No hidden agenda, just pure, honest, down and dirty truth.

"Me too." *And it scares me.* No man had ever owned her, ever tamed her or controlled her. Bo could do it all and ruin her defenses in the process.

Bo's strong arms locked her to his hard, hot chest. "You're overthinking things. Stop."

Tina clenched her eyes closed. She wasn't used to being

this honest with a man. For the first time in her relationship history, she spit out exactly what she was thinking. "I'm afraid we're going to lose this on Monday morning."

"We won't. Trust me." It was a command, one made with the authority of a man who owned his woman. "I've wanted you in my arms since the first time I laid eyes on you and I've worked for you just fine."

Tina pulled back. She touched his cheek. "You say that now. What happens when I make you mad at work? Will you take it out on me afterhours? Or if something happens and we break—"

"Don't say it." He touched her lips and her heart kicked over. "Get this straight now. Either you're mine or you're not. It's all or nothing. You'll trust me and surrender your heart, or we aren't doing this. I'm not going to be like these other pricks you've dated where you keep your distance and only come around when you feel like it."

"Is that what you want?" she whispered, swallowing hard. "My surrender?" Tina took a deep breath when he nodded and stared at her lips. "What if I want you to surrender to me?"

"I will, every moment we're on the jobsite. Just like I do now, boss." Those delicious lips pulled back in the corners and melted her into a puddle of goo.

Tina pursed her lips and narrowed her eyes at him. "We'll see, Bo Galloway. I think you might just surprise me."

"I will." Bo sprang up and jumped backwards, sending them flying back into the water. Tina yelped and came up laughing. She splashed him, loving his tendency to be full of surprises.

There was a part of her, a huge part, that just wanted to fall into him like she fell into the lake—free and uninhibited.

To let Bo deeper into her heart than she'd ever let anyone. If she did that, he would have the ability to break her so easily.

She'd been betrayed. She'd walked up on a man she thought loved her to find him with another woman. As much as she hid behind her antics and pride, Steven had broken her heart. Behind closed doors, she'd cried her eyes out and cursed herself for being young and stupid and naive.

Maybe Bo would be different. Maybe not. Maybe she would fall even harder and hurt even deeper. Or maybe she would fall and find love they wrote songs about.

Four words kept coming to mind as they spent the day together. *He's worth the risk.*

Chapter Seventeen

ABOUT TWO THAT AFTERNOON, HE MADE A PHONE call to his grandmother to check in with her. He usually called every day, so this was nothing new. With the phone on speaker, he asked his beloved Nan how her day was going and if she needed anything.

"I'm fine, Bo darling. Are you having a nice time?"

"Yes, ma'am," Bo replied. Tina, however, wanted to tell her all the details. Bo leaned back on the truck and settled in.

"How about you kids come here for dinner?" Nan suggested. "I put a huge roast in the slow cooker this morning and it's nearly falling apart, smells wonderful."

"Yes, ma'am."

"That would be great." Tina's face lit up. "We have to drop off Dixie. Do you want me to pick up some salad? Maybe some garlic bread?" They then had a conversation about the menu for the evening and why Tina's dad couldn't join them. That flowed into talking about the fishing season and how Nan wanted Bo to work on her old boat so they could take a trip upriver.

Bo held the phone out so the two most important women in his life could chitchat. Damn, the women could talk. It was pleasing that they conversed so easily and seemed to get along. That would make his life better—right up until they ganged up on him.

"She's great." Tina smiled when Bo hung up the phone. "Really chatty, huh?"

Bo's head fell backward as he barked out a laugh. "Pot, meet kettle." He wiggled his phone at her.

Tina's mouth hung open. "Are you saying I talk too much?" The glimmer of challenge in her eyes and the way she licked at her lips made him happier than he ever thought possible. He adored her playful side.

"No." He chuckled. "Not too much. You can talk, though." He put his arm around her shoulders and pulled her to his chest. "I like it. All I have to do is listen."

"Well, you're a man of few words. Someone has to pick up the slack or we'd sit in silence all day." Her justified haughtiness made him smile. "I'm surprised you don't get sick of me talking at work."

"Actually, you sing all day. That never gets old." Even though they'd been swimming, when he nuzzled her hair, he could scent her shampoo.

Tina smiled up at him, her hand settling on his cheek. "Why don't we run back to my place and clean up?"

Bo nodded and used his shirt to dry off. When he turned to help Tina down, she had this look in her eyes. He couldn't place it. "What?"

"I've had fun today." She pushed her hair behind her

ears, a sexy blush painting her cheeks red.

"Surprised?" He rested his hands on her thighs as she sat on the tailgate.

"No. I knew beneath that quiet exterior you were a total nutcase." She smiled and Bo leaned in. Tina didn't hesitate to kiss him, which was good. She needed to get used to him touching and kissing her at will.

He swiped his tongue into her mouth and moved in between her thighs, then buried his hands in her hair, angling her head to deepen their kiss. Her mouth was pure heaven, warm and lush, bitable. The way she sighed and wiggled her body to the edge of the tailgate to get closer to him just ramped up his desire. She was right there with him, needing but not knowing how much to take.

"Damn, baby," he mumbled against her neck. His hips nestled between hers, heat coming off of her in waves. "I haven't even touched you and you're burning up." He brought her leg up over his hip, opening her thighs wider. His large hand traveled up the back of her thigh, cupping her bottom under the frayed shorts. Tina gripped his shoulders and neck. Everywhere she touched went up in flames.

"Well, I'm a bit attracted to you," she panted.

"What's a bit?" He nibbled on her ear and lightly nipped at her neck. All the while, he kept his hips aligned with hers. There was no way she could mistake his arousal.

"Enough that I'm dry-humping your leg like a damn Chihuahua. We have to separate. This is ridiculous."

He dropped his forehead against her shoulder and his whole body shook with laughter, which made her giggle too. "You'll say anything, won't you? No shame, no filter."

"Honest to a fault, that's what Daddy says. Sorry."

"Don't be. You make me laugh."

"And you make me...dizzy." She fanned herself.

"Good." He wanted to keep her wanting and needing. It took time to bridle a filly and he was a patient man.

Chapter Eighteen

NAN HAD SET OUT HER BEST DISHES AND MADE UP THE table by the time Bo and Tina arrived. Tina was freshly showered, but he needed to run upstairs to change into dry clothes. When he came back down, Tina and Nan were in the kitchen laughing like old pals. He leaned against the doorjamb and watched their interaction. Tina was so damned lovable, how could his Nan resist? He hadn't, not from day one.

The ladies lifted the lid of the crockpot and Tina bragged on how great the roast smelled.

"You know, it takes a lot of food to keep that grandson of mine fed. But I don't mind. It's been so long since I've had someone to cook for and God knows he didn't get good food in—" Nan paused and cast a glance to Tina.

"It's okay, Nan. He told me everything."

"He did?" That surprised his grandmother. She placed a hand over her heart. "Well, you must be one special young lady."

"I hope that's what it means. I'm pretty crazy about him." Tina bit her lip and tilted her head, almost like asking permission.

Her declaration knocked the wind out of his chest. She cared enough to confide in the one person who mattered most in his world. This morning Bo had faced her father, and now Tina had faced Nan. Parental approval—*check.*

Nan smiled and took Tina by the shoulders. "My cup runneth over."

They noticed Bo standing there and Tina instantly came to his arms. "I'm pretty crazy about you too, baby," he said in her ear.

"All right, lovebirds. Let's eat." Nan brought the roast to the table.

Their dinner was fantastic; the food and the company. Tina and Nan were an unending stream of conversation and laughter. He fell more in love with both of them as the night went on. They finished the meal, played a couple rounds of cards, even whipped up some brownies before they decided to call it a night.

Nan kissed and hugged Tina, begging her to come back soon.

"I will. This was fun, Nan."

"Don't wait up." Bo kissed his grandmother's temple and hugged her close.

"You two kids use protection, okay? I want great-grandbabies, but y'all need to get married first."

"For real? You just had to go there, oh my God." Bo stood dumbfounded and completely mortified. Tina nearly fell off the porch laughing.

Nan put her fists on her slender hips. "You're spending

the night with a wonderful young lady after four years in the slammer. Do I look stupid to you?"

"No, ma'am." Bo shook his head and hurried off the porch. He grabbed Tina—who practically brayed with laughter—and tugged her to the truck.

They were both chuckling as he drove her home. Tina scooted over on the bench seat until she was right under his arm. Her head rested on his chest. "I absolutely adore that woman," she said, kissing him on the cheek.

"She's a damn riot." He rolled his eyes with affection. Nan was one of a kind for sure.

"You're lucky to have her."

"I know." He smiled down at her. "What happened to your mother?"

Tina snuggled closer. "She died right after I was born. She had a blood disease. Daddy says it's a miracle she even carried me. They both knew it would be tricky, but Mom wanted a baby so bad and as much as Daddy hated to risk her, he hated to deny her even more."

"He knew his wife might die and he let her get pregnant anyway?" That blew his mind. What was wrong with her father? How does a person find something so beautiful and then throw it away? Then again, Bo would give Tina the moon and stars if she asked for it.

"My mom wasn't going to live a long life anyway, Bo. Eventually, the disease would've killed her. Then who would my father have? He says Heaven had to trade angels."

"Not that I'm complaining about his choice, but if I had to choose between my wife and a child that may or may not exist…" He shook his head. "Don't know if I could make the right decision."

"I honestly don't know if I could either, but like you

said, I'm not complaining. I rather like this whole existing gig."

"I like your existing gig too." He pulled her close and kissed her head. How the hell had he gotten so lucky? He put in applications at other businesses in town and yet the billboard advertising Foster Construction had called out to him, caught his attention immediately. He'd searched the internet for other companies that were actively hiring, which Foster's wasn't, but a small voice in the back of his mind told him to try. With a little phone call from his praying grandmother and some divine intervention, he'd gone with his gut.

He rubbed his cheek against her soft, blonde hair. Thank God, he'd listened.

Tina's house was dark when they arrived and went straight to the side of the building where a tall staircase led to her second story entrance.

"I don't use this entrance often, but if you ever come over and don't want to disturb my dad, you can come this way."

"Like if I want to sneak into your bed in the middle of the night?"

Her eyes danced with mischief. "Exactly."

The industrial, loft-style apartment was massive. The lower level of the metal building held the offices, Duane's two-bedroom home, and a garage. The second story was all one big open space with the exception of the bedroom and bathroom in the corner.

"Wow. This is big."

"Twenty-two hundred open square feet." Tina set her bag and keys down on a table by the door. "This was the old cannery. Fruits and produce came in from the fields, were packed up in here, and sent down river."

Her design style married corrugated tin walls, brick, and stainless steel. Recycled barn wood framed her office area straight ahead of him. A stainless-steel kitchen lined the west wall to his left. The long island featured the sink and a row of bar stools on the opposite side. Two brown leather sectionals created a U-shaped seating area facing a giant flat screen and entertainment center to his right. Bo went to check out the brick that covered the entire south wall behind the television.

"It's tile. Thin. But it looks like real brick, right?" She grazed her hands over the wall.

"Did you lay it yourself?"

She nodded, proud. "Dad and I did everything ourselves."

"Not surprising. You can do anything, I swear."

"Pot, meet kettle," she said, throwing his words back at him.

"I've had an amazing teacher the last couple months." Bo took her into his arms and smiled down at her.

She linked her hands behind his head. "Would you like a drink?"

Bo nodded. He tried to act otherwise, but he was nervous as hell to be in her home. This was her personal space, not the jobsite. For months, he'd watched her disappear after work and now he was getting to peek behind the curtains and see her sanctuary.

"Beer or something stronger?" She opened an armoire that acted as her bar, her fully stocked bar.

"Drink much?" he teased.

She elbowed him in the ribs. "I happen to have a lot of visitors who enjoy the gaming center and bar, thank you very much."

"Men type visitors?" Bo growled, his territorial streak coming out.

Tina raised a single brow. "Jealous?"

Bo took her hips in his hands and pulled her back to his chest, glancing over her shoulder at the mounds of her breasts. "Maybe. I don't play well with others, and I don't share."

"I bet you were *no* fun on the playground." Tina lightly slapped his leg behind her. He liked her feistiness, admired the fact that she didn't take his overbearing desire for her lying down. She would eventually, but in her own time.

"Bear and his brother visit. They bring friends. Men and women. Jayden, Keri, and Marshall. I do have a social life outside of work, you know?"

"As long as I'm included in that life now, I'm good."

Tina swallowed and handed him a beer. "If you're lucky." That little smirk on her face only made him more determined to hang on for the ride. "Come on, I'll show you my favorite place."

She led the way out to a balcony that extended the length of the brick building and over the water of the river. Across the Sanguine was downtown Riverview and the shopping center where Bear's place lit up the night sky.

"You can hear the music."

Tina smiled. "Yep. I come sit out here almost every night." She leaned on the rail beside him. "I love hearing the water below and the party across."

"Ever jump off?" He leaned over, guessing the water was a good thirty feet below them. The retaining wall that held back the river was part of the foundation of the building. He didn't see any rocks around the building. The river was wide enough at this point that the water calmed and spread out, unlike upstream where it fought for every sliver of space.

"Never had a reason to jump. Don't think I'd want to. I know the water is deep here, because the boats would dock to load. But no, I've never jumped. I'm not sure how you'd get out except to float downriver to the banks somewhere." She pointed south, where the retaining wall ended and the natural riverbank began.

"This town has changed a lot since the last time I was here." Bo pointed across the river to the shopping center. "That's completely new."

"It went up last year. They're going to expand it to accommodate a few other businesses." Tina leaned her back on the iron railing. "That's where Jayden's future store is. I mean, she hasn't bought it yet. I'm really excited for her." The smile on her face and the twinkle in her eyes let him know how important this news was to her. "She deserves some happiness, you know? As much as I loved Christopher as a friend, I can't imagine her pain of losing her husband. I don't know how she gets out of bed."

Bo trailed a knuckle down her cheek. "She has friends like you, who rush to her side and give her strength."

"She's one of my best friends. I'd do anything for her or Keri, or Meg, or Holly. They're my girls."

"You're lucky to have each other."

"Yeah, we are." Tina turned back to face the river. She closed her eyes and took a deep breath of the night air. The lights from Bear's Bar danced over the water behind her, creating a picture of her Bo wished he had a camera for. He burned that image into his brain and would take it with him the rest of his days. He sank deeper and deeper in love with her every moment they were together. For months, he'd observed from a distance, keeping his thoughts to himself, not saying a word when she looked so radiant it made his heart ache. Tonight, he didn't have to hold his tongue. Tonight, he could tell her all the things he'd wanted to say since the moment she walked into her father's office and introduced herself. Did she have any idea how insanely he longed for her? Could she comprehend how he arose each morning with the joy of seeing her and working for her?

He found his mouth went dry and he could hardly breathe. "You're so beautiful."

Tina's gaze darted to his, a shy smile spreading across her face. "Thank you, Bo." She leaned in and kissed him, gentle and soft. "I like being beautiful in your eyes."

"You always are. Even covered in sawdust and sweat, you're a beauty."

He could see her blush in the soft lights.

Her phone rang inside the house and her eyes lit up. "That's Meg's ringtone. You might be able to see my Noah." She took his hand and pulled him along with her as she practically skipped to the phone. "Hey, Me—Cole?"

Tina froze and so did he. Her body went from loose and free to frigid and stiff in an instant.

"He what? That's impossible. What happened?"

Bo could barely hear the words on the other end of the line over the sobbing in the background. All he heard was a man's voice.

Tina dropped his hand and walked into her bedroom. When he followed, she held up her hand to stop him and closed the door in his face.

"Tina?"

She didn't answer and he pressed his ear to the door.

"I just saw him last night, Cole, I talked to Meg. There's no way he… they call it what? I've never heard of that. What caused it? Yes, I'm coming. I'll catch the first flight I can. No, be with Meg. I'll tell the others. I'll be there soon."

Tina threw open the door, her eyes ringed in red and her face pale. Bo startled her and she clenched her eyes closed. "I, I have to go. You need to, I need you to leave, please," she stuttered almost incoherently.

"What happened?"

Tina blew past him and headed for the stairs. "I can't do this right now, Bo. Just… please leave. I have to go to Boston and call the others and I—" She reached out and braced herself on the wall and covered her mouth with her other hand. "Oh, God."

Bo touched her shoulder. "Tina."

"No!" She pushed him off. "Sorry, I, I have to get to Boston."

"Tina, let me help. What do you need, baby?"

She wheeled on him, her eyes studying his for a moment before they darted around, her mind running in circles. "I don't have time to—I have to get to Boston."

Fuck. He cupped her cheeks and bent to get her attention "It's okay. Let me help—"

"It's not okay." She pried his hands from her face. "I don't need your help. My best friend just lost her baby boy. I want you to move out of my way so I can get to Meg." Tina covered her mouth with the back of her hand, tears cresting over and spilling down her face. "Shit, I can't do this. Meg needs me. I can't…." She wiped her tears away and steeled her spine.

"Do you want me to book your flight? Get a rental car?"

"It's easier for me to do it myself." She turned and bolted

down the stairs, already dialing the phone. "Jayden, pack a bag, now. We're headed to Boston. It's an emergency. Call Keri. I'm going to book the flights and call Holly…"

Bo stood in her apartment and watched the woman he loved turn away from him in the middle of a crisis. Instead of leaning on him and letting him help or letting him in, she pushed him away.

"I see," he whispered to the silence. Not one to stay where he wasn't wanted, Bo grabbed his keys and left out the back stairs.

Chapter Nineteen

TINA CAME BACK UPSTAIRS AFTER SHE BOOKED FOUR tickets to Boston on the earliest flight they had and made all the necessary phone calls. The drive to the airport was about two and a half hours, giving her about three hours until she needed to leave to pick up Jayden and Keri and swing by and nab Holly on her way north.

Tina opened the door from the inside stairs and was met with silence. Bo was nowhere to be found.

Oh God. What have I done? She crumpled to the ground and buried her head in her hands. Of all the things she could've done, she'd sent him away like a dog. Now she was alone in her grief with not even her father to comfort her. She'd called him, but only to give him the news and assure him that he didn't need to come home early. She would be halfway to Boston by the time he arrived.

Her strength failed her and she curled into a fetal position.

Noah was gone. An innocent, precious little boy was gone from this world. Meg had said last night that he had a fever, but she never imagined it could kill him. Febrile Seizures, that's what Cole said.

Tina thought about Noah's precious face, his laugh that she loved so much, the day he was born, the first time he smiled at her on the screen of her phone. *Never again.* How could this be happening? He wasn't a sick child. He was happy and healthy and loud and wonderful. He played hard and grew fast, never getting more than the occasional sniffles.

Sweet Noah. Please don't go. This can't be real.

She cried until she was screaming. Why? How is this fair? The pain was too much. Her heart couldn't contain it and she didn't know how to process it. She pounded her fist on the floor until it bled, screaming and sobbing. The floor turned redder with every punch.

He's gone. He's gone. He's gone.

My Meg. Oh! My poor sweet Meg. Only the thought of her friend's need gave her the strength to get up off the floor and move to the sink to rinse her hand and find a bandage. Shit. She didn't need a bandage; she needed to wrap her knuckles.

I need Bo. She cried harder, knowing she'd done damage to their budding relationship. She's slammed a door in his face, literally and figuratively. She could only pray he forgave her. Right now, she had to get to Boston.

At two in the morning, Tina threw her backpack in the bed and cranked up her truck. She drove to Jayden's house, her heart crushing under the pressure as she passed Bo's house. There was a single light on in an upstairs window.

Not now. You have to get yourself together. Jayden

had already had a mental breakdown not long ago over Christopher. God only knew what this was going to do to her. Tina had to put Bo in a mental box and set him aside for right now. Her friends needed her to be strong and she would. By the time they picked Keri up and headed upriver to get Holly, Tina had gained her composure. A good thing, because Jayden sat in the passenger seat softly crying the entire trip. Keri didn't fare much better. Noah was around the same age as her daughter, Misty. As the only other mother in their foursome, she knew better than Tina or Jayden how devastated Meg must be. When they finally picked Holly up, they all started crying again. Holly had once been engaged to Meg's brother, Lance. Losing Noah was pretty close to losing her own nephew.

Tina had to focus. She could fall apart later. Not now.

Meg would need her and she couldn't let her down. Tina had to shut off her emotions and focus on what had to be done.

Before she flipped that switch, she sent a simple text to Bo. *I'm sorry*.

His only response was, *Me too*.

Chapter Twenty

Bo didn't sleep that night. He lay in bed, holding his phone, staring at the ceiling, praying Tina would call him.

When her text came, he knew those two words were all he was going to get. Tina was in support mode. Except for helping her friends, Tina wasn't thinking about anything, not even him.

Tina had to be hurting. He remembered walking in on his second day and seeing her making silly faces at Noah over the video chat. She loved that little boy. Every week she sent him something: toys, diapers, treats, noise makers, whatever she could find. Not to mention the regular phone calls and video chats. Tina had made every effort to be a part of his life, short of moving to Boston.

Now her beloved boy was gone. Bo wiped his wet eyes and blamed it on being tired.

He couldn't imagine the pain of losing a child, especially

one so young. Those poor people. Their lives were altered forever. All their hopes and plans for his life were ripped away in an instant.

Bo wished he could talk to Tina. Hell, he didn't want to deal with the death of this child alone and he didn't even know him. He padded downstairs and found the bottle of rum his Nan kept in the cupboard.

For baking, my ass. He turned it up and took a swig right from the bottle.

"Easy, son." Nan tied her robe and emerged from her dark room. "I won't have any for cake if you drink it all."

"I didn't mean to wake you. I'm sorry."

"It's all right. You look like I need a drink too." Nan grinned and pulled two shot glasses from the cabinet. "I'm going to go out on a limb and say you're not drinking because your dry spell was broken?" One thin, gray brow raised in question.

"First of all, Nan, that was so inappropriate. I love you, but, yeah, let's just not go there. Ever." Bo downed a shot. Nan poured him another.

"I promise nothing." She took her shot, he poured her another one.

"I love her."

"I know."

"She isn't ready."

"I know."

"Her friend lost her little boy, and she has to get to Boston. She shut me out. Literally. Kicked me out. She didn't want my help, no shoulder to cry on, nothing. She was so upset, and in her grief, she didn't want me." Bo did a shot before his bottom lip quivered.

Nan didn't take her shot. Instead, she placed her hand

over her heart. "Oh my goodness."

"I'm an idiot."

"Bo Allen, don't you say that. Why would you say such a thing?"

He huffed a sardonic laugh. "I finally find a strong, respectable, wonderful woman... and she slams the door in my face."

"She's upset, honey. Women do weird things when we're upset. Don't be too hard on her or yourself. The death of a child is every parent's worst nightmare, and Tina wants to be there for her friend, as she should. It says a great deal that she would drop everything and fly up there."

"I know." Bo nodded, but his heart still ached with the sting of her rejection. "But who's going to drop everything and be there for her, Nan? What happens to her when her friends are neck-deep in their own problems and she has shut everyone else out?"

Nan put her hand on his. "That's when you must be the last man standing there. When all others fall away, you stand like a tree rooted by the water. That's love, Bo. Right now, you have a choice to make. Can you love her even when she's hard to love? Can you love her even when she needs you but doesn't realize it? Will you fight for her?"

"What if she doesn't want me?" Bo slammed another shot, finally feeling the effects of the alcohol. "I'm not sacrificing any more of my life on people who don't want me."

Nan looked away, her lips pinched together. "Tina isn't anything like your mother and you know it. Don't punish her for your mother's sins. You've already suffered for them, paid for them. Why should Tina?"

"What do I do, Nan?" He scrubbed his hand over his face.

"Only you can answer that, Bo Allen." She sighed and rose to go back to her room.

"Nan?" Bo called, his mind on the little boy. "Does that Bible of yours say anything about what happens to children who die?"

Her face softened and she nodded. "A child is innocent, free from sin. Until they're old enough to understand the choice between right and wrong, they're pure-hearted. Don't worry, Bo. That child rests with the Father."

Bo nodded, resting his elbows on his knees to hide his face. He almost broke down when he felt Nan's lips press a kiss to his head. "I love you, Bo. You're a good man."

Bo watched his phone Sunday. Nothing.

He went to work Monday, only to find Duane had talked to Tina multiple times. Tuesday brought no relief from the drought.

"She's taking it hard, Bo. Give her time." Duane clapped him on the shoulder and tried to reassure him.

Each day that went by without her chipped away at him the same way he chipped away at his wooden sculptures each night. The difference between him and that piece of wood was evident. As he was carved, he wasn't becoming something beautiful. He was doubting everything. He missed her, God how he missed her.

Thursday evening, he was in his shop using his chisel to take out his frustrations on a rough log. His radio blared the local country station. Every song that came on made him think of her, until he stomped over and ripped the cord right out of the socket.

"What did that radio ever do to you?"

He swirled around to see Tina standing in the door, her arms crossed over her chest protectively. Bo swallowed the excitement of seeing her again. He wanted to be mad, he wanted to teach her a lesson about pushing him away, but all he could think about was holding her again.

"Makes me think of you."

Her face tightened and she lowered her gaze. "I can see how that would anger you." She looked tired; exhausted, actually. She'd lost weight; it was evident in the hollow of her cheeks. Her eyes were still swollen and her hair was up in one of her messy buns.

"How's Meg?" He turned his back to her, going to work on his destruction. If he kept his eyes on her, his hands would follow.

"She's a wreck, just…taking it one day at a time. They had to give her something to help her sleep."

Bo nodded and made a blind scrape across the wood. "And your other friends?"

"About as well as they can be. Everyone's home now."

Bo nodded again. "You?"

"I'm holding up."

"Of course you are." He kept his tone matter of fact. Tina wouldn't show weakness, vulnerability; it wasn't in her DNA.

Tina meandered around the workshop and touched the various pieces and carvings he'd been working on for the last couple months. "I didn't know you were into carving."

"My grandfather taught me."

"He did the benches in town, didn't he?" She pointed to one of his practice logs. "I recognize this one." When he just nodded, she walked over to stand where he could see her. "Bo, I'm sorry. Please understand. I was upset and—"

He threw his tools down and braced his fists on the table, startling her into silence. "You're not an easy woman to break into, Tina Foster. Do you know that?" He met her eyes and saw them gathering moisture. "I've dealt with murderers easier to get along with than you."

"I'm sorry." She nibbled on her bottom lip to keep from crying. "I had to—"

"All I want is to love you. Is that so fucking hard? I'm—" He stood up and lifted his face to the ceiling. He'd been brooding, pouting the whole time she was gone, preparing what he would say. It suddenly didn't matter. "Damn it. You needed me, like it or not, and instead you pushed me away."

"I didn't—"

"Yes, you did. I know what rejection looks like. I went to jail because of it." He was almost shouting, so he took a deep breath to calm down. "And you know what absolutely sucks about this whole situation? I can't even be mad at the reason why you did it. You had to get to Boston. You had to be strong for your friends. I'd expect nothing less. But, damn it, Tina, for once in your life, let someone help you. Let someone be strong for you."

"I don't know how!" Tina's voice filled the barn, bouncing off the metal walls. Her leg twisted about, and she was going to gnaw her bottom lip right off if she didn't quit. "I don't know how, Bo. I've always had to be the rock, setting the course of the river. I don't know how to be the water, following it. I don't know if I can do what you're asking of me."

"How would you know? You've never tried. You run in, guns blazing, commands flying, and you never once stop to think if your way is the best way." Bo leaned over the table on his fists again and sighed. "Even a great stone can be moved by water given the chance."

Tina swiped a tear from her cheek and turned her face away. She was quiet for a moment and he took that time to gain his composure.

"Am I just too much for you to handle? Are you done with me then?" Her shaking voice almost broke him.

"That's not what I want." He met her blue eyes and saw the pain she was holding in. "But I'm not the one who's in question here. What do you want, Tina? And before you answer, make damn sure you mean it because I'll never have another door slammed in my face. I promise you that."

Tina came to his side and raised a hand to touch his cheek. "I can't... I'm sorry, Bo."

He closed his eyes, fear and anguish flooding him, leaving him cold. Of course she didn't want him. He was an ex-convict with abandonment issues and a desire to be the center of her universe. He had nothing to offer her as far as money or prospects. Hell, she was his boss; she knew exactly how much money he made. He lived with his grandmother and drove a beat-up, broken down truck. As far as arm candy, she would've been better off sticking with the fancy engineer.

Yet he had hoped that, for once, his heart would be enough for a woman. Many years ago, he'd given everything for his mother. When they lived alone, things were good, not great, but he tried to treat her with respect and love, and make up for the fact that she'd left her husband in order to raise him. He'd been a foolish child, unknowing of his mother's deceptions. When the police were hauling him away and she clung to the very man who had just beat the hell out of her, he realized that his best never would've been enough.

Tina was nothing like his mother, and yet the sting of her rejection felt the same. He wasn't enough.

His jaw tensed under the palm of her hand and he tried not to let her see him react.

"I'm sorry…I shut you out."

His gaze went to hers and the desperation he saw there broke his heart.

"You're right, I'm hard to deal with. No one has ever given me a reason to try harder. I never cared to with Trey and, God knows, Steven broke all kinds of things inside me that I didn't bother to fix." She took a deep, shaky breath. "I want to try…for you, I'll try. Just…" she closed her eyes. "Don't give up on me."

Bo's breath whooshed out of his lungs from holding it. He pulled her into his arms and locked her in his embrace. Tina clung to him for dear life, like she would float away if she didn't.

"I thought about you," she said, hugging him tight. "I tried so hard not to. I wanted to put you in a box and not think about you when I had to be away. It didn't work. I wanted to call you every five minutes. I worried you'd hate me forever."

Bo's world turned around so fast he was dizzy. "I missed you too. From the moment I left your place, I missed you. Why the hell didn't you call?"

Tina leaned back but didn't leave his arms, making him happy. "It was so awful, Bo. When Meg's brother Lance died, it was rough. Then when Christopher died, I almost couldn't get out of bed. But this…this is—" She closed her eyes and shook her head. "I don't want to ever lose a child."

Bo held her close again, soaking up the feel of her. "I'm sorry, T. I would've been right there with you if you—"

"I'm thankful you're here now." Tina's blue eyes turned upwards to his and a tired grin flashed on her face. She cupped his face with her hands. "Forgive me for being an ass?"

"Always." Bo leaned in and felt a sweet release when his lips touched hers. *Home.* Was there anything more perfect in the world than having her in his arms, her body melting into him and her mouth following his?

"Will you do something for me?" she asked between their kisses.

"Anything."

"Can I borrow a shirt?"

Bo pulled back. What the hell was she talking about?

Tina's eyes sparked with mischief. "To sleep in. Here. If that's okay?"

"That depends," Bo pursed his lips, "'cause if you're planning to curl up in bed with me, I plan to at least get to second base, maybe steal third."

Tina chuckled and rolled her eyes. "As long as I don't have to drive home and you let me sleep, that's fine by me." About that time, she let out a huge yawn that made her laugh. "Sorry."

Bo ushered her out of the shop with his arm around her shoulder. "Come on, beautiful. Let's get you to sleep."

At any moment, he was going to wake up. *This is a dream.* He pulled off his boots and jeans as Tina moved around the bathroom next door getting ready for bed and humming. She still had her bags from her trip in her truck and he wondered if she had gone home first or come straight to him. The thought made him smile. Either way, she was here and she was *his.*

He picked up his room, gathering up the few dirty socks

and shirts lying around and threw them in the hamper. Nan kept clean sheets on his bed, thank God. He grabbed an extra blanket from the hall closet and tried to slow his drumming pulse. She was exhausted, and though he joked, she needed rest not sex. It didn't damper the excitement of getting her into his bed. At least she was here.

Chapter Twenty-One

TINA TOOK A DEEP BREATH AND SLIPPED INTO BO'S room. She'd sent Duane a text letting him know she was crashing over here. She'd gone home earlier just long enough for her father to rip her a new one for being rude to Bo. Apparently, while she was gone, Bo and Nan had brought Duane dinner one night, cupcakes the next, and stayed to play cards each time they came by. Duane reported that Bo asked about her every morning and worked his butt off to cover in her absence.

She didn't deserve his affections. No matter how she justified her actions, she kept coming back to feeling guilty. Instead of repaying her with anger, he'd taken care of her father while she was gone. Instead of slacking off at work because the boss was away, he'd worked double hard to do his work and hers.

Tina leaned against the inside of his door and marveled at him lying in the bed, shirtless and waiting.

"Come on, baby." He threw back the blanket and Tina's stomach filled with butterflies. "You need some sleep."

What she wanted and what he said she needed were two different things. What she wanted was to climb on top of that muscled, tattooed body and ride hard. Bo's delicious lips curved into a warm smile that beckoned to be kissed.

Dear Lord.

Unfortunately, she yawned again, making him laugh. "Yeah, I know. There's a lot more interesting things we could do, but you're exhausted and I can see it. I'm staying on my side and you stay on yours."

Tina sighed and crawled into the bed, instantly liquefying into the mattress. "Oh God, this feels so good." She wiggled and moved the pillow, getting comfortable. She faced Bo, both of them settling in. He stayed safely on his side, only crossing the invisible line to brush her hair off her shoulder. The softness of his touch gave her chills. "You're trying really hard to be good, aren't you?"

"Yes, I am." Bo grinned. "You're temptation personified right now."

"So…you don't want to come over here and see what's under this shirt?"

Bo closed his eyes and took a deep, deep breath. "No. You need to sleep."

Tina liked this game. She loved seeing the effect she had on him. "What if I told you I'd like to run my lips over every inch of your bare chest?"

"Tina." Bo clenched his teeth and his sharp jaw tensed. "I will go sleep in another room if I have to. Don't push me."

"Did you have a girlfriend in jail?" Tina bit the inside of her lip to keep from laughing when he gave her a dirty look.

"You're a brat." He turned on his back.

She started giggling and was so deliriously tired that she couldn't stop. "Screw the treaty line." Tina cuddled right up next to him and nestled into his side. Bo took another deep breath, but put his arm around her and held her close. "Mmm. Now this is wonderful."

"You're too damn hot for your own good, Tina Foster. Now go to sleep." He reached over her and turned off the lamp, pecked her lips, and went still beside her.

Tina closed her eyes and listened to the rapid beat of his heart. It made her happy to know she wasn't alone in her nervous delight. The drumming slowed with each breath he took.

"Bo?"

"Yeah?"

His rough, sleepy voice curled her toes. "Have, um, have you been with anyone since you got home?" *Please say no. Please say no.*

"As soon as I got out, all I wanted to do was get to Riverview. As soon as I got to Riverview, I was focused on getting a job. And then I met this feisty, sexy blonde who gave me said job. I've been concentrating on those two things ever since; the job and the girl." He trailed his fingers down her back and made her shiver.

"How long has it been?"

"About five years."

Tina popped up and looked down at him. "Holy shit! You need to get laid, man."

Bo chuckled. "Don't worry, I plan on making a move on that feisty blonde soon. She has to be well rested first. After five years, I might break her."

Tina couldn't contain her giddiness as she leaned down and kissed him. "Good thing she's tough. Unfortunately, she's not well rested." Tina yawned again and settled back into the bed.

"Good night, baby."

"Good night, Bo." Tina closed her eyes and focused on breathing him in, the scent of his skin, the beat of his heart, the rise and fall of his chest. It was easy to relax into him and drift off.

She woke at some point during the night with Bo curled around her and happily went back to sleep.

The morning sun came far too quickly. Tina rolled over on to a piece of paper crinkling beneath her. She grasped it and propped herself up.

T,

You were too peaceful to wake. Stay as long as you want. Nan made breakfast downstairs. I have to get to work, my boss is a task master. Get some rest. You're going to need it.

-B

P.S. I want to wake up with you every day.

Her body sang at the thought of what she might need that rest for. Of course he went to work. He would do double the work just so she could sleep. Everything Bo did secured her heart more and more.

I want to wake up with you every day.

She read the words over and over again, each time letting them sink deeper and deeper into her heart and soul. Did that mean what she thought? He wanted to be with her...*forever*?

Tina couldn't stay in bed. She was restless and, if she wanted to admit it, she wanted to be working with Bo. She dressed and pulled her hair up in a bun. There was no noise coming from downstairs and she casually meandered around the house, examining the structure, looking at the pictures on the wall, taking in the trinkets and books.

There were pictures lining the staircase of Bo as he'd grown up. Once Tina saw the picture of him on one knee dressed out in his Riverview Pirates football uniform, she recognized him.

Jail had changed Bo a lot. He used to be thin and lanky and had had an odd haircut. It made her giggle. He looked nothing like that awkward kid in the picture. Now his body was beefy and ripped with muscle. He traded that long brown hair for a barely-there buzz cut. The main reason she remembered him was that he would fall asleep in class and still make straight A's. The teachers would gossip about how smart he was and how far advanced he was for their lessons.

Damn, and she had him screwing up sheetrock and painting walls every day. He could go back to school, get a degree, be making more money somewhere else. What if she was holding him back? *Hmm*.

Tina hit the bottom stair and nearly jumped out of her skin when Nan popped her head around the corner of the kitchen. "Morning!"

Tina gasped and clutched her chest. "Sweet Jesus, Nan. You scared the hell out of me."

Nan chuckled and went back to washing dishes. "Sorry, honey. Come on and get some food in you. Did you get some sleep?"

Tina slid up into a stool at the serving counter and watched Nan's able hands work. Did she think that Tina had sex with Bo?

"Yes. Your grandson was a perfect gentleman." She couldn't meet the older lady's eyes.

Nan leaned a hip against the counter and dried off the

cup in her hands. "Don't worry, honey. I know you two kids didn't fool around. He was wound tighter than an eight-day clock when he left this morning."

"Good. I hope he stays that way all day long." She exchanged grins with Nan, who winked at her.

"I hate to make it sound like you were on vacation, but how was your trip?"

Tina didn't know how much Nan actually wanted to know, so she answered as honestly as possible. "Miserable. I pray I never have to attend another child's funeral ever again."

"It's horrible, isn't it? I bet that poor girl is devastated."

"She is." Tina took a bite of eggs, needing a moment to get Meg's wailing screams out of her head. Nan kept quiet and continued drying her dishes. "That baby was her whole world. She married Cole because they got pregnant and Noah has been her reason for living. God knows it isn't Cole. I told her she needed to come home."

"Do you think their marriage will survive this?"

Tina met her eyes and shook her head. "Cole loved Noah. He was a lot of things I wouldn't say in polite society, but he loved his son. He loved Meg because of Noah, not the other way around. I don't see what'll keep them together now."

"That's a shame. I hate to hear that." Nan poured a cup of coffee. "You're all so young to be going through such tragedies, and divorce on top of that."

"I don't know if they ever had a real future. They weren't stable when they started dating, much less now. I never understood why Meg moved to Boston with him in the first place." Tina scraped her fork across her plate. "Then again, how does anyone know? Everything can change in an instant."

"For worse or better." Nan smiled. "Wonderful things happen in an instant too."

"Yes, they do." Tina brought her plate to the sink and washed it, then turned to face Nan. "Is he happy? Is Bo happy working for me, us, my company?" she corrected herself.

Nan's knowing eyes crinkled in the corners. "Why do you ask, honey?"

"Because, I finally remember him from school. He's smart, like, brilliant kind of smart. He can't possibly be happy painting for a living. He's capable of so much more."

"He was capable. Now the world has labeled him as a convict, a stain on society, all because he fought an abusive son of a bitch and didn't fight his crackhead mother." She sighed. "Your daddy was the first person he interviewed with who didn't take one look at him and judge him on what society says. Trust me, after the first two interviews, he's happy to work, period."

"I want him to be happy, Nan."

"Good. Then go work with him. That's all it takes to make his day."

Tina swiveled her leg nervously and chewed her bottom lip.

"What's wrong?" Nan took her hands and led her to the table. "Come talk to me, child. I don't always give the best advice, but I know my grandson."

Tina sat at the table and accepted the coffee that was offered. This was so new. She was used to venting to her father. Since she'd never had a mother, heart-to-heart talks were usually done over beer not coffee. It amazed her how nervous she was in front of Nan. Her hands got sweaty and she tapped her foot under the table. It took her a moment to gather her thoughts and to form what she wanted to say. Nan casually poured sugar into her coffee and waited.

"Bo is… It's just…" Tina sighed. "I don't want to disappoint him. He's had so much heartache in his life. I don't want to be one more. I'm so absorbed in my work, and half the time I forget to eat, much less communicate with other people outside of my crew. Jayden and Keri tell me I'm the most antisocial social butterfly they know. I don't even know if that's an insult or a compliment."

Nan laughed and so did Tina.

She closed her eyes against the emotion welling up inside her. "I care for him so much it scares me. What if I mess up? I'm a pain in the ass. He said so himself."

Nan leaned her head to the side, her wavy, gray hair falling to her neck. "And what did he do when you asked for forgiveness?"

"He took care of me."

"He did. And trust me, honey, he was very upset. Not angry at you, but upset that he couldn't be there for you."

Tina put her elbow on the table and held her hand over her face. "I was rude. God, I was so rude to him. I don't know why he was so merciful."

"He adores you."

Tina's hand slowly fell and she met Nan's gray eyes. "Really?"

Nan reached up and touched Tina's chin, a loving smile on her face. "He adores you, honey. His grandfather, God rest his soul, used to look at me the way Bo looks at you. Bo has respected you from the beginning. That respect has grown into admiration and now that you've taken the relationship outside of the workplace, he's getting to know you more intimately. The question is, do you feel the same?"

Tina pushed the stray tendrils of her hair off of her face. "He has me all turned around and messed up." She let out a nervous huff. "Even in all the drama and tears and chaos of Boston and the funeral, I wished I could have him with me. I picked up the phone at least a dozen times and was too scared to call him."

"And what would you have said?"

"That I was sorry for being an ass, that he was right, that I love—" Tina froze. The realization of her words hit hard and heavy to her chest, knocking the air out of her. "Holy shit." She blinked back the emotion before it turned into tears. "I love him."

"Take a breath, honey. You're turning green." Nan chuckled and put her hand over Tina's. "It's okay."

Tina took a gigantic shaking breath and tried to calm her erratic pulse. "I...have to go." Tina stood and went upstairs to grab her bag. She hurried back down the stairs and kissed Nan on the cheek in passing. "Don't wait up for him."

"Use protection," Nan called out as Tina bounded down the front steps and to her truck.

Happiness flowed through her at her revelation. She was in love with Bo Galloway. It all made sense when she admitted it. That was why she couldn't get him out of her mind when she was in Boston. She never imagined in her wildest dreams that she would fall in love with a man like Bo, not after the track record she had. Yet here she was, contemplating crazy things like *forever*.

Her heart lurched when she saw his red and white truck at the jobsite. What was she going to say? What was she going to do, walk up and drop the L-word right in the middle of the work day?

"Be real, Tina." She slid out of her truck. No, she had to

be chill on the site. Her rules.

Bo walked by the door of the house with a long piece of lumber in his hands. Just the sight of him left her breathless. *I'm a sunken ship.*

As she passed various crewmen, they offered their sympathies and told her how glad they were to have her back. Uncle Terry gave her a big hug and kissed her head.

"Glad to have you back, kiddo. These guys cry like little girls when you're not here."

"Thanks, Terry. I'll remember to buy them some pacifiers next time I go out of town." Tina winked at him and listened as he told her about the progress of the house and the various tasks being performed.

The Ragland house was coming along and they were picking out interior finishes.

"Can you spare Bo today? I want to take him to Jayden's house to look at some spindles. We're going to have to replicate them."

Terry's face wrinkled up even more than usual. "I guess. He can do that?"

Tina grinned, thinking about all the beautiful carvings in his workshop. "Yes, Terry, and much more."

Terry scratched his beard and narrowed his eyes. "I know that look in your eyes. That's the same look your mother gave me when she met your father."

"I don't know what you mean." She shrugged and walked off, then stopped to glance over her shoulder at her mother's big brother.

Her uncle tipped his head, giving her his blessing. Everything was falling into place.

As she approached the house, her heart sped up like it always did when Bo was around. Today, it kicked into fifth gear. He was wearing his usual attire, tee-shirt and jeans, nothing special, and yet he never looked better.

Bo's eyes met hers and she sucked in a deep breath. *Incredible.*

He smiled and dipped his head. "G'morning. Did you get some re—"

Tina didn't let him finish. She wrapped her arms around his neck and tiptoed up to plant a kiss on his lips, right there in front of God and everyone. She didn't care that the guys were whistling or clapping or making dirty comments. She didn't care that this was the workplace and she had strict rules about personal matters interfering with their progress.

This was her man and she loved him. Every single one of those guys needed to know it.

When she released him, Bo's eyes were the size of dinner plates. "Whew."

"Just saying thank you." Tina winked at him.

"That was a hell of a thank you." He grinned and let out a deep breath.

Jason came over and put his hands on their shoulders. "It's about time. Seriously. If I had to listen to another day of Bo acting like a love-struck little girl, I was going to quit."

Tina chuckled and let the happiness fill her heart and soul. Bo knocked Jason in the gut and blushed.

Jason, who was taking this opportunity to give Bo hell, raised his voice like a woman and started fluttering his eyelashes. "Oh, Tina's so pretty. Tina's so talented. Oh, she's so smart and wonderful and she shits rainbows and rides unicorns."

"I'm getting Tina's nail gun." Bo pretended like he was reaching for the tool as Jason walked off, still cackling like a hen.

"Come on. I have a special project we have to plan." Tina took his hand and led him to her truck.

"Um, T. I have some stuff I need to finish here. I'm not done today." He hesitated and glanced back to the house.

"It's okay. Terry has you covered."

He leaned in and whispered, "We can fool around later, you know."

Tina grinned. "As much as I would like to say that's where I'm taking you, I actually need you to look at Jayden's house."

"Oh." He rubbed the back of his neck. "You're making me nervous, boss lady."

Tina couldn't hide the smile on her face as they drove through the countryside to Jayden's old house.

Bo leaned against the passenger side door but kept his eyes on her the whole ride. Tina stole peeks at him as heat crept up her neck. "What?"

"I'm taking you out tonight. We need to go on a date."

The thought made Tina's insides spin. "We slept in the same bed, Bo. I think we might have skipped a step."

He turned his head to the window, like he didn't want her to see his expression. "Nope. We're going to dinner. Nothing too fancy, but you and me, alone."

"Yes, sir."

Bo's head swung around to her. "What was that?"

A giggle escaped her lips. "I can obey, thank you very much." She reached over and took his hand in hers. "Sometimes."

True to his word, when they pulled into Jayden's driveway, Bo was all work. Jayden met them at the door, and they walked through the house room by room. Bo took notes on a clipboard as Tina talked and described to Jay what all needed to be repaired on the house. Tina was thorough in her inspection of everything from the pier and beam foundation to the attic. She drew out the floor plan, took measurements of the various rooms, took pictures of the moldings and trim, and then pointed Bo to the newels on the staircase.

"See where they've been replaced?" She pointed to the mismatched posts. "We need to match the original."

"I can do that." Be nodded and snapped a picture with his phone.

The evaluation took most of the day, especially since Tina and Jayden liked to chat. The great thing about having Bo there was his ability to take her ideas and expand on them. He had a creative mind and even Jayden made the comment that she liked his ideas on materials and textures for the walls.

"You know," said Jayden, studying Tina and Bo. "You guys make a really good team."

"I think so too." Tina smiled at Bo and he winked back.

Jayden gasped. "Wait, are you two...you know, *officially* together now?"

As hard as she tried to keep her composure, Tina couldn't help but smile. "Yeah, something like that."

Bo leaned in beside her and took her hand. "I've been warned not to anger her around the nail guns."

Jayden made a snorting noise in the back of her throat. "You think staying away from nail guns will protect you? Just don't piss her off and you're fine."

Tina looked at her watch. "Oh, look at the time. I have a hot date tonight."

"Yeah, you do." Jayden winked at Bo. "Better go get ready."

Tina and Bo headed back to get his truck. He leaned over to take her hand and brought it to his mouth. "That's going to be a fun project."

"I can't wait. I'm so honored to work on it, you know?" Tina's heart sang with excitement. "It's like I get to give Christopher one more gift."

"You have a beautiful heart, Tina Foster."

She felt Bo's compliment from head to toe.

I love this man. She expelled a happy sigh. Now she just had to figure out how to tell him.

That evening, she took her time curling her hair, putting on her makeup, and picking out a dress that would drive Bo mad. The best part about tonight was the fact that she actually didn't have to do any of it. Bo had fallen for her while they worked together. He'd seen her sweaty, smelly, covered in dirt, and grumpy as hell. They'd spent hot days in the Texas sun working together until they were give out. She'd belched in front of him and he never blinked. For a while, she thought he would see her as one of the guys, the way the rest of the crew did. And yet, he still wanted her, still found her attractive.

It only made her want to impress him more by dressing up like a real woman. Just before she went downstairs to talk to her dad, her phone chimed. Tina answered the video call from Meg. Her friend looked rough. Meg's eyes were sunken and her cheeks hollowed. Even her usual shiny red hair appeared dull and unkempt.

"Wow," Meg said at seeing Tina. Her voice lacked her usually chipper rise and fall. "You look lovely."

"Thank you. How are you? Are you okay?"

Meg faked a smile. Tina had known her since high school; she knew a fake smile when she saw it. "One day at a time. Cole's mother came over to help me clean out Noah's room."

"What?" Tina sat down on her bed and clenched her heart. "So soon? Are you kidding me?"

"Cole's sister is pregnant and his mother came to scavenge my baby's things." Meg's bottom lip trembled. "You would be proud of me though, I grabbed up that toy hammer you gave Noah and hit her with it."

Tina's mouth fell open. "You didn't?"

Meg laughed even while she wiped a tear. "I did. I knocked her right in the head until she ran out of the house screaming that she would tell Cole."

"Meg! I'm so proud of you for standing up to her. And with a tool!" Tina grabbed her heart dramatically. "That's my girl."

Pride filled her chest. Even in Meg's pain, she'd stood up against her raving lunatic of a mother-in-law. Her sweet Meg had used a tool as a weapon, even if it was bright red and plastic.

"I just wanted to tell you that. I won't keep you."

Bo entered her bedroom, standing inside the threshold. Tina opened her mouth, but nothing came out. He had on nice slacks and a white button-down shirt with the sleeves rolled up. He'd traded his tool belt for sexy suspenders and his work boots for shiny leather loafers. Bo could've stepped out of a men's fashion magazine.

He shook his head and waved his hand, not rushing her off the phone.

"No, Meg. I have time." Tina told her friend all about fixing up Jayden's house and other town gossip. Meg needed a distraction and Tina gave her one for the next thirty minutes.

"I can't thank you enough for coming up here, Tina. I love you so much."

Tina smiled at her over the phone. "I'd do anything for you, you know that."

"I know. Go have fun on your date." Meg blew her a kiss and hung up.

Tina stared at the blank screen. Meg needed to come home. Period. She needed people around her who would help her heal and be healthy again. What she didn't need was Cole's crazy family who never cared for her in the first place.

"Is she okay?" Bo asked, taking a drink from his water glass. He'd gone into her living room and waited patiently.

"I don't know. I was just thinking that she needs to come home."

"She will, when it's time. She loves you. You can tell in her voice she misses you."

Tina stood and stepped in front of him, running her hands up the suspenders to his chest. "Thank you."

"For what?" His eyes narrowed, like he truly didn't know.

"For being amazing. Today with Jayden, you were kind and patient when we got off topic. Now, with Meg, you didn't rush me off the phone."

Bo wrapped her up in his arms. "You'd do anything for your friends. I'd do anything for you. We're no different in that aspect, T."

Tina pressed her lips to his, drowning in the sweet relief of their kiss. His lips moved softly and gently against hers, coaxing a sigh.

"We don't have to go out," Tina said, between kisses.

"Yes, we do." Bo gave her one last, deep kiss and pulled away. "With you looking this hot, I need to show you off." He held out her hand to assess her from head to toe. "Damn, baby, you're a little too hot right now."

"Pot, meet kettle." She wiggled her brows and popped one of his suspenders.

Luckily, she had on flat shoes because Bo decided to take a stroll across the bridge and into downtown. He held her hand and the simple gesture made her feel like a million bucks. They meandered downtown as the sun set and the street lamps flickered to life.

Fran's Front Porch sat right in the middle of downtown Riverview. Along the row of stores, the café was set back off the sidewalk, allowing for a lovely, quaint patio area lit with strings of lights. Fran made the best Italian food in town, and Tina didn't mind admitting that since Bear's didn't serve Italian. She and Bo were seated at one of the outdoor tables right by the street.

They ordered a bottle of wine and Bo lifted his glass. "To revitalization, for houses and us."

"Cheers." Tina sipped her wine and wished like hell they had stayed at her house. The wine went straight to her head and mixed with the high Bo gave her. She was clenching her thighs together and watching his lips as he sipped from the glass. She licked her lips out of stark and gnawing hunger.

Chapter Twenty-Two

THE WAY TINA RUBBED HER LEGS TOGETHER IN THAT short skirt had Bo wishing like hell he'd taken her up on the offer to stay home. She was too beautiful with all that blonde hair spilled over her shoulders and her big blue eyes shining every time she looked at him.

"Have I ever told you how beautiful you are?" Bo didn't mean to sound so corny, but she made him do things that he didn't understand.

Tina blushed and pushed her hair behind her ears. "Are you just saying that because I'm wearing makeup?"

"Nope. I thought you were drop dead gorgeous the first time I saw you. You were dirty as hell and I still thought you were a dream."

Tina studied him through narrowed eyes, nibbling on her bottom lip to contain the smile. "You didn't say a word."

Bo shook his head. "Wasn't the right time."

"Now is a great time." Tina linked her fingers with

his on the table. She took a deep breath and met his eyes. "What are you working on right now in the wood shop?"

"One of Nan's customers asked me to carve the school mascot for her son's graduation." He cringed, thinking about how cheesy she wanted it. "It's not glamorous, but she's paying me and it's good practice."

"Why the face?"

"Because she wants a cartoon pirate carved in wood." Bo shook his head. "It's not exactly challenging."

"You like a challenge, don't you?"

Bo took a drink. "You and I have that in common."

Tina tilted her head and lifted her glass. "Guilty."

"I've got other projects I'm working on. Taking on something like that isn't a big deal."

"It sucks that you have to work two jobs. That first one not paying enough?" One of her brows kicked up and her lips pursed.

"First one pays fine, and the benefits are…" Bo licked his lips and intentionally lowered his eyes to her breasts and then those sexy legs. "Well, the benefits are looking better and better every day."

Tina blushed red and messed with her hair. He'd never seen her nervous. He'd never seen her fidget. Usually, Tina Foster was composed and not too much rattled her.

Tonight…not so much. She took a relieved breath when the waitress delivered their order and every time she came back to refill their glasses or take away dirty plates. They talked like normal, laughed like always, bounced from subject to subject, and never lost physical contact, whether they were holding hands or she was rubbing his leg with her foot.

By the time they ordered dessert, her foot was tapping.

"Why are you nervous?" Bo asked, taking her hand in his.

"I'm not." She chuckled, only proving she was nervous.

Bo frowned and pulled her chair around the table, closer to his. "Talk to me."

Tina stared at him for a long moment and finally reached up to touched his cheek. "How is this possible?"

Bo leaned in to her palm. "What?"

"How is it possible for you to be so… so *easy*."

"Hey," he blanched, "I haven't let you take me to bed yet."

She threw her head back and laughed, then put her arms around his neck. "See, this. *This* is what I mean." Tina let out her breath and kept her hands on his neck. "This is effortless. Why? How?" She blinked, trying to clear out the moisture that had gathered in her eyes. "Is this what I've been missing? Because this…this…this thing between us is just…perfect. And nothing is perfect. Right? So if nothing is perfect, but this is perfect, then—"

"Shh, okay, you're overthinking right now." Bo brought her knuckles to his mouth. "Why is it so hard to believe we work? We're good together. Accept it, T."

"You're so certain, so sure of yourself." One side of her lush mouth pulled back. "Cocky little thing, aren't you?"

"Cocky, no. Confident, yes." Bo leaned in and kissed her hard, staking his claim right there in the courtyard of Fran's Front Porch. "You're mine, Tina Foster. Period. Stop trying to talk yourself out of it. We work. You and me."

"Bo, I have something I want to tell you." Tina closed her eyes and took a deep breath, letting the air out of her mouth. "Today, when I was talking to Nan, I realized that I, um, I mean, I know it hasn't been long and this is our first official date as a couple, and we, um, had that argument."

He tried to follow along her train of thought, but it didn't go in straight line. She bounced all over the place and he grinned, trying to figure out what in the world had her scatterbrained. It was kind of cute.

"We really haven't worked together as a couple, so I think this might be premature. But I really think that I'm fall—"

"Tina?"

"Bo?"

Tina's rambling was cut off. Bo turned to see Rodman on the street with a couple other guys. They were walking by the restaurant and apparently stopped when they saw Bo and Tina.

"Sean, hey." Tina stood up and leaned over the railing to hug one of the guys. "I miss you, man. How are ya?"

Bo would recognize a Harris boy anywhere. He had the same facial structure and big blue eyes as Bear. His hair was a little darker, not the dirty blond of the other brothers, but he was definitely a Harris.

"Hey, sweetheart." Sean hugged her and gave Bo an obligatory head nod in between the puffs of his cigarette. "I'm glad to see you too, baby girl." He touched her cheek briefly, a sad smile on his face.

"That's the guy who took my job," Rodman sneered. "He took my job and apparently my cousin's girlfriend."

"No, Rodman," Tina pointed her finger at him and used her *kiss my ass, I'm the boss* tone, "you threw away your job. He just cleaned up the mess...for both you and Trey."

Rodman stepped forward. "Mouthy bi—" Sean put a hand on his chest when Bo rose from his seat.

"Hey, that's my friend. Back off, Rodman." Sean held up

a hand to Bo. "It's cool, man."

Bo glared at Rodman. "It's good to see you, Sean, but y'all should keep walking."

Sean nodded and gestured the others on. "Yeah, yeah, you guys have a good time."

Rodman, however, wasn't budging and crossed his arms over his chest. "You're not going to do shit, jailbird. I'll have your parole officer on your ass so fast it'll make your head spin."

"Is that supposed to scare me?" Bo gripped the railing, leaning on the iron fence that separated the patio from the street. He knew he was fearsome; he'd had to become a hardened criminal to survive in jail and this loser didn't intimidate him a bit. "Care to see if I won't chance it?"

"Don't worry, baby," Tina said from their table, "I'll hire you a good lawyer. Kick his puny butt six ways to Sunday."

Sean gulped in air. "Come on, man. Let's not ruin a good night." He pulled Rodman down the sidewalk.

That lowlife didn't quit. "You two are quite the pair. Wait until Trey hears you downgraded to this loser. You'll regret it."

"I wouldn't put money on that pony." Tina waved them off and turned her back to the street.

The group of guys sauntered off, chests puffed like they'd done something. Bo sat back down and glanced over at Tina, who chugged the rest of her wine. "You'll hire me a good lawyer?"

They both cracked up, letting the tension of the moment float away.

Tina threw up her hands. "Okay, not my best comeback. I don't exactly have a nail gun handy."

Bo laughed and pulled her over for a kiss. "You're a

funny woman." He tossed back his drink, sensing that she was ready to leave. "What is Sean Harris doing with a piece of shit like Rodman?"

Tina sighed. "He took some emotional hits; first Lance, then Chris. His best friend and his brother dying within a year of each other, he has…lost his way. One day, he'll figure out the drugs won't fix what's wrong. Hopefully, someday soon. I miss the guy he used to be." Tina's expression fell with a deep sadness. She'd been close to all the Harris boys as a teenager and Bo knew how much she adored Bear. It couldn't be easy for her to see someone she loved turning to drugs.

"Let's get out of here, Bo." Tina leaned her chin on her palm, her blue eyes sparkling with mischief. "I'd like for you to take me home."

"Yes, ma'am, boss." He paid the check and they walked down Main Street hand-in-hand back towards the bridge. He kept his eyes peeled for the group of guys. "Should we get a cab? I'd hate for Rodman to start something I'll finish."

"Sean won't let him do anything. I'm not worried. It's a beautiful night and they can't ruin it." Tina looped her arm around his waist and kept walking. That didn't stop Bo from being on alert. Druggies were unpredictable and Rodman already had a big chip on his shoulder.

They stopped right in the middle of the bridge and looked downstream at the view. To the left, the lights from Bear's Bar glittered on the water. To the right was Tina's home. The tall brick building sat off the road but overlooked the river. It was a beautiful view and a beautiful person enjoyed it with him. Tina leaned on the rail and he stood behind her, holding her close.

"When I was a kid," he said, opening up the

discussion of his mother, "my mom and her boyfriend were having another fight. She grabbed me up and drove me into town. She stopped right before the bridge and got out of her car. Mom threw her engagement ring off the bridge and I thought it was over for good. I was so happy. Even as a little boy, I knew everything that she tried to hide from me. I knew about the drugs, the men, and the crap she took from the men to get the drugs. When she threw that ring in the river, I felt hope for the first time in my life. She pulled me to this spot and said, 'Take a good look, Bo. Even the water wants to get out of this damn town. The river runs to get the hell out of here.' I thought about that a lot when I was in jail. For a long time, I thought she was right. When I got out and came back here, I came to this bridge and stopped, walked to this spot, and remembered her words again. I realized something; it's all about where you choose to stand." Bo took her hand and guided her across to the other side of the empty bridge. He wrapped Tina in his arms, her back to his chest. "You can choose to look at the world and see the bad or you can choose to change directions and see the good. From this perspective, the river rushes to get here. It's why the river runs, T. It loves Riverview so much that it spreads out in the creeks and coves and tries to stay a while. I promised myself I'd always have a better perspective than my mother. That I'd focus on all the good things I have."

"I'd like to get my hands on that woman, and maybe a nail gun or two." She turned in his arms and faced him. Tina's brows pinched together. "I'm sorry about what Rodman said."

"Why are you sorry? That jerk can't hurt me. He's

nothing. Unless he hurts you, then we'll have problems."

She grabbed the collar of his shirt and made him look at her. "Bo, don't ever risk yourself for me, please. I can handle it. You don't have to defend me. I'd like to think this is one of those reasons we work. You can't afford to risk it and I don't need you to."

"Trust me, baby, now that I have you, I'm not eager to break my parole. That doesn't mean I'm going to cower while some douchebag insults the woman I love." *Oh shit.* The words slipped right out of his mouth and he tried twice to speak again while Tina stared. "That wasn't exactly how I was going to tell you." Bo stepped back and put his hands in his pockets.

Tina didn't move. Her mouth hung open and her eyes were huge.

"I'd actually planned a more romantic delivery. It just slipped."

Her lack of response worried him and the seconds turned into hours waiting on her reply. Was it too much too soon? Should he try to take it back? Not that he wanted to deny it, but it might make her feel better. "Tina?"

"I love you too. That's what I was trying to say when Sean walked up." Her chest pumped hard with each breath. "I love you too. I realized it this morning when Nan and I were talking."

Bo's relief and joy had him huffing out the breath he'd been holding. She loved him. Tina Foster loved him and he loved her.

Her smile grew wide and his probably matched. She stepped into his arms and linked her hands around his neck. "I promise you, Bo, I'll love you better than any woman ever has. I'll be like the river, always running to you and I'll stay a lot longer than a little while."

Bo's heart danced in his chest as Tina rose and placed a sweet kiss on his lips. Each time he was with her, she set the bar higher for the happiest moments of his life. Whatever he'd done to win her heart, he prayed he did it every day.

"Take me home, Bo," she whispered against his lips. "I don't care what we do, I just want to fall asleep with you tonight and wake up with you tomorrow."

"Yes, ma'am." Bo held her hand and walked over the bridge and down the long gravel driveway through the woods leading to Foster Construction and her home. They hit the top of the stairs leading up the side of the building and he scooped her up, kissing her like crazy. She was so soft, so incredibly silky in every way. He gripped the back of her head, her hair wrapped around his hand, deepening their kiss.

Tina fumbled with the key while still trying to kiss him. Bo finally turned her around so she could see what she was doing. While she opened the door, his lips trailed her neck and shoulder, his hands roamed her stomach and her hips, loving the way she pressed her body against his. Once he got her inside, he all but lost control. It had been at least five years since he'd been with a woman, and back then, he'd barely known what to do.

The one good thing about having so much free time in jail was he read...*a lot*. Now all he could think about was putting some of his knowledge to work on Tina. He kicked the door closed and never lost contact with her mouth. She was wrapped around him, climbing him like he was a damn post. Her purse and keys hit the floor right where they stood. Bo ran his hands up under her dress and up her thighs, lifting her from the ground. Tina was a petite woman, and she fit perfectly in his grip.

Her mouth was heaven, pure, sensual heaven. Never in his life had he dreamed such pleasures could be his. And Tina Foster was definitely his.

Chapter Twenty-Three

TINA DROWNED IN BO. JUST LIKE HE PROMISED, HE took over her body and soul. Bo's hands ran up her thighs and cupped her bottom, lifting her into his arms. His strength only turned her on more. How in the hell could one man drive her insane with only his hands and his kiss? Even if all they did was kiss until the sun came up, she'd be satisfied.

That was not his plan.

Bo carried her to the bedroom and laid her on the bed. His weight pressed against her and his lips traveled down the sensitive skin of her neck and then farther south. Tina closed her eyes and let him do whatever he wanted. For the first time in her life, she felt safe enough in bed to surrender. It was easier than she expected, allowing him to pleasure her in any way he wished. Maybe it was his air of confidence as he brought her to a climax, maybe it was the way he whispered how much he loved her in her ear as her body quaked and writhed under his. Maybe it was the way he was right there with her, staring at her as he took her over and over again, or the way his big body felt inside hers. Maybe it was all of it mixed together and multiplied by her love for him. Whatever it was, it was the best night of her life.

When they both collapsed from exhaustion, Tina and Bo laughed about what a damn mess her room was. She'd never been giddy after sex, another first. There were clothes everywhere, and all her blankets and pillows littered the floor where they'd kicked them off. His clothes made a trail to the door. Her dress was inside out and thrown across a chair in the corner.

"I'm thirsty. You want anything?" Tina hopped up from the bed and searched under the scattered blankets for his button-up shirt.

"Sure, baby."

Damn, her body was humming and pleasantly sore. She slipped into his shirt, pressing her nose into the cologne-scented collar.

She heard a clicking noise and turned to see him with his cell phone, taking a picture. "Bo!"

He grinned at his screen. "Hot damn, that's a good picture of you." He shook his head and sighed. "I can't believe you're mine. I'm the luckiest bastard on Earth."

Tina crawled on the bed and kissed him again. "I love how much you love me."

He ran his knuckles over her breast. "I'm just getting started."

"Then I definitely need a drink." Tina couldn't contain her joy as she padded to the kitchen.

There was one thing she'd learned about Bo during

their working time together; he was a determined man who paid attention to details. He was no different as a lover. Every little whimper made him more attuned to what she liked. In a matter of minutes, he'd figured out her sensitive spots, her weaknesses, and her deepest pleasures. More than anything, he'd not only made her quiver with delight, he'd made her laugh.

Tina leaned against the sink and sipped her glass of water, smiling to herself, when he came out of the bedroom in nothing but his briefs.

"Dear Lord," she whispered, taking in his rock-solid body. How the hell had she ever thought she was attracted to any guy before Bo? No one could compare.

"What's wrong?"

"We have a problem," Tina said and sighed, playing him.

He put his hands on her hips and frowned. "Are you okay?"

"I think we've crossed a line, and I'm afraid this is going to turn into a very physical relationship. I think I want to use you for a sex toy."

Bo smirked and swatted her bottom. "That's fine, as long as you don't mind me obsessing over you and spoiling you rotten in the process."

Tina's cheeks hurt, he made her smile so much. "Deal."

"By the way, I'm leaving that shirt here just so you can walk around in it." He dipped his head and took her mouth in that powerful way that he had.

It was an odd feeling, letting a man take control and not only being okay with it, but wanting it, desiring for him to take her any way he wanted. Then again, this wasn't just some guy. This was Bo; her rock, her soft place to fall, her greatest strength and her biggest weakness. Each moment they were together, she lost more and more of her heart to him.

What happened when she lost it all? Did she lose herself? Did she become Bo's woman and not Tina Foster? What if she lost her entire heart to him and he realized it was a mistake?

"Bo?" She swallowed hard and met his eyes.

"You're overthinking again, aren't you?"

"Maybe." She bit her bottom lip and shrugged. "I'm sorry."

Bo cupped her cheeks and looked her deep in the eyes. "I love you. Period. I didn't fall in love with you just now because we had sex. I've wanted you in my life since the first day I met you. You know how hard it was to see you with Trey? To know he didn't make you happy and I could? The first time I heard you sing on the jobsite, I knew I'd never be able to appreciate that song again unless it came from your lips. When you sang at Bear's, I knew I was sunk, worthless to any other woman in the room. So I waited. I prayed to have you. I gave you space when you needed it and felt the loss every day you were gone to Boston. I'm not going anywhere, Tina, not until you tell me to leave."

"Never again." Tina shook her head and blinked the moisture from her eyes. His words were just as much making love to her as what they did with their bodies. "I love you, Bo. I'm scared of how much I want you in my life. It's a new sensation for me, that's all."

He pulled her to his chest and she hugged him close. "It's okay. I'm a patient man, T. You process it however you want, but you're mine and I'm yours. I didn't spend four years in Hell just to have Heaven pass me by."

"You know what I will never get over?" Tina leaned back and tilted her head upward. "How a man who said a grand total of four words in the last two months suddenly has so much to say."

Bo's deep rumbling laughter warmed her from head to toe. "You're the only person worth talking to, well, and maybe Jason."

Again, Tina found herself laughing and happier than she'd ever been. They spent the rest of the night cuddled up on the couch watching movies and talking until they fell asleep.

She woke the next morning to Bo making coffee. Another first for her. Trey never stayed the night. He always left so he could use his own bathroom to shower. He was a freak about hygiene. Tina slowly stretched and made her way to the bathroom to brush her teeth and do something with her mass of hair.

The last thing she expected was for Bo to barge right in with her.

"Um, hello," she said around her toothbrush.

"Morning. You might want to get naked. I plan on doing you in the shower." He shut the door behind him and kissed her head.

Tina's mouth dropped open, nearly drooling toothpaste, and she scoffed. "Tell me what you really want, why don't you?"

"I just did." He winked at her and dropped his drawers.

Holy shit. Bo started the water, giving her a fabulous view of his naked backside. She finished brushing her teeth, awed at how relaxed he was around her. Was this what it would be like to live with him? Totally at ease with him being in her private spaces?

It wasn't as bad as she imagined.

She shrugged internally and went with it. "You need a toothbrush? I have extras down here." She moved aside to let him search the lower cabinets.

"Why do you have so many? Good gracious, woman."

"Daddy prefers we shop in bulk."

Bo popped to his feet. His face went pale. "Oh my God. Your dad. He's right downstairs, isn't he?"

Tina laughed and rinsed her mouth. "Please don't tell me that just now dawned on you. He was down there all night, Bo."

His eyes rounded. "He's not going to shoot me, is he? I mean, I didn't exactly ask permission to—"

"Bang his daughter?" Tina giggled and unbuttoned her shirt until it slid to the floor. "Better to ask forgiveness than permission."

Bo tickled her sides and made her squirm. "If he kills me, I'm haunting you."

Their laughter continued through the shower. Both of them got a lot dirtier before they washed each other off.

"By the way," Tina panted, leaning her head against the shower wall, "since you didn't ask, I assumed you figured I am on the pill, and I am."

"I didn't care either way." Bo soaped up a sponge and washed her back.

"And if you knocked me up?" She huffed and turned around. Did he seriously not think about using protection?

He waved her off like it was no big deal. "Then I'd have two angels instead of one. I'd make an honest woman out of you and we'd have a baby."

Tina froze, staring at Bo. Her heart had just started to calm from their lovemaking, now it hammered hard again.

She pushed her hair back off of her face. "Shit, Bo. You act like you'd marry me today if you could."

"I would." He rinsed himself off. Since she was unmoving, he gently brought her under the spray of water and rinsed her off too. "Don't act so damn surprised. I told you, I went through four years of Hell. I'm not letting Heaven pass me by. You, Tina Foster, are my Heaven."

Tina blinked rapidly, wishing her blurry eyes were from the shower. She cursed under her breath and turned her back to him. He was intense, that was all there was to it. Bo was a no bullshit kind of man and while she respected him for that, it was overwhelming.

Bo put his hands on her shoulders and rubbed gently. "I love you. Those aren't words I throw around, Tina. They aren't a pickup line or a tool to get you into bed. I love everything about you, so much that the thought of having a baby with you or spending the rest of my life with you doesn't scare me. It excites me. Being with you excites me. I know it's going to take you longer to get there, but you're worth the wait."

Bo kissed the back of her head and got out of the shower, leaving her to her thoughts. Tina stood under the water contemplating how deeply he cared for her. It made her shiver with awareness. He made it sound so simple. She was his. He was hers. And they lived happily ever after.

Except that wasn't how the world worked. Husbands died. Wives died. Boyfriends cheated. Girlfriends cheated. She'd seen it all before; ugly divorces and exes that hated each other so much they couldn't live in the same town. What if they did have kids? Did she really want her children going through that?

Love was a risk, a huge risk.

He's worth it, whispered a voice from deep inside her.

Tina sucked in a breath. Now that she'd found Bo, now that she knew her heart could soar so high, could she live without him? She didn't want to. *Hell no.* She might not have much faith in love as an ideal, but she could have faith in Bo.

She wrapped up in a towel and dried her hair.

Bo was sitting on her couch, dressed in his slacks and shoes, nothing else. He twisted his shirt in his hands and stood when she came out. "I freaked you out, didn't I?" He rubbed his temple with one hand and hit his shirt on his thigh with the other. "Tina, I'm sorry. I know you're not anywhere close to thinking about mar—"

"Were you going to leave?" Her breath caught in her throat.

"What? No, I just don't have any other clothes. Unless… you want me to leave?"

Tina shook her head quickly. "No."

He stood there, looking down, twisting the shirt in his hands.

"You're wrinkling my shirt." Tina approached slowly and took it from his hands, pressing it to her cheek. "It's my new favorite."

Bo's chest relaxed and he grinned. "I didn't think this through. Now I don't have a shirt."

"I have an idea. Why don't we get you some clothes, not that I don't enjoy the view, but it's my view and no one else's. And we can just hang out, do whatever you want to."

Bo nodded. "On one condition; you have to sing at Bear's tonight."

Tina frowned. "Not you too."

"Number one fan, right here." He pulled her into his

arms and satisfaction lit her from the inside.

They spent the day together, happy and laughing and kissing. Tina suggested a movie, so they hit a matinée, went driving through the country, met Keri at a piece of land she wanted to develop, and ended up having an early dinner with Keri, Marshall, and their daughter, Misty. The day flew by and Bo dropped her off in time to get dressed up and meet their friends at Bear's that night.

Being with Bo was effortless. They danced, they drank, they talked about life, and got to know each other better. This was the easy part. Tina had no hesitation about their relationship outside of the worksite. The real challenge would come Monday morning.

After a fantasy weekend with Bo, Tina hated to kiss him goodbye Sunday night. He insisted on going home to get some laundry done and get ready for the work week. She had to admit, there were plenty of things she needed to do as well. Bo was a beautiful distraction.

It probably wouldn't hurt to see if her father was still kicking too.

Tina came downstairs and had a late snack with her father. Late snack meaning a beer on the back porch.

"So, I guess you two are pretty hung up on each other, huh?" Daddy said.

"Something like that." She took a swig of her beer, the only way she could disguise the perma-smile on her face.

"You love him?"

"Yep."

"You sure?"

"Yep."

"He love you back?"

"Oh, yeah."

"Did he say so?"

"Yep."

"He scared to talk to me about it?"

"Yep." Tina grinned at her daddy, who grinned back.

"Good. Means he's smart."

"He is."

Daddy leaned back and narrowed his eyes, making his brows dip together. "You're sure enough in love with that boy, aren't you?"

"Yes, Daddy. He's…incredible."

"That's not an adjective you use when referring to most men."

Tina's smile spread wide and she pulled up her knees to her chest. "He's not most men, Daddy. He's intense and honest and determined. He's been through some tough shit and he's a survivor. We started talking about politics at Bear's the other night and he was explaining parts of the law I didn't even understand. It's like," she shrugged and shook her head, "it's like, he let jail make him a better person, not a criminal. He read and studied and learned another language. Did you know he speaks Spanish? Two dialects: proper Spanish and the local Mexican dialect. He and Keri were going back and forth at dinner like it was no big deal." Tina let out a deep breath. She glanced over at her father, who stared at her like she had sprouted another set of eyeballs. "Sorry. I'm sure you don't want to hear me gush like some love-struck teenager."

"Actually, I was just thinking how nice it is to see you gushing like a love-struck teenager. You've never done that before." He took a swig of his beer, still staring at her. "I wondered if you'd ever find someone who made you all silly and happy like this." One side of his mouth pulled back into a smirk.

"I told you, Daddy. He's different."

"Good. Tell him I want him to come to poker at Terry's Thursday night."

"Fine, but keep one thing in mind." Tina finished off her beer. "He's probably not going to cower to the whole 'cleaning my gun' speech."

"Eh…" Daddy waved her off. "I'm not going to do all that. Give me some damn credit, woman. I already know what his intentions are."

Tina scoffed. "Oh, yeah? And what's that?"

"I imagine he means to be a more permanent part of our lives. I just think we need to discuss what that looks like."

"Oh, no." She shook her head and sighed.

"And I think it needs to be mandatory that when he comes over, he brings beer."

Tina frowned at her father. "No. No blackmail. No demands. No threats."

Daddy sagged his shoulders like a disappointed kid. "Now you're taking all the fun out of it."

Tina rose, laughing, and kissed her father's cheek. "I'm going to go look at the schedule for the week."

"I, uh, put Bo on your crew all week. That okay, or do you want some separation at work?"

Tina hesitated opening the screen door to the house and met her father's knowing eyes. "That's fine. I'd rather find out sooner than later if he can't handle it." The very thought of Bo turning into another Steven made her chest ache. Trial by fire was the only way she'd ever know.

Chapter Twenty-Four

MONDAY MORNING, BO KNEW THAT THIS WAS THE real test of his and Tina's relationship. She was scared to death that he would be like that other guy, and he had to prove her wrong. He had to act like nothing had changed with them behind closed doors. She might've kissed him in front of the crew last week, but then she whisked him off so she didn't have to deal with the questions.

This week was the gauntlet. He had to make it through the next five days to prove to her he could submit to a female boss. What she didn't know was that for two years, he had a female jailor on his block. Having a woman boss him around all day was nothing new. He just happened to know what this cute blonde looked like naked.

Bo had never been a religious man, and yet, he said a little prayer that his love for Tina would be evident, even if it meant not showing it at all.

As soon as Bo arrived at the Ragland house, he found

Terry and started to work like normal. Tina arrived with a truck cab full of wallpaper. She waved him over to help her unload it.

"Have you ever done wallpaper before?"

"No, ma'am. Today seems like a fine day to learn if I need to."

Tina crinkled her nose. "This is some of the most expensive wallpaper I've ever bought. No offense, but I might get Gary and the prophets to help me until you get the swing of it. I can't afford to fuck this up."

"Understood. I can finish the trim out painting while you get prepped and then I can come watch and learn."

"Oh, okay, then." Tina's smile was a quick flash, contemplating for sure.

"Baby," Bo leaned in so none of the other guys could hear, "I love you."

She closed her eyes and a genuine smile stretched across her face. "I love you too, Bo."

"Now go teach me something." He grabbed an arm load of the paper and a five-gallon bucket of the glue, ready to follow her lead.

The rest of the day, Bo was her most attentive student. He watched her lay out the first couple of runs of the wallpaper, careful to match up patterns and not put down too much glue or crinkle the delicate material. By lunch time, he was helping cut. By the end of the day, he put up a piece by himself.

Tina had made the Ragland house her priority and it became just as much a priority to him. Nothing was too good. By Wednesday, the rest of the house was ready for the sheetrock. The electrical had been updated and brought to code the week before and they were set to start on repairing the walls.

This was Tina's most dreaded part of the job. Sheetrock days wore her out and they had at least a week's worth of work in the huge house. Wednesday night, Bo sent his Nan a text about quitting time. Then he found Tina screwing in the last piece of rock for the day.

"Done, thank fu—hey, babe." She turned to see him and hopped down off the ladder. "I'd kiss you, but—"

"The rest of us would gag," Jason said, slapping Tina's legs with his work gloves. "See you love birds tomorrow." He stopped in his tracks and narrowed his eyes at Bo. "Does this mean our Friday beer nights are over? 'Cause I'm not cool with that. You're the only DD I have."

Tina rolled her eyes. "I can spare him for one night of the week. Two if you count poker nights with Dad." Tina grinned and wiped the white dust off her hands.

"Good. You know, too much of a good thing is still too much. Unless it's getting laid, then there's no such thing." Jason wiggled his brows.

"Tell your doctor that the next time you get tested for STDs," Bo said and punched him in the arm.

"Funny." Jason flipped him the bird and sauntered out to Tina's and Bo's laughter.

Bo put his hands in his pockets to keep them off of her. She was tired and she didn't like to be touched when dirty. "Nan is making dinner for four. Your dad is going to head over in about an hour or so, and there's a jetted tub with your name on it."

Tina's shoulders slumped. "Bo, I'm exhausted. I might not be great company and I'll want to be asleep by eight."

"Join the club, sweetness. Water's running. Come on. Go grab Dixie and an overnight bag. I'll see you at the house." He kissed her cheek and left.

When he arrived home, Nan had once again outdone herself. The table was set, the whole house smelled like cookies. "Bo Allen, will you go out and check the grill, honey?"

"Yes, ma'am." He rotated the chicken and came back inside.

Nan wiped her hands on a rag and leaned a bony hip on the counter. "Now, I don't mean to be nosy, but I'm old and my heart don't handle surprises well. You're not going to propose or anything crazy, are you?"

"Hell no," Bo said and laughed. "I'm not trying to scare her off, Nan. She'd never talk to me again if I did that. I just want this, us all getting together, to be natural. You know? You're all the family I have, and Duane is the most important family she has. I just want this to become normal."

"You're planning. That's wise. Warming her up, warming her dad up." She shook her finger in the air. "Smart, Bo Allen. Smart."

He chuckled and kissed her cheek. "I've got to keep this one, Nan. No letting her go."

"Agreed. Now go get clean. You smell, son." Nan shooed him out of the kitchen.

Tina arrived about the time he stepped out of the shower. She was still in her work clothes and looked like she was about to fall asleep. "You said something about a tub?"

Bo slipped on his pants and walked her downstairs to Nan's room.

Tina sighed when she saw the claw foot tub, filled with bubbles and steaming. "Oh my God, you're *so* getting lucky tonight."

"Not why I'm doing this."

Tina wrapped her arms around his waist and laid her head on his chest. "I know why you're doing this and that's what makes you so wonderful."

"Enjoy. I'm going to help with dinner." Bo closed the double doors to the bathroom and left her to it.

Nan smiled at him when they heard Tina singing a few minutes later.

Bo kept on cutting up tomatoes for the salad. "She sings when she's happy."

"Keep her singing, son. Keep her singing." Nan danced around the kitchen, humming in harmony with the lovely melody coming from the bathroom.

Duane arrived about an hour later with a jug of sweet tea and a six pack. Duane was having trouble with his legs cramping, so he traded his canes for a wheelchair once he got inside the house. He had to tell Nan all about his accident and how Tina stepped up to take the reins. He was a man proud of his daughter. No one could blame him. Bo was pretty damn proud of Tina too.

The four of them had a great dinner. Nan even made Dixie her own casserole so she could eat too. Nan and Duane had a lot of mutual friends and acquaintances in town, so there was no lack of conversation, even though Tina wasn't in a talkative mood. There were three generations sitting around that table, and Bo took a hard look at Duane. Until he was next to Nan, who was well into her seventies and had the head of white hair to show for it, Bo never realized how young Duane actually was. He was in his early fifties, old enough that he could have been remarried after Tina's mother died, and young enough to still have a chance at it. It made Bo wonder why Duane was still single. Tina never mentioned him dating and only once had she ever hinted around about the possibility.

Before Duane headed home, he turned to Bo and stretched out his hand. "You coming tomorrow night?"

"Yes, sir. At Terry's?"

"Yep." Duane kissed Tina's hair. "Does Dixie need to come home?"

"She can stay," Nan said from the kitchen. "She's helping me clean the dishes."

Duane shook his head. "All right, then. Thank ya, Nancy."

"Have a good night. I'll make sure these kids behave."

Duane muttered something unintelligible under his breath when Bo tried to help him down the stairs.

After they cleaned up and locked the doors of the house, Bo and Tina headed up to his room. They were both so exhausted, they could barely see straight. Tina fell into bed and only moved to cuddle to him when he joined her under the covers.

Bo never thought to make a move on her. Sure, she was temptation, especially when she backed her bottom right into his crotch and sighed. However, his woman needed sleep, and he needed to occupy his brain with something else. It took three repetitions of the National Anthem in his head before he finally relaxed.

This was what he wanted every night. How could life get better than this? Their families joined together, having a meal after a long day of working, and their bodies joined together, even in rest. He'd been alone for over four years, without friends and family. Under this roof right now were the two women who meant everything to him. Well, three, including Dixie, who hopped up on the foot of the bed and settled in for the night.

This was what heaven was made of, and an angel slept by his side. Bo drifted off, finally at peace with the world.

Sometime in the middle of the night, he stirred awake, his body aching with need. The dreams that filled his mind were coming true. He was sprawled out on his back and Tina knelt between his legs, bringing his fantasies to life. His muscles strained and his control went out the window. Her mouth was a miracle and it drove him straight through the clouds and into space.

"Sweet Jesus, woman. That's a hell of a wakeup call." He panted as his body relaxed into the bed afterwards.

"You've earned it." Tina grinned.

"I'll draw you a bath every day. I'd also be happy to reciprocate." Bo licked his lips in anticipation.

"Not my motive," she said, throwing his words back at him. "Now go back to sleep, baby. We have a busy day tomorrow."

Tomorrow.

And the next day.

And the next week.

And the next month.

Bo and Tina worked side by side for the entire summer. Before he could blink, it was July and Tina soothed her heartbreak over Noah by celebrating Misty's birthday. The two kids' birthdays were close together and while it was painful in one aspect, celebrating life helped them all.

A month later, it was his turn. Bo walked into Bear's on a Wednesday night expecting to have a nice quiet dinner with Nan to celebrate his first birthday as a free man in five years.

"Surprise!"

Bo's mouth dropped open at all the people who

crowded the restaurant. All of the guys from work, their families, Tina's friends that he'd gotten to know over the last couple months, and even a few of his customers who had bought carvings from him all cheered when he entered the doors. Bright-colored balloons dotted the room and a huge birthday cake sat on the decorated stage. A sign hung behind it, exclaiming "Happy Birthday, Bo!"

Nan covered her mouth and had tears in her eyes as Bo just stood there, stunned. *Friends*. He actually had friends and people who cared enough to come out on a Wednesday night and celebrate *him,* of all things.

Right there, in front of them all, was his beautiful lady, her smile shining brightly and her blue eyes lit with happiness. She clapped and cheered, her face radiating all the joy he felt inside and had no clue how to express.

Bo shook his head, intense heat rising in his cheeks as he smiled and rubbed the bridge of his nose. *Holy shit*, if he didn't man-up, he was going to cry.

Tina threw her arms around his neck and jumped into his arms. "Happy birthday, baby."

Bo lifted her off the ground and buried his head in her neck. "Did you do this?"

"I had help. Daddy and Nan were in on it too."

"This is… This is…" *Shit.* Where was the testosterone when he needed it?

Tina took his face in her hands. "You didn't think I'd let you celebrate your birthday without me…and a few of our friends, did ya?"

"I'd hoped," he joked and winked at Nan, who giggled. "Well, hell. Let's have a party."

Jason shoved a beer in his hand and they escorted him to a special table right by the stage. Bo was in awe of all the balloons and streamers. It must have taken hours to string all that crap across the beams of the ceiling and get all these balloons in place. "Thanks in advance to whoever has to clean this place up afterwards."

Nan lifted her glass of wine. "I'll take credit for putting them up, but I won't take responsibility for taking them down. I'm too old for it."

Bo relaxed into the laughter; he drank it up, swimming in it until his entire being was so content he didn't know what to do with himself. Was it legal for a man to be this happy, to have his family, his woman, his friends, and a night of celebrating a life that had been in question at one point?

They ate cake and oohed and ahhed as Bo opened the first birthday presents he'd had in years. He didn't know if there was a limit on personal happiness, but he figured if there was, he would've blown it sky high tonight.

Tina took the stage with a familiar band behind her. When she started singing, it was like living in a dream. She sang a couple fast songs and then broke into country ballads that melted him to the core. She was a Siren, a goddess who wrapped him up and enslaved him with the sound of her voice.

He put his arm around Nan's shoulder. "If my heart wasn't already hers, it sure as hell would be now."

"I got news for you, son. If you don't hang on to 'er, I just might." Nan crinkled her nose when she chuckled, a sign she was half lit. "Damn, that child can sing." She swayed her head back and forth to the beat and clapped when Tina finished. "That's my girl," she hollered out.

Tina winked at her and started another song, perfect for the two-step. Bo extended his hand to Nan. "May I?"

Nan grabbed at her chest and swooned. "You may."

He'd never had so much fun in his life, dancing with his grandmother while the woman he loved and needed more than his next breath sang a country song. It was by far the best birthday of his life. No man was more blessed than he was; they just couldn't be.

It was odd, the way time flew on the outside. When he was behind bars, the hours seemed like days and it was easy to lose track of time because everything felt delayed and in slow motion.

Now, every hour seemed like a minute and he lost track of time because it zipped right out from under him. Working with Tina was as easy as breathing. She was a natural leader and Bo didn't mind falling into step with all the other soldiers. After work, however, he was the general. The crazy part was, as much as she loved to control things, Tina also appreciated not having to be in control.

She didn't argue when he told her where they were going for dinner or if they were going to stay in. Bo always asked her opinion, but nine times out of ten, she would let him decide what movies they would watch. Tina put up a fight for which sports they watched and what team she rooted for, but that was pretty hot and Bo loved the competitive side of her.

The deeper their relationship went, the deeper his love grew. Tina Foster was a great boss and a great person. But she was more than that to him; she was inspirational and worthy of so much more than what Bo could ever offer her. Each time he saw her smile or heard her laugh, his heart softened more. They went for walks, discussing their personal philosophies and thoughts on everything from cereal brands to politics, tools to celebrities, and everything in between. Some things they agreed on, some things they agreed to disagree.

When Bo took her to bed...*fireworks.* Tina was just as passionate about making love to him as she was about fixing up old houses. They had nights where they could barely get their clothes off fast enough and nights where one of them would pleasure the other just to be giving.

The best parts of his day was waking up to her. He loved the way her body fit tucked into his, the way her hair smelled, and way she hummed in her sleep. The nights they spent apart were agonizing but necessary. In order to keep some healthy distance, he made sure they didn't spend every moment together. He still had work to do on Nan's house and his woodworking projects that he wanted to keep going. Tina had joined up with the local band who played at his birthday and they had practices two nights a week, so he planned to be away from her those nights. Jason had been kidding when he mentioned too much of a good thing, but he had a valid point. Bo was well aware of Tina's ability to quickly shift gears. She was the queen of compartmentalizing and, so far, he was a welcomed presence in both the work and personal compartments. He didn't want to wear out his welcome in either.

Chapter Twenty-Five

TINA HELD THE PHONE TO HER EAR AS SHE DROVE home from band practice. "Holly, please come," she pleaded. Tonight was one of the few nights Bo wasn't with her and she could have a serious conversation. Holly was younger, closer to Meg's age, and during their couple of years on the cheer and drill team together, they'd become close friends. She was dating Lance, Meg's brother, when he'd run off the road and into river. He'd been drinking and was ejected from the car, his body found downriver, washed up on the banks in another city. Holly couldn't stand to see Meg suffer and she'd felt responsible because she and Lance had had a fight before he left. She moved into her half-brother's cabin over an hour upriver.

"I can't. You know I can't." Holly spoke in staccato beats on the other end of the phone, her voice tight and unyielding, just like her will.

"It's his birthday, Holly." Tina sighed. Justin and Holly

had once been attached at the hip, part of the reason Lance was angry the night he died.

"I'm aware."

"Justin wants you there."

"Did he say that?" Her uncertain tone showed Tina where the crack in her armor was.

"He told me to invite you this weekend. You were one of his best friends. He misses you, Holly. We all do."

"I miss you too." She cleared her throat. "I don't think it's the best time for a reunion, okay?"

Tina gnawed on her bottom lip until it hurt. Maybe she needed to try the bad cop routine, since the good cop got kicked to the curb. "Do I have to come up there and drag you out of that cabin? Is that what it's going to take for you to realize no one is shunning you? No one blames you, Holly. No one points a finger at you. You heard Meg at Noah's funeral. It's not your fault. Stop taking the blame for Lance's poor decisions. It's been three years. Enough is enough."

"I need more time."

Tina gripped her cell phone so hard she thought it might crack. "Fine, but I'm not giving you long, Holly Combs. If you don't get your shit together, I'll come up there and—"

"I'm not one of your houses, Tina." Holly's firmness startled her. "You can't fix me with a hammer and nails or threats. I'll come when I'm ready. Tell Justin I said happy birthday." Holly hung up the phone and Tina's heart tore in two.

She drove her truck over the Main Street bridge and she looked to the left as she passed by her house and kept driving. She needed to talk to someone, but who? Her father was a good listener when it came to non-emotional situations. But this was an emotional reaction she was having.

Nan.

That was where she was heading, even if her brain hadn't acknowledged it yet. Tina didn't hesitate to put on her blinker and turn onto the county road that led to Bo's house. He was finishing up a project for one of his customers, so maybe they could have a heart-to-heart while he was busy. Nancy was wise and had been so good to Tina in the last couple months.

"Well, hello there, kitten!" Nan opened the door and smiled.

For some reason, Tina couldn't hold it in. Her bottom lip trembled and Nan's chipper countenance fell.

"Oh, honey, come to me." Nan opened her arms and Tina fell into the safety and love she offered. "Is this a woman thing, or do you need Bo?"

"You."

Nan tightened her hold. "You've got me. Come inside and let's talk. I have booze or chocolate, pick your poison."

"I don't want Bo to worry."

Nan turned her around and headed right back out the front door. "Front porch it is."

Tina chuckled through her tears. Of course Nan would understand. They curled up in the front porch swing and Nan listened as Tina unloaded all about Meg, Lance, Holly, Justin; the whole story from the time they were in high school to the moment Holly hung up on her. Nan listened and took in every detail, asking questions so she had all the information.

"I fix things, Nan," Tina said, wiping her tears away. "It's what I do. So why can't I fix this? It's like Holly doesn't want anything to do with us anymore."

"If you could fix hearts, people would be praying to you, not the Lord." She patted Tina on the knee. "People have to process in their own way. Holly does want your friendship, otherwise she wouldn't have taken off to Boston with you in the middle of the night." Nan smiled at her. "You know, there have been a lot of times in my life when I've wondered why I couldn't fix my daughter. Trust me, I've had years to try to make sense of her actions, to comprehend where I went wrong as a mother. Like you're doing now with Holly. I'm a fixer too," she whispered conspiratorially, "so I understand your pain. Are there things I should've done better? Sure. I could list them off and badger myself every day if I wanted to. At the end of the day, people make their own choices. You're not responsible for Holly's guilt any more than Holly is responsible for Lance's death. Focus on what you *can* fix."

"Easier said than done." Tina shrugged and tried to muster a smile.

"Yes, child. It is, which is why I'm going to ask you to focus on something else." Nan frowned and her gray eyebrows pinched together and dipped low. "Belinda contacted me today."

"Your daughter?" Sickness rose in Tina's throat. *Oh no.* "Does Bo know?"

Nan nodded. "I keep nothing from him. He's had enough people lie and betray him. I won't be a name on that list. He loves you, Tina, and if we can protect him from her, we have to. I've already contacted the sheriff about restraining orders and such, but it's not that easy. She technically hasn't done anything wrong yet. She was apologizing and saying how much she missed her family. Said she's been clean for a year." Nan's gray hair shook with her head. "But I've heard it all before, then she does something horrible."

A switch clicked in Tina's mind. Bo was hers. Nan was hers. She would do anything to protect those she loved. "What do we do?"

"We make sure he knows who loves him and who won't betray him." Nan held her hand and Tina noticed it shaking. "Bo has to make up his own mind about his mother."

"Nancy?" Tina whispered, sensing the fear in the older woman.

Nan's eyes filled with moisture. "I just got him back, Tina. I don't want her to hurt him again."

"She won't," Tina promised with a deep and unwavering conviction. "I won't let her. You're not alone in this, Nan. Daddy and I will fight for him too."

"You know the hardest part?" Nan touched her mouth and gazed out over the gardens and fields she labored in daily. "She's my little girl. The moment I heard her voice on the phone today, it broke my heart. Even after everything she's done, I'm still her mother and she's my child."

"Bo says you always look for the best in people. I don't imagine your own daughter would be exempt. Guard your heart, Nan. It'll work out."

Nan's wrinkled lips pulled into a smile. "He's so blessed to have you, kitten. So am I."

Tina hugged Nan, finding the comfort she needed and hopefully giving some. She left Nancy, in search of her man. Bo was in the workshop, gently carving a statue of a bear. He had earbuds in and had no idea she'd come into the door. Tina took the opportunity observe him in his natural habitat.

Bo was meticulous, using his hands with masterful skill

and ease. He bent to get close to the bear's face and picked up a different tool to etch out details of its eyes. Bo was so strong and yet delicate in his work. His broad back twisted and stretched as he repositioned himself. Tina loved the roundness of his shoulders, the thickness of his bulging biceps, and the way those arms felt when he held her. Bo was her safe place, and even before she knew it, he did.

He stood up and turned to examine his tool in better lighting and saw her at the door. Bo yanked his earbuds out and his face lit up, then fell. "You're crying." The tool fell from his hand as if nothing in the world mattered more than her. "What happened?" Bo came to her, touched her cheek, and wrapped his other arm around her waist.

All it took was his touch, and she felt grounded, centered, at peace. Her body relaxed into his hold and she laid her head on his chest. The mixture of the scent of wood and Bo had become her favorite cologne in the world. "Holly and I had an argument. I needed to talk to Nan."

"Is everything okay?"

"I hope it will be. How are you?"

Bo tensed up. "Fine. Why?"

Tina peered up into his eyes. "I know about your mother, Bo. You don't have to pretend."

His jaw worked and his nostrils flared. "I don't want you to worry about her. I won't let her near you."

"It's not me I'm worried about." Tina cupped his cheeks with her hands. "I'm not afraid."

One side of Bo's lips turned up. "Of course you're not. You're the bravest woman I know." He dipped his head and kissed her. "I didn't think I'd see you tonight."

"Surprise." Tina turned her gaze away.

Bo tilted her chin up and ran his thumb over her bottom

lip. He leaned in and whispered, "Baby, what do you need?" He kissed her nose. "Do I need to hold you?" Bo gently dotted kisses on her temples. "Do you need sleep? Food? Target practice?"

"I just wanted to come get some advice. I'm going to go so you can finish up. I just wanted to say goodnight."

"You'll see me in the morning, lover." Bo kissed her lips and Tina sighed when his soft, velvet tongue slipped past her lips. Her body hummed to life. Bo's lips were pure sin and pure salvation.

Yet her mind was on Holly and Bo's mother possibly being around and having to explain to Justin that Holly wouldn't come to his birthday.

"Bo," Tina gasped as he kissed his way down her neck, his hands working loose the buttons of her shirt, "you know I love getting you naked, but that's not why I'm here."

Bo stopped kissing her and narrowed his eyes. "I knew it. You're not okay. That neck bit always works."

Tina slapped his chest. "I'll see you in the morning, brat." She pushed him and headed for the door.

"T?" The urgency in his voice made her spin around.

"Yeah?"

Bo didn't meet her eyes. His hand tapped on the work bench in front of him. He was hesitant about something. "You know that I love you, right?"

"Of course I do, Bo."

"I'm here if you need me."

Tina remembered what he'd said a while back about having abandonment issues. She could just wring his mother's neck. Hell, if the bitch was in town, Tina might just get her chance. Bo was the strongest man she knew in so many ways, and yet he was scared to death of losing her.

"I'm not going anywhere, Bo. You have my heart and I can't very well live without it."

He nodded and turned back to his work. No man wanted to be needy, Tina knew enough to understand that. And she wasn't going to baby him when he had moments of doubt. Thanks to his mother, Bo would always have moments when the scars from her betrayal were ripped open Tina was more than happy to mend his wounds and assure him of her love.

Chapter Twenty-Six

RAIN WAS OFTEN A PAIN IN THE ASS WHEN IT CAME TO construction. No one liked to work in the rain, and even though they could, Bo was a bit relieved when he received the group text message from Duane letting the guys know they had the day off. He peered out his bedroom window and could barely see the outline of the barn through the sheets of water coming down.

Nan, also unable to work in the rain, had fixed him a nice breakfast and coffee. "Mornin', sugar. Guess we're both S.O.L. today, huh?"

"Yes, ma'am. Tina sent me a text to let me know she was going up to see Holly, so I think I'm going to run over to Dalton and see if I can find the chisel I need."

"If you'll gather up your sheets, I'll—"

Tap. Tap. Tap.

Nan and Bo froze when they saw the silhouette in the frosted glass of the front door. The black-headed woman puffed on a cigarette and leaned over to one of the windows.

Bo's heart sped up until he was panting. He met Nan's eyes. "Nan, would you like me to get the door?"

"I've got it." She walked over to the door and opened it wide. "Give me one good reason I shouldn't slap your face and slam this door, Belinda May?"

"Mama, please don't." Her voice cracked.

"Put out that damn cigarette." Nan's voice was sharp and hard, a blade that sliced right through anyone in her path.

"Yes, ma'am." Belinda stepped off the porch and rolled the tip in a puddle on the ground, then came back to the door. Nan didn't let her pass.

Bo stood behind Nan and met the hazel eyes of his mother. She was different than the last time he'd seen her. Her face was fuller, healthier. There were no bags under her eyes and her cheeks weren't hollowed out. She'd gained weight. Her hair was long and shiny, even under the dim lights. Her clothes were clean, almost new looking. Her eyes were clear, not hazy and bloodshot. But when she met his stare, they filled with moisture. She whispered his name and cupped her mouth.

Bo didn't move. He barely breathed. Two pieces of him warred inside his mind. Part of him wanted to physically hurt her, give her every ass-whipping he'd received in prison, let her see what that place did to him. Part of him wanted to slam the door and pretend like she didn't exist. This wasn't the woman he loved. This wasn't the woman who raised him. This was the woman who had betrayed him in the worst possible way. He didn't care about her emotional reactions.

"Say what you have to say," Nan said, leaning against

the door.

"Can I come in?" Belinda gave Nancy big puppy dog eyes, but they had no effect on this crowd.

"No."

Belinda took a deep breath and lowered her head. "I'm sorry. I know you have no reason to believe me. I've done nothing but hurt you. I've been clean for a year and I'm really trying this time."

Bo rolled his eyes. "I've heard this story before, then the dean of my college called me in because you were stealing money. I don't need to read this one again."

"Bo, please," she pleaded. Belinda's bottom lip trembled and she stretched out a trembling hand. "Please. I'm sorry. I know I ruined your life. I hurt you and I hurt Mama. But I've cleaned up; there's no drugs, no alcohol, no men. I've held down a job, I've paid off the college, I've even rented my own place in Dalton for the last few months. I left all of it behind for you."

Bo turned his head away. He couldn't believe her. He didn't want to. Why should he take stock of anything that came out of her lying mouth? He'd heard it all before... right before she had him arrested.

"That's great, Belinda," Nan said, her voice flat and lacking her usual warmth. "You're finally acting like an adult. It only took your son rotting away in a jail cell to wake you up. Unfortunately, I'm not willing to risk another four years of his life on your word alone. If you've cleaned up, time will tell."

She held out her hands. "I'll prove it. I will. I'll take a drug test, my boss can tell you, my landlord, whatever you want. I swear it on a stack of Bibles."

"Child, if you're gonna put your hands on the holy

book, I suggest you read it before you swear on it."

"Yes, ma'am." Her wide hazel eyes begged them to buy into her words and if Bo had to base his decision on her appearance and sincerity alone, he would almost be tempted to think she was telling the truth.

However, the memory of her clinging to his stepfather's arm, her face covered in an inch of makeup to hide the bruises, shaking her head in disgust as the bailiff escorted him from the courtroom and to jail quickly evaporated any belief in her words.

"I don't care to hear any more," he told Nan and turned away. Belinda repulsed him. There was no way he was going to forget and forgive all her sins.

"Bo! Please, son. I'm your mother. Doesn't that mean anything?"

He slowly pivoted and tilted his head, narrowing his eyes. "No. And you know who taught me that lesson?" He lifted his finger and pointed. "You." He shifted his hand to point to Nan. "That's my mother, right there. That's the woman who stood up for me, who fought for me, who sent me cards on my birthday, who called me three times a week, and visited when she could afford it. That's the woman who welcomed me home and loved me when I thought I was unlovable. She prayed for me when I didn't think there was a God to listen. She never gave up on me. Because that's what a mother does. You think DNA gives you the right to that title? No. Sorry. I forgive you, Belinda. I do. We've both made mistakes. But being called mother is a privilege and you threw it away a long time ago."

"You're right. You're absolutely right." She cried in earnest now, causing tremors in her shoulders. "I'll never deserve your forgiveness. I can only make it up to you, somehow, some way. I'll earn your love back."

"I wish I could believe that. But I'm not big on pipe dreams." Bo shook his head and took a deep breath. He'd heard enough. Life was finally looking good and he wasn't about to let his mother back in to sabotage it for a fourth or fifth time—he'd lost count. Now he had Nan and Tina to protect.

"It's okay," Belinda said, gathering herself and wiping at her eyes. She even tried to smile. "You don't have to believe me, not today. I'll be around and, in time, you'll see. I'll make it up to you…both of you." She nodded her head and backed away, heading out into the rain.

Nan and Bo stood in silence as Belinda drove away.

Nan let out a heavy, uneven breath. "I'd give my left arm for all that to be true."

"It'd be hard to kick butt like you do with only one arm." Bo grinned, hoping to lighten the heavy weight that had settled like the thick, wet air outside.

"I never said I'd give 'er my *good* arm." Nan winked at him and went back to the kitchen. "Be smart and let the parole officer know she came by and nothing happened. Then go on about your day, Bo. We have to keep moving forward."

"Yes, ma'am."

As much as he tried, Bo couldn't keep his mind off of his mother. He drove to Dalton, found his tools, went by Andrew Buchanan's house to check on his dad, stopped by Charlie Ray's automotive shop to ask Justin for some advice on his truck, and ended up making some business phone calls for Duane, who'd taken the day to go fishing downriver. Bo was determined to keep his mind off of Belinda, but the more he tried to distract himself, the more he thought about that morning.

Belinda looked healthy. She spoke with a clarity she hadn't had in his entire life. But his mother was a con artist, pure and simple. How many times had he bought into her lies and forgiven her, only to be hurt again? This time, he knew better.

In the very recesses of his heart, he wished he could forget all the horrible things she'd done, all those days he'd spent in jail because of her lies. Maybe he was a sucker? Maybe every son desired his mother's affections until the very end? Who knew?

"If it makes you feel better," Tina said as they cuddled up in her bed together that night with Dixie at their feet, "I'm incredibly proud of you, Bo. You amaze me all the time."

He kissed the top of her head and inhaled a deep pull of her scent. This was his own personal miracle, right here. This was a woman who loved him without strings attached. For all the shit that had gone wrong in his life, Tina was like repayment from the universe.

"That's what matters to me." He kissed her head again. "What's up with Holly? Justin asked me about her when I went to the shop today."

"Holly is…holding on to things she needs to let go of and not grabbing hold of what she needs. Or who."

"Justin?"

"Yep."

"Not everyone bounces back like you, T."

Dixie's head popped up and a crashing sound came from downstairs.

"What was tha—" Bo's words were cut off by a glass breaking in the living room. Dixie bolted out of the bedroom and they scrambled to see what was going on. Bo slipped on his jeans and Tina threw on a robe.

As they stepped out of the bedroom, a flaming coke bottle hit the floor in front of them and shattered. He dove to shield Tina. The accelerant spilled out onto the floor, igniting with a whooshing hiss and blasting hot glass all over the room. Bo bellowed as it hit his back. He and Tina fell back into the bedroom as gasoline spread over the hardwood of her kitchen area, igniting as it reached outward.

"Extinguisher!" Tina yelled and pointed to the fire extinguisher above her fridge.

Bo surveyed the way the liquid fire moved towards the couch and towards the wall of the bedroom. "Get out of here. Once the fire hits your liquor cabinet, we're screwed."

Tina shook her head and he could see the rebellion in her eyes. She opened her mouth to argue and he pulled her off the bed. "I said *go*, woman!" He practically pushed her to the stairwell and ran for the extinguisher.

The fire ate up everything it touched. The couch was gone and the curtains were flaming, the rug sped up the crawl of destruction. This was too much for a simple fire extinguisher. The blaze moved too fast. He made a split-second decision to just get the hell out, especially since the entire second story was filling with smoke. Crouching beneath the haze, he made it over to the stairwell.

When he opened the door, smoke from the first story came up. He closed the door, knowing the oxygen from below would only give further life to the flames above.

The sirens of the fire trucks blared outside. They would handle it from here.

Now he just had to get out.

The back door was completely blocked by fire. The

stairwell was out. What was he going to do?

The balcony.

He belly-crawled over to the bedroom and his heart sank when he found Dixie huddled in the corner and whining. Shit.

"Come," he screamed at her. Dixie didn't move.

Each inhale burned his lungs and his vision blurred. By the time he reached the dog, he could hardly see her. His eyes stung and his head swirled. It would be easy to close his eyes and make the world stop turning. But if he could reach the balcony, maybe he could at least breathe.

"Bo...Bo..." From a long distance, he heard her calling. His angel. His life. He had to...

Chapter Twenty-Seven

"Bo!" Tina screamed his name at the top of her lungs, kicking and yelping as Bear and her father held her back.

"Tina, stop it, you can't go in there!" Bear held on to her shoulders.

Tina thrashed in his grip, reaching for the house. Tears streamed down her face. "Let me go! He's still in there, damn it. Let me go, you bastard!"

"You're not going to die trying to go get him." Daddy held an arm across her chest. "Let the professionals do their job."

They stood in the parking lot of the cannery with the fireman scrambling about, pumping water into the windows of both stories. Black smoke billowed out of the open areas and a team of men were suited up to go in, knowing there were victims inside.

Tina watched in horror as the flames lit up the night

sky and ate her home. Bo! Oh God.

Please don't let him die, she prayed. *Please come out.* He couldn't die. Not like this. Bo had survived over four years in jail, he had survived an abusive step-father and a horrible mother, only to come out stronger on the other side. If all that hadn't killed him, he had to survive this.

Tina crumpled to the ground, the gravel of the lot jabbing into her knees, but it didn't matter. Bo!

What if she lost him? What if he was already dead? Oh God!

Tina sobbed and Bear held her close. He had seen the fire from across the river and literally ran over the bridge to help while his staff called for help. "They'll find him, Tina. Don't worry."

"I can't lose him, Bear. I can't."

"It's okay. It's okay." Bear's voice sounded far off, like he was in another room.

All Tina could think about was Bo. It didn't matter that her home was damaged. She needed Bo.

"Holy shit." Bear stood up and brought her with him.

Tina followed his gaze to the balcony of her room. "Bo!"

He stumbled out of the French doors, smoke billowing out behind him. His head hung to his chest and in his arms...was Dixie. Tina cried out as they tumbled over the iron railing and fell into the waters of the Sanguine.

"No!" Tina took off running, uncaring if the gravel of the lot sliced into her bare feet. Bear and two firemen ran in front of her as they rounded the building and disappeared into the woods that backed the river. Tina jumped over fallen trees and waded into the water, searching for any sign of Bo or Dixie. She screamed his name at the top of her lungs.

She coughed, not realizing until that moment she might have some smoke damage herself. She'd helped her father out of the bottom story of the warehouse. There was a bottle bomb thrown into his apartment too.

"There!" Bear trudged through the shallow waters by the bank then swam out to where Bo floated.

"I've got the dog," shouted a fireman, lifting Dixie from the water. They carried her off and Tina knew her dog would be in good hands. Dixie hadn't floated far and, surprisingly, she was conscious.

Bo, however, was not.

Bear hauled him up to the shore and the first responders started CPR. Bear scooped up Tina. "Your feet are bleeding."

"Put me down, no, stop it. I need to be with him." She was strong, but not nearly strong enough to battle Bear Harris.

"Let the EMTs handle this, Tina. You're coughing your head off."

His words didn't mean anything to her. They didn't register as logical thinking in her mind. All she could comprehend was being with Bo. Men rushed passed her with a stretcher and oxygen tanks. Daddy was talking to police officers and the fire marshal. Most of the flames seemed to be gone and the tone of the entire scene had calmed somewhat. Neighbors and onlookers crowded the street.

Bear sat Tina on a gurney, pulled out his phone, and stepped away.

Tina didn't pay any attention to the woman attending to her feet and slapping a mask on her. She just stared at her home and inhaled the oxygen. It was like watching a car wreck, except this disaster didn't end with one big bang. This nightmare kept going, and there was nothing she could do about it. The warehouse had stood the test of time and hopefully it would survive this too. How much of the fire had reached their offices? What pictures were left? Where were they going to stay while they rebuilt?

Nan. Crap!

"Bear, you have to call Nancy." Tina coughed and sputtered.

"I'm on the phone with her. She's on her way. I also texted Jayden to bring you clothes." He finished his conversation with Nancy and hung up.

The fireman and EMTs came out of the woods carrying Bo. He was strapped on the stretcher with a brace around his neck and a huge oxygen mask over his face. *Oh God.*

Everything in her world slowed down. She couldn't move as the men carried Bo across the Foster Construction parking lot. Their heavy steps kicked up the gravel. Those men didn't realize they carried her heart on that stretcher. Her pulse beat in her ears in time with their footfalls. Her life was in their hands and they didn't even know it.

Now that she'd found him, Tina didn't want to live without Bo. He'd brought light and laughter, joy and passion to her life. The idea of living without that seemed impossible.

She rose and tried to get to him. "Bo," she screamed through her oxygen mask.

"Miss Foster, please." The woman restrained her and gave her a kind smile. "They've got him. He has to be taken to the burn center, Miss Foster. If you'll allow me to check you over, you can go with him."

"I have to be with him. He can't be alone." Tina pushed the woman off and reached for her mask to remove it. "Why isn't he moving?"

The nurse wrestled with Tina and won, pushing her back down and securing her mask.

"Miss Foster, he's been sedated for the intubation, he's going to be fine—"

"So am I, damn it. Let me up!"

Daddy stepped up and grabbed her arm, like he used to when she was in trouble. "Tina, behave and let this woman look at you or I'll make them sedate you too." He used that stern tone of voice that instantly turned her into a child again. "I mean it."

"Yes, sir." Tina's mind went numb. She allowed the medic to bandage up her feet, slip on some socks. Usually, Tina was the one taking charge, she was the one giving orders and fixing everything.

Bo.

Nothing else registered. Not the tote bag Jayden shoved into her hands or the sentimental words Tina forgot as soon as they hit her ears. Even Nan was out of it and holding on to Tina's hand like a life raft. Thank God her father and Bear took control.

I need Bo.

Daddy stayed back to deal with the mess and make sure Dixie made it to the emergency vet. Terry and his wife came over to help, so Tina didn't feel bad running out on her father.

Riverview passed by the window as Bear drove her truck behind the ambulance. The flashing lights only added to her disorientation. She should be in the ambulance with Bo, holding his hand, not following along.

It was even worse that the ambulance wasn't taking him to the local county hospital, but to rendezvous with a helicopter that would take him to a burn care center three hours away. They met up at the local emergency clinic helipad to transfer him into the helicopter. Since Nancy was his next of kin and knew all his important information, she was the one they hurried into the chopper with him.

Bear drove like a bat out of hell down to Carreyville, the nearest major city with a burn unit.

"Does this mean he's going to die?" Tina hated the unknown, hating the fear that ran in her veins like arctic water.

Bear kept getting phone calls and text messages. He knew something and he needed to talk to Tina. "Alex Moody, the fire marshal, is a friend of mine. He said there weren't any major exterior burns that they could see, but they worry about smoke inhalation, plus the fact that he did have some water inhalation as well. They're taking him to Carreyville because they specialize in this sort of injury, not because he's dying." Bear's calm and firm voice made her hopeful. Then again, not too much ruffled big, bad Jake Harris.

The entire drive, Tina and Bear tried to figure out who in the world could've done this. Who hated them so much that they were willing to destroy their home and possibly even kill them? As hard as it was to admit, Tina had a tendency to piss people off with her big mouth, but she couldn't think of anyone who would be angry enough to purposely try to hurt her or her father.

"Any suppliers or homeowners mad at you?" Bear asked, grasping at straws.

"Not that I can think of." Tina shook her head. "I mean, I doubt anyone would try to burn down my home over a messed-up supply order."

"What about Bo's mother? Didn't you say that she was

in the area?"

Tina pinched her temple. "I was really trying not to go there."

"T," Bear said, taking her hand, "someone just tried to blow you up and nearly killed Bo. I think your mind needs to go anywhere it can to figure this out."

"But why would Belinda give a rat's ass about us?" Tina shrugged, throwing up her hands. "I can understand wanting to get to Bo, but why in the world would she care about me and Daddy?" She shook her head. Belinda wasn't out of the running, but she wasn't Tina's prime suspect either. "Whoever it was knew to aim at the back of the house to reach Daddy. They didn't throw the bombs in the front windows. It was someone who knew our business was up there. I've never even seen Belinda, much less let her into our home."

"There's thousands of people who know Duane lives in the back of the first floor. That doesn't narrow it down."

"True." Tina groaned. They rode in silence for a moment before she realized Bear had walked out of his restaurant to literally run to her aid. "I'm sorry to pull you away from work. Is someone closing up for you?"

"Do *not* worry about that, seriously. How many times have you dropped everything for someone else? I'm happy to help. Hell, I'm glad I noticed the dirty table in front of the window so I could see the fire."

"I feel bad. I didn't really speak to Jayden." Tina raked her hands through her hair and leaned her head back on the seat.

"Don't worry. She knows all too well what shoes you're in." Bear's lips pinched together.

Tina covered her hands with her face. "Oh God. Please,

God, I hope not. I can't lose Bo."

"You're not. Don't think like that."

"How can I not?" Tina pulled her legs up into her seat. "If the fire didn't get him, that damn river will."

The Sanguine harvested people. First Lance, then Chris— "Sean." The thought hit her loud and clear. Sean Harris was with Rodman the night she and Bo went out. Rodman said she would regret firing him.

"What about him?"

Tina uncurled her legs as the pieces clicked into place. "He's friends with Rodman. Rodman is Trey's cousin and he worked for us. We fired him."

Bear took out his phone and immediately dialed his little brother's phone number. "Sean? Where are you? Good. You been there all night? Good. Where's your buddy Rodman? Why? Because someone lit up Tina's place like a fucking battlefield with Molotov cocktails. Yeah, she's okay. Duane too. But Bo was there and he's being airlifted to the burn center in Carreyville. Yes, I'm serious and if I find out you had anything to do with this—"

Sean's voice rose high enough on the phone Tina heard him from the passenger seat. "No! Hell, no. Tina is my friend too."

"I'm not the one with the loyalty issues. What do you know, Sean?"

"Nothing."

"Sean?" Bear growled into the phone. "I'm your brother, and I love you, but if you're lying to me, I'm going to beat the shit out of you and then help the police throw your dope-head ass in jail. If Rodman did this, he's up for prison time. You want to join him?"

"No, man. Come on. Tina's my girl."

"Well, *your girl* was nearly killed tonight."

"I'm sorry, man. I'm sorry, okay. I don't know anything."

Bear pulled his phone away from his head and threw it on the dash of the truck. "Son of a bitch just hung up on me."

"He knows something, doesn't he?" Tina's blood was boiling now.

Bear nodded and grabbed his phone again. "Alex? Hey, it's Bear. I've got someone you need to check in on." He gave the fire marshal all the information they could on Rodman. Alex would take it from there.

Her mind kept focused on Bo. That drive south had never felt so long. Once people found out she didn't have her cell phone and she was with Bear, his phone lit up every five minutes with calls. Some of their neighbors who also knew Bear called to check on her, along with other friends in the community. Jayden, Keri, Holly, even Meg made sure to check on Tina.

"Are you okay?" Meg cried out over the line when Tina answered Bear's phone. "Keri texted me and, oh my God, is your dad okay? What about Dixie? Was Bo with you?"

"Take a breath, Meg." Tina smiled, so happy to hear her voice. She didn't react when Bear leaned over slightly as if to hear their conversation better. "Right now, Bo is the only one in question. Daddy and I are fine. Dixie is at the vet. Bo got the worst of it."

"Oh," Meg gasped. "Tina, I'm so sorry. Do I need to come? I'll make Cole buy me a plane ticket right now."

"As much as I'd love to see you again, I don't think there's a need. Thank God."

"Well, that's good, I guess." Meg hesitated. "I'm glad Bear is with you."

Tina smiled over at her driver. "Yeah, me too."

"Tell him—never mind. Do you know what started the fire?"

She would overlook that slip, this time. "Not what. Who."

Meg sucked in a breath. "Someone set your house on fire?"

After telling the story fifteen times, she gave Meg the watered-down version before Bear's phone ran out of battery. She was blessed to have so many people who cared about her, but after the adrenaline rush of the last couple hours, Tina was starting to crash.

Meg promised to call later and demanded that if anything happened, she was to be notified so she could fly down.

"Or steal the car; those were her words." Tina recited them to Bear. "She doesn't even have her own car to drive. Cole won't allow it."

"Does that stupid asshole know if Meg had a car to take their kid to the hospital, Noah might still be alive?" Bear gripped her steering wheel so hard she heard the leather creak under his palms. "I swear to God, the next time I see that bastard, I'm going to rip his dic—"

"Bear," Tina yelled to get his attention. "Stop trying to break my truck."

He let out a heavy breath and loosened his grip. "Sorry."

Tina reached over and placed her hand on Bear's shoulder. "We'll get her back, you know that, right? Cole isn't enough to keep her up there."

"Yeah." He didn't say more. Meg was a subject he often left untouched. Tina had never understood the dynamic between the two, but there was something there.

It felt like an eternity before Tina and Bear found Nancy. She sat in a waiting room with her elbows on her knees, one leg bouncing up and down. When she saw Tina, she immediately rose and pulled her into a hug.

"He's going to be okay, sweet girl. Don't you worry."

Tina had lived her entire life not knowing what it was like to be held by a mother...until that moment. For the first time, she was safe to just be a scared little girl, crying to her mom. The shelter Nan provided was enough of a safety net that Tina knew she could fall apart, and Nan would be there to catch her.

All her strength crumbled as she embraced Nan. She released all the fear she'd bottled up on the drive there. Walls came crashing down and, for once in her life, Tina didn't have to be the rock.

"I gotcha, honey," Nan whispered and kissed her cheek. "I'm strong enough for the both of us. You just let it out."

"I love him so much." Tina buried her head into Nan's neck.

"I know you do. You can tell him as soon as he wakes up."

Tina nodded and stepped back, taking a steadying breath and trying like hell to get herself together. "Sorry."

"No apologizing. If crying were a sin, we'd be neighbors in Hell." Nancy handed her a tissue. "You good?"

"Yes, ma'am." Tina sniffled and Bear put his arm around her shoulder.

"The doctor is doing some internal scans and chest x-rays. They intubated him as a precaution because they didn't want his air passages swelling during transport. He's got a pretty nasty cut on his head, which is what they think knocked him out when he fell in the water. So far, nothing life-threatening, okay, honey? Take a breath; you're turning green again." Nan waved her hand around her chest and inhaled, indicating Tina to do the same. "Good girl."

Nan sat Tina down beside her and they waited…and waited…and waited some more.

Tina checked her watch. It had barely been fifteen minutes. This was going to be a long night.

An hour later, Tina was greeted by a tall, lanky doctor. She didn't catch his name. But he spoke to Nan about Bo's condition. "We want to monitor him for at least the next twenty-four hours to make sure his lung function is optimal. Thankfully, we didn't find any external burns. He did need stitches across the back of his head, again, minor injuries, given the events that brought him here." The doctor met her eyes. "You must be Tina?"

She nodded.

"He's asking for you…quite insistently." He smiled and guided her down a corridor into a room. "Bo sustained limited injuries, but he is having some difficulty breathing and has some throat soreness. His blood oxygen levels are lower than average, not dangerously, but we do have him on high concentration oxygen. He woke up agitated from the sedatives. Please encourage him to calm down and not to speak."

"Calm down?" Tina asked as they walked in the room.

"Get this crap off my face!" Bo's voice didn't sound right. It was hoarse and clogged, as if he strained to speak.

The doctor immediately had to step in and help the nurse. "Mr. Galloway, keep the mask on!" Bo pushed both of them off and wouldn't lie down.

Then his bloodshot hazel eyes met Tina's. He froze. The nurses turned to see what had enraptured him.

Moisture formed in the corners of his eyes. Tina smiled and took a deep breath. Without a word, she slowly came to the side of his bed and took the oxygen mask from the nurse, whose mouth fell open as Tina slid it over his head without any fight at all. The room was still and quiet, except for the machines. The hospital staff didn't understand, but Tina did.

Bo belonged to her just as much as she belonged to him. He needed her and she needed him. Right now, he was the water, and she had to be the rock.

Tina gently ran her knuckles over his cheek and down his neck. Bo cupped her cheeks, and a single tear slipped down his face. She wiped it away and pressed his shoulders until he leaned backwards on the bed. His eyes were zeroed in on hers as if she were the oxygen he needed to survive. Tina sat on the edge of the bed. He barely blinked. She trailed her hand over his head, down his cheek, and across his jaw slowly. With every pass, his pulse slowed and his body relaxed against the pillows.

A nurse tapped Tina on the shoulder and handed her a small white clamp with a wire attached. "On his finger," she whispered, not wanting to intrude.

Tina recognized the oxygen monitor and did as the nurse instructed. She couldn't take her eyes away from Bo's. From the day they met, his intensity had scared her and made her feel things right down to her toes. How could she not love the way he loved her? His eyes told her everything.

He needed her.

He wanted her.

He loved her.

Tina kept skimming her fingers over his skin, thankful that there were no burns. She knew the nurses were waiting patiently behind her to continue their work, so she bent down close to his face. "I'm not going anywhere. I'll be right here." She winked at him and pursed her lips. "Behave, Galloway, or we'll sedate you again." Joy flowed from his smile through to her heart. "I love you."

Bo touched her cheek and nodded once.

Tina moved off the bed and stepped back so the staff could do what they needed. Bo kept his gaze on her.

"I can do that to men too," said an older nurse. "But I usually have to inject 'em with something first." She winked at Tina, who slapped a hand over her mouth to cover her teary laughter. The nurse clapped Tina on the shoulder. "There you go, sugar. Keep that smile on your face. He's going to be fine now."

Chapter
Twenty-Eight

Two weeks later, Bo was released. Two miserable, awful, depressing—okay, maybe that was being dramatic, but Bo hated hospitals. He hated the way the nurses came in every five minutes to take his blood or make him breathe in some stupid tube. He hated the way the machines beeped and kept him up at night. The bed was uncomfortable and the wires bothered him.

All of that was minor compared to the way his chest burned, like he'd run a marathon in the freezing cold and breathed through his mouth the whole time. It hurt to inhale too deeply or cough or laugh even. His head finally quit hurting in time to have the stitches removed. He had a rocking bald spot where they shaved him.

The pain and the bald spot were tolerable if it meant being at home with Tina instead of being in the hospital. He was happy to get home and start helping Foster Construction get back to being Foster Construction. The fire had ruined Tina's apartment upstairs. Duane's apartment downstairs was damaged, but salvageable. The office area had smoke and water damage. Most of the important papers and cash were in a fireproof safe. Work had to keep going, the crews still needed a paycheck, so life didn't stop to work on the warehouse. Bo was ready to get back to work, get in there and get his hands dirty on one of their many projects. Which would be great, if Nan and Tina didn't have him on house arrest. By the time Bo snuck out and went over there, a month after the fire, it was nothing but a block shell.

Tina saw him and immediately scowled. She stomped over to him, angry as a wet hen, that blonde ponytail swinging behind her. "Bo, you should *not* be here. The doctors said any chemicals you inhale—"

"Tina, stop. I had to get out of the house. Nan is about to smother me and Belinda is calling every damn day to check in." He pulled Tina into his arms. "I need you and I need a distraction."

"You're so hard-headed." She hugged him back and everything good and whole in the world settled into place. "I'm glad to see you up and moving, but you have to at least wear a mask while you're here. That's an order from the boss, not your girlfriend. This is a construction site, after all." Her sexy, cocky smirk turned him on like never before.

"Yes, ma'am." Bo slipped the dust mask over his face, secretly thankful, not wanting to inhale anything that might irritate his lungs or throat. He was finally getting to the point where he could breathe deeply again.

Tina walked him through the building, rambling, like she usually did, about all the things they were going to do. The canning warehouse was technically a historical building. The insurance on it covered whatever it took to keep the building standing, not to mention the various policies that Tina and Duane carried for the business and personal effects. His woman had great ideas, as always.

They would rebuild. Foster Construction would rise from the ashes, literally, and be better than ever.

That night, Tina and Bo sat on the front porch of Nan's house cuddled under a blanket. The October nights were turning cold and the chilly air was good for the soul after a long, hot Texas summer.

"I have a confession," Tina whispered, gnawing on her bottom lip. "When you were in the hospital I, um, well, I might've done something stupid."

Bo raised a brow. "Might've?"

"Okay, I did do something stupid and rash and maybe even illegal." She played with her hair, twirling it around her finger in a way he'd never seen her do. "Nan made me come home after I'd been down there a couple days and Bear told me the fire marshal was having a problem locating Rodman to question him. So I...I may have gone to Trey's office..."

"Oh no."

"...and I may have taken a nail gun..."

"Oh God."

"...and I may have nailed his tie to his desk."

"You didn't." Bo scrubbed a hand down his face.

"There's a possibility that Trey will press charges."

"A possibility?"

"Okay, Trey pressed charges." Tina swallowed and lowered her gaze.

"Tina..." Bo sighed and his head fell back with a groan.

"It's okay. He dropped them when Rodman was

arrested…right after I was."

Bo pinched the bridge of his nose and shook his head. "He was still wearing the tie, wasn't he?"

"Maybe." Tina cringed and bit her bottom lip. "Yes."

"Oh my God, T."

She crinkled her nose in the cutest way. "Just think, we can have matching mug shots on our Christmas card this year."

Bo busted out laughing. He couldn't hold it in. The very thought of that little firecracker marching into Trey's engineering firm with her tool belt on and nail gun loaded just sent him to cackling uncontrollably. They laughed so hard they both had tears in their eyes and Bo started coughing. He hadn't laughed that deep in months and it was worth every bit of burning in his chest.

"This is why I love you," he said, pulling her into his arms. "Our life will never be dull."

Epilogue

Bo had everything ready. He'd been planning this night with Duane and Nan for months now. Everything was in place. Sweat dripped down the back of his neck and his palms were clammy. He tried to take a deep breath to calm himself, but it only made him dizzy.

Bear's was decked out with St. Patrick's Day themed décor, except for one portion of the restaurant area decorated for Tina's birthday.

Their friends and family were gathered to celebrate not only her, but the reopening of Foster's Construction in the warehouse. It was truly a big night for all and especially for him.

He hid his nervousness through the toasts and through dinner. But Bear was about to bring out the cake and Bo was about to shake his skin loose. Nan found his gaze and winked at him, reminding him this was the right thing.

Duane, who must've sensed Bo's nervousness, stood and quieted everyone down. "Tonight we celebrate the re-opening of the cannery and the birthday of my incredible daughter." Everyone cheered and Tina blushed, her smile beaming from ear to ear. "In honor of both, a young man I have come to know and love like a son has a special gift he would like to present. Bo?" Duane lifted his beer.

Taking one more deep breath, Bo stood and walked over to the corner of the room, where a sheet covered his first gift to Tina. "Foster Construction has been a place of refuge for me in the last year. Duane and Tina are good people to work for and good friends to have by your side."

Jason held up his beer and yelled, "Hear, hear!", inciting many others to do the same.

Bo chuckled and put his hand on the sheet. "I'd like to give you guys a token of my appreciation." He pulled the white sheet off of the statue. It was almost like being naked in public.

Underneath was a four-foot-long sculpture he'd been working on for months. One hand, on the left, was palm up and open, giving a flowing stream of water to another hand on the right.

"The word 'foster' means to encourage growth and development or to bring up. This is what Duane and Tina do in their business and their personal lives. They openly give of themselves so that others may receive."

Everyone cheered as Tina and Duane stood to examine his artwork. Tina's mouth hung open, while Duane shook his head like he couldn't believe what he saw.

"Spectacular," he said. "Just spectacular, son." Duane shook his hand and pulled him in to clap him on the back.

Bo blew out a breath as Duane gave him a head nod.

He knew what Bo was about to do and moved out of the way.

"If everyone will indulge me one more moment," Bo said over the oohs and aahs. Bo took Tina by the hand and looked her right in those big blue eyes that had captured his heart from the beginning. She raised a brow and glanced out at everyone who was anxiously awaiting what Bo had to say. "It's been almost a year since I walked through the doors of Foster Construction, hoping and praying for a second chance at life. You and your father gave me that chance and so much more. Whether you knew it or not, you owned a piece of me from that moment on. As the weeks went on, I came to admire you as a leader, as a boss, and as a woman."

"Bo," Tina gasped, the light bulb pinging to life above her head. Moisture filled her eyes and she gripped his hands so hard, he almost lost his train of thought. She bit down on her quivering bottom lip.

"You are the most inspirational woman I've ever met, Tina. I'll happily follow you for the rest of my days, if it means we get to travel this life together." Bo knelt in front of her on one knee and reached into his pocket to pull out a black velvet box. "More than that, I promise to lead you as your husband, your friend, and always strive to be your hero."

Tina covered her mouth with her hands, her tears now overflowing.

"Tina Foster, will you do me the greatest honor and marry me?" Bo opened the box, his heart stuck in his chest, awaiting her answer. He couldn't breathe. His hands shook as he held out the ring and offered his heart.

Tina's chin quivered so much, he almost didn't hear her whisper, "Yes."

Bo let out the breath he'd been holding and rose to slide the gold ring on her finger. Tina jumped into his arms and he twirled her around. Happiness and cheers vibrated the room, and the entire restaurant erupted into one big party. Bear cranked up the music as a waitress handed out shots.

Tina wiped off her face and met his gaze. "You really want to marry me?" She smiled through her tears.

"Sure do, with one stipulation."

"What's that, Mr. Galloway?" Tina tiptoed up and put her arms around his neck.

He rested his hands on her hips. "When we argue, you can't be within reach of a nail gun."

Tina threw her head back, laughing, and then jumped into his arms, wrapping her legs around his waist. She planted a kiss on him, right there in front of half the town.

Bo had never been happier than that moment in Riverview, Texas, at Bear's Grill and Bar, surrounded by his friends and family, and holding the woman he was going to marry. He was home in every way.

Check out *The Roles We Play* by JoAnna Grace, a contemporary romance.

CHAPTER
One

Kelly rolled over in bed and picked up her cell phone. Mark's face smiled back at her as his Bon Jovi ringtone blared. What could he possibly want at three in the morning? Was he insane?

"You'd better be bleeding, jackass," she mumbled.

His deep chuckle filled the silence of her studio. "Damn, you're grumpy in the morning."

"It's not morning yet. It's that time of day even Jesus hates. What do you want? Where are you?"

"I had to work the late shift, remember?"

Kelly vaguely recalled that the night guy at the airport had quit and Mark had to fill in for him for a couple weeks. "I'm really sorry for your luck. Again, what do you want?"

"I need a favor."

Ah hell. The last time Mark needed a favor, Kelly ended up watching three little girls—scratch that, three little terrorists—all under the age of six so he could go bang their mom. "If this involves you getting laid, I'm not interested. Try that website for nanny services."

"Don't be bitter. It doesn't suit you."

"Point, Mark. Let's get to the *point*." She rubbed a hand

over her messy hair and down her face. People should not be awake at three a.m., especially people like her.

"Remember that actor that had his plane serviced a couple months ago?"

Kelly answered with a grunt. She had to admit, it was pretty sweet that Mark had spent an entire afternoon chauffeuring around a big time celebrity while his plane was checked out. They went to lunch and spent the afternoon driving around and chatting like old friends. That was just Mark, though. He had the best luck of any person she'd ever met.

"We were having lunch and he starts telling me that he likes to hide out, right. No cameras, no interviews, just shootin' the shit. We got along, so I offered for him to stay around here when he needed to."

Kelly cursed. She knew exactly what Mark had offered. "What did you promise and how screwed am I?"

"Let me finish." Mark sighed, his nerves clearly shot. "So I *might* have led him to believe that I knew someone with a private bed and breakfast type place that is way off in the hills."

"Damn it, Mark. You know Pops doesn't like strangers."

"Well, here's the thing. He might have told his girlfriend about this little hidey-hole."

Kelly groaned. "Might have? God, you make me want to hold your head under water until the bubbles quit."

"Plane lands in an hour, private runway H."

Kelly was already pulling on her jeans because this was Mark. Even though Mark was a pain in the ass, he would give his left nut for her. "Do you mean to tell me that now I have to play hostess to some stuck up actress in hiding because she's in trouble and needs her publicist to smooth things over?"

"You know I love you, right?"

"Ha! This is why I don't do the whole *love* thing. Men are pigs."

"All but me, babe. You're a freaking angel. Private run—"

"Runway H, got it, got it. Bye."

Kelly stood in the hangar at four in the morning. She was freezing. The November winds cut through her hoodie down to her bones. The private runways on this side of the small airport were lifeless. If this was another one of Mark's jokes, she would hang him and beat him like a dirty rug.

Mark enjoyed playing jokes, particularly on her.

As unfair as it was, he had to be the luckiest guy on the planet. God only knew how many pictures he had with famous people who flew into the airport and happened to land in the private hangar where he worked. The photos lined his wall. Movie stars, rock stars, even a porn star. Kelly didn't ask how he knew who she was. Some things needed to remain a mystery between friends.

The likelihood of this being real was high. As a small plane came in for a landing, Kelly took out her phone to see exactly who she was hosting.

"Mark?"

"That's his plane."

"*His* plane. It's a guy? You said your friend told his girlfriend."

Mark chuckled mischievously. "And she turned around and told her friend—an actor."

"Why won't you tell me who he is? Is this one of your pranks?" Kelly looked around, expecting to find Mark watching and laughing. "I will have your testicles."

"No pranks. This is honest to God the luckiest day of your life."

"Come on, Mark. Seriously, will I even recognize this guy? Have I seen any of his movies? What is he, extra number one hundred and fifty—" She stopped mid-sentence when her eyes locked on to the man stepping out of the private jet. "Holy. Shit. Please tell me that is not…"

"Your very own guilty pleasure, Trevor Jacobs. Happy Thanksgiving, Merry Christmas, and Happy Birthday for the next twenty years."

"If you ever need a kidney, I'm your girl. Gotta go." She hung up to Mark laughing and saying, "You're welcome."

Kelly watched her ultimate celebrity crush shoulder a duffle bag and head in her direction.

Damn, he was even hotter in person. From the first time she'd seen him on the big screen, Kelly had been a closet junkie. He was the definition of gorgeous. Tall, lean but built, dark hair, brown eyes that made her libido stand up and salute. Those eyes were as famous as his name. Women had been arrested for trying to sneak in to his hotels, hack his social media accounts, and track his cell phone. Not that Kelly was that obsessed—well, she was, just not in a *get-out-the-straightjacket* way.

But she remembered from an interview that he preferred when women didn't act crazy. He'd insisted that he was just another guy who enjoyed hamburgers and lazy Sundays.

Yeah. Just another guy with the body of a god, the face of an angel, lips of sin, and a voice that made her knees weak.

Yep, he could enjoy a burger at her place on Sundays all he wanted…as long as he did it naked.

"You Kelly?" asked a baritone laced with honey and spice.

"Yep." Kelly stuck out her hand. "Nice to meet you." She tried not to even smile as he slid his warm hand into hers. Her heart fluttered fast as her brain stalled out.

"Trevor."

"Yep."

He stuck his hands in his pockets and rocked back on his heels. "So." He smiled. "You're my ride?"

"Yep." Kelly nodded and Trevor chuckled.

He looked around at the dark and empty hangar. Clearly her lack of intellectual conversation made him uncomfortable. "Well this is the only bag I have. So…if you're ready?"

He was trying to set her at ease. All she did was nod and say, "Okay." Her sedan wasn't much, but it was clean and the interior was nice. It was nothing compared to the jet he had just flown in on. He couldn't really complain, right?

They rode in silence for a few minutes. Kelly had no idea what to say and the fragrance of him nearly made her drunk. It was sexy and sweet. If she licked his skin, would he taste the same?

"You in some kind of trouble?" The words spilled out of her mouth before she considered tact.

Trevor threw his head back and laughed. "Not exactly. But getting away for a while is a good idea. A friend told me about this place in the mountains that was nice and quiet."

"Okay."

"You don't believe me?" He looked over and smirked. Kelly shrugged. "Truth is I got caught selling drugs with a hooker in my hotel room. We tried to run from the cops, bad deal."

The inflection in his words made her turn to look at him. Never in a million years would she have agreed to this if—damn, he was pretty.

After a few seconds, a goofy grin spread across his face and he laughed. He was totally messing with her. "You should see your expression."

"You're one of the top paid actors in Hollywood. Naturally I should assume you're full of shit." Thank goodness it was dark and he couldn't see the bright red of her face.

Trevor was absolutely floored. Usually he didn't get this level of honesty, especially from women. This one didn't seem to care one bit about who he was.

"You don't believe I simply needed a break?"

After a deep exhale she tiled her head. "Nope. Not if you're flying in at four in the morning before the first commercial flights start. This wasn't a planned vacation. You're running."

Trevor nodded, seeing the logic in her words. "I'll admit, I did want to leave at night and it was last minute. I recently finished shooting one movie and the director was going to throw me right into another. I told them I needed time to look at the script before I agreed."

"You getting burned out, Hollywood?"

Trevor looked out the window at the forest as it passed by. "Yeah, I guess you could say that." He didn't want to think about it. It was easier to focus on his cute hostess. "Tell me about your place."

"Um, about that. Mark lied his ass off. I don't have a B and B."

That's kind of important since he was traveling to God only knew where. He cleared his throat. "Care to elaborate?"

"My grandfather owns a historical plantation house. It's been kept up quite well, and in our neck of the woods I guess you could call it a famous mansion. We usually don't keep guests."

"Mark said—"

"Yeah, I can imagine what Mark said and what it became by the time it hit your ears. It's fantastic; you won't be disappointed. There's not exactly a wait staff, so don't try to call in room service. Catch my drift?" Kelly yawned with a sigh. "Sorry, I'm not a morning person."

"Me either. And four thirty isn't morning. It's evil."

She laughed, actually laughed. It was a beautiful sound, slightly husky.

"I agree. I'll get you set up in a room and if you'll let me catch a couple hours of shut eye, I'll take you out for breakfast."

Trevor smiled. There was something refreshing about her honesty and outspokenness. She was *real*. It'd been a while since he'd been with a woman who was comfortable enough to call him out. Was there more to this woman? What made her act differently towards him?

Funny, he was rather excited to find out.

Kelly was right. The mansion was fantastic. Three stories of plantation perfection complete with white columns holding up the wrap-around balcony.

"Wow." He stepped out of the car and walked up the lit path. "You don't have weddings here?" He couldn't believe that a house so grand didn't get a lot of traffic. A place this majestic could be a gold mine.

"When my grandfather was a child, his parents threw parties. The place was crawling with people every night of the week." She didn't walk to the front door, but around to the side entrance of the mansion. "Turns out, his parents were both cheating and used the parties as cover for their affairs. When they found out, it tore their family apart. He was an only child so they lived together for his sake, but it was rough to say the least."

"That could screw with a kid. No need to carry on that tradition." Trevor nodded.

"Occasionally I do photo shoots. We have friends and certain family members that come and visit, but since it's just Pops and me left, we don't draw a big crowd."

Trevor followed closely as Kelly led him through the house, her voice lowering to a whisper. "We have one lady that keeps up the house as well as a gardener."

"Why don't you try to bring in more traffic? You could make a killing off this place," he whispered as they went up a set of old stairs that must have served as a staff entrance decades ago.

Kelly never stopped climbing the stairs. "People cause problems."

He couldn't argue about that. That's why he was here to begin with.

Did you enjoy *Why The River Runs*?

Did you know that authors need many reviews to help sales and boosting of their pages online? Reviews can be two sentences to multiple paragraphs.

Please consider leaving a review for this book where you purchased it from.

Thank you for thinking about helping an author. We really appreciate reviews from readers and fans. You're awesome!!

About The Author

JoAnna Grace lives in a world of alpha males and strong females where true love conquers all—at least in her writing! A proud indie, she has published The Divine Chronicles, the Blake Pride Series, and more. Joanna loves paranormal and urban fantasy romance novels. She's a romantic at heart.

From the time she started holding a crayon she began to create magical worlds. Living in the real world was never an option. JoAnna's tales are spun at her home in East Texas where she lives with her Prince Charming, three kids, and a couple dogs. When not hiding behind the computer screen chugging coffee, you can find her shopping. singing with the radio, or speaking on behalf of Y&R, a public relations and publishing company.

JOANNA GRACE
Giving Wings to Words

BOOKS BY JOANNA GRACE

DIVINE CHRONICLE SERIES:
Divine Awakening
Divine Destiny
Divine Judgment
Divine Encounter
Divine Pursuit
Divine Escape (Coming Soon)

The Roles We Play

BLAKE PRIDE SERIES:
Pride Before The Fall
Break Her Fall
The Harder They Fall
Divided We Fall (Coming Soon)

THE RIVERVIEW SERIES:
Why The River Runs

OMEGA OFFICE ROMANCE SERIES: *(Coming Soon)*
Crossing The Lines
Blurring The Lines
Erasing The Lines

FIND JOANNA ONLINE

Find JoAnna's Books online: www.authorjoannagrace.com
or www.yandrpublishing.com

Website: www.authorjoannagrace.com
Join JoAnna's group for monthly giveaways: http://bit.ly/
JoAnnaGrace
Email: JoAnna@AuthorJoAnnaGrace.com

Social Media
Twitter: @JoAnnaGrace4ya
Facebook: Jo Anna Grace Author
Pinterest: JoGraceAuthor
Instagram: AuthorJoAnnaGrace

Businesses for Authors & Readers
Reader's Boutique: www.readersboutique.com
Y&R PR: www.yandrpr.com
Y&R Publishing: www.yandrpublishing.com